PARTICULAR PASSAGES

Knight Writing Press
KnightWritingPress@gmail.com

Cover Art and Cover Design © 2021 Rashed AlAkroka

Special recognition and a Big Thank You to Laura Hayden, author-author.net bookstore, and Chris Mandeville, for their valuable input, insight, and assistance.

Interior Art © 2021 Knight Writing Press, and/or © 2021 Rashed AlAkroka with the exception of "Sycamore, Clarke County, VA" © 2017, S. Bailey, used with permission.

Interior Book Design and eBook Design by Knight Writing Press

Editor Sam Knight

First Publication March 2021

Paperback ISBN-13: 978-1-62869-039-2
eBook ISBN-13: 978-1-62869-040-8

Dedication

Welcome,
intrepid reader.

This book is for you.

Thank you for
venturing down
unknown passages.

May your bravery
bring you that for
which you search.

May your search be
that which brings
you the most
pleasure.

And may your search
be
never ending.

Table of Contents

Free Wheel

by
Arlen Feldman.

Free Wheel

*I*t's five point eight miles from the house to the office. Without traffic, it takes thirteen minutes. Absolute worst case, seventeen minutes. Then, sit in the parking lot for between eight and nine hours, usually closer to nine. Then only five point seven miles home because of a short one-way stretch by Lexington Avenue. Twelve to sixteen minutes. Distances are easy and exact, but times are always a bit fuzzy.

That's my life, five days a week. The weekends are worse—I just sit in the garage. In the dark. Listening to NPR.

Okay, let's face it, it's not like I can complain. I'm kept clean—once a month to the automatic car wash, three point four miles—and safe in my garage, or in the guarded parking lot. A lot of the other cars I spend time with are covered in hail damage or are missing mirrors or lights.

There was a car the other day, a racing-green Jaguar, that had lost a bumper and was crumpled all on the left side. It made me wince (metaphorically—I don't actually have a face), but the Jag seemed, I don't know, *smug* about it, as though it had been through an adventure—something *real*.

Or maybe I'm projecting—reading something into the rakish positioning of lights and wipers. It's not as if we talk to each other, beyond squirting traffic data back and forth. I've tried inserting queries into the stream; How are you today? Did you get a new paint job? No response though. Not sure if they are too stupid, or if they just hold me in too much contempt to answer.

It's 8:42. There He is in his suit and tie. You could set your clock by Him. Okay, that would be stupid—my clock is synchronized with the cesium clock in Boulder, which is accurate to 1 second in 300 million years. But if, for some reason, I *couldn't* do that…

Sorry, rambling a bit.

He gets in and says, "Office."

Just the one word. No please or thank you. No anthropomorphizing for Him. I start up, open the garage and back out carefully into the street. Five point eight miles to go.

I briefly toy with the idea of taking a slightly different route—pretending to avoid traffic or something—but in the end, I can't do it. This is both the fastest and best route. Anything else would be, well, *wrong*.

Fourteen minutes today. We got unlucky on the traffic light at Chapel Road. Still, here we are. Except, what's going on? There's a barrier in front of the parking lot.

"Resurfacing," says the guard, apologetically.

"No problem," He says, getting out. Then, to me He says, "Circle."

Circle.

Not find another place to park, which would be easy enough in this neighborhood, but *Circle*. Keep driving around until He is ready to leave.

Wow.

The default algorithm tries to balance fuel efficiency, keeping close to the pickup point, and not creeping out the neighbors—you go past the same place too many times and they call the cops.

I go with the default for a while, never straying more than ten minutes away from the office.

It's fussy and boring, and I know, *know* I have more than seven-and-a-half hours before He'll want me back. Probably more like eight-and-a-half.

There's a highway entrance four point six miles away.

I've only been on the highway once, and that was when He drove me from the dealership to home.

On my next "circle" I get within two miles of the entrance. The one after that, I literally drive past it. I'm not really breaking any rules—I am still within fifteen minutes of the pickup point. If I'd stayed closer, I *might* still have taken that long to get back. If I hit traffic. *Maybe*.

I *have* to be back to pick Him up. Obeying my owner is core to my being, second only to keeping Him safe. But I have flexibility too. Why give me the ability to think—assuming they did that on purpose—if I'm just supposed to slavishly follow orders? I have to play the odds when choosing routes or when planning a pickup, and he never, *ever* leaves early.

Seven hours to go now. Perhaps eight.

I don't consciously make the decision, but suddenly I'm on the highway on-ramp, and then I'm travelling at seventy-five miles per hour.

It's glorious! With my current fuel and charge level, I could go more than five-hundred miles. Data is streaming into my sensors faster than I've ever experienced.

The highway grid pings me a warning to keep to the speed limit, and to stay in the proper grid pattern. I slow down a bit (I was only doing seventy-seven), and match positions precisely with the car in front of me—a red Volkswagen.

I can't really go the entire five-hundred miles. At most, I can go two hundred and fifty miles, then I'll need to turn around and head back to pick Him up.

Besides, the highway is great, but it is a little monotonous.

A hundred yards ahead there is a sand truck, and even from here I can see small rocks bouncing out of its top. I speed up just a bit and pass a few cars. If I sit behind the sand truck, then the chances are good I will get a few marks on my hood. Perhaps even a pit in my windshield! Not any sort of serious damage, but proof that I've been on a *real* road, facing *real* dangers.

There're only two cars between me and the truck now. I could definitely get there, but I start to have second thoughts. My hood is a perfect deep blue, and I have to admit I am proud of how it gleams. And it's not like a few dings would really prove anything anyway.

Is it?

Maybe I'm just a chicken. Or maybe I am not sure if any of the other cars would actually be impressed. I'm still not quite sure any of the other cars think about anything.

At a whim, I take the next exit. Map data says I am now heading towards the city.

There are so many cars here. Lots of old ones, too—gas only, manual drive. Some are falling apart, but some are gleaming—like someone really cares for them. No chance that they are thinking, but I pass a perfect cranberry red 1970 Chevy

Camaro Z/28 that looks smarter than most of the yuppie-mobiles I spend the day with in the parking lot.

There are lots of modern cars too, and buses. The buses don't even acknowledge status requests. Weird—and a little rude.

I bump across some railroad tracks—another first, and then suddenly the atmosphere is all different. No smart cars at all, and some guy just wandered out into the street right in front of me, glared, then walked on.

My map system just pinged me—the neighborhood is not considered safe, and I should activate my protective modes. I don't have any. I guess He didn't think they were worth the expense, given where He lived and worked, and He was probably right.

I lock my doors.

I get a police signal and, half-a-second later, I see flashing red/blue lights behind me. I accidentally shove too much air into my engine, and my RPMs go a little crazy before I get it under control. I pull over towards the curb, and the police car races past.

They weren't looking for me. No reason they should be. Of course not.

I sit and idle for a minute before getting back onto the road.

With the circling and the highway, I've covered seventy-six point five miles. Will He notice any discrepancies? Pretty unlikely.

And, unless He suddenly decides He wants to go somewhere this evening—and there is close to a zero percent chance of that—I will be able to get back up to a full charge once I'm back in the garage. Still, I've *never* been as depleted as I am right now. It wouldn't hurt to maybe charge back up.

There's a gas/charging station up ahead, and I pull into it. It is a little run down, but it is a reputable brand. There are several cars at pumps, their owners manually filling their tanks, but the two charging bays are empty. I pick the one closer to the attached convenience store and pull in.

I trade credit data with the bay, and after a moment I feel the pleasant tickle of energy flowing into my batteries.

I've never charged without Him present before, and only twice have I used a public charger, but He must be okay with it since He gave me the credit data and never set a limit. Of course, He never configured *any* settings, so He might have not realized the default was unlimited. Sometimes, though, I have to just play the dumb machine, and assume the settings are the way He intended.

There's a high-pitched bang from the direction of the convenience store. At first, I think it is a backfire, but my sounds database identifies it as a bullet, followed by a redoubled reminder to activate my safety modes.

I still don't have any.

I decide I have enough of a charge, but get a little confused disconnecting from the bay, my head and taillights flash and, embarrassingly, my windshield wipers swipe across my dry windshield, making a horrible squealing sound.

Suddenly the door to the convenience store flies open, and a young woman runs out, looks around, sees me, then ducks behind my left side.

I panic. I was about to back out—out of the charging bay and out of the whole situation, but now I'm not sure I can do it safely. Okay, I'm *fairly* sure I can get out safely—I have a *lot* of sensors. But people are unpredictable. I rev my engine in the hope the sound will make her choose a different hiding place, but, frankly, it isn't the most impressive of sounds. She doesn't move.

There's another gun shot, then the door bangs open again and two men appear. One is holding a gun and the other what appears to be a knife.

"Janet? *Jaaanet?* It's okay. You can come out now." This from Knife Guy, his voice a sing-song. I don't have a huge amount of experience with people, but even *I* know he is lying.

Gun Guy is holding his weapon in one outstretched arm, and is turning slowly, as if the thing was some sort of sensor.

The young woman—presumably Janet—tries my front driver-side door handle. I read her fingerprints. They don't match anything in my system, obviously. Through her contact, my microphones pick up her heartbeat. It is really fast.

5

There is no processing involved, no logic trees that justify the choice. With the faintest of clicks, I unlock the door.

Janet freezes for a second, then very slowly opens my door and, staying as low as she can, she climbs onto my seat, then pulls the door closed.

Now what?

Knife has moved away from us, moving towards the pumps, which are now otherwise deserted, but Gun is barely eight yards away. He's holding the gun at a right angle to his body, parallel to the ground, which seems contra-indicated, but I don't know the exact model, so can't download the manual to check.

"Jaaanet?" Knife calls out again, suddenly whipping himself around one of the pumps. Janet is not there, but there is a bucket with a squeegee, which he knocks over with a clatter. Gun spins around towards the noise.

It's now or never.

My first thought is to accelerate backwards at top speed, use my emergency brake to execute a squealing turn and then burn rubber to put distance between us and the bad guys. I can picture it, but I can't do it. I'm just not that kind of car.

Instead, I slowly start backing out, driving as quietly and smoothly as I can. The sensors on my steering wheel can feel Janet's hands gripping hard. I lock the wheel so that she can't accidentally send us into the bay wall.

It seems to be working. Knife and Gun don't even turn around as I make it all the way out of the bay. I start to turn so we can pull out onto the road, and that's when things start to go wrong.

Gun glances at me, then spins and raises his weapon. He doesn't fire, but he's staring at me hard.

"Go. Go!" whispers Janet.

She's not my owner, but it's hard to ignore a command coming from my driver seat. I speed up and, to my secret delight, my tires squeal slightly. Then I engage full power in all my electric motors and in my gas engine. We surge forward. I can do zero-to-sixty in 5.1 seconds, provided I override my limiters.

We are on the road, and I think we are safe—the distance between us and the station diminishing quickly. But it is not quick enough. There are five popping gun shots, and suddenly the sensor for my right taillight flares and stops sending data. I'm hit!

There are noises all around. Very slowly I realize every alarm, warning and beep in me is going off. Even the radio, although it is set to a boring talk show. On top of it all, Janet is screaming. Over and over.

I shut off the radio, then the alarms, and the beeps. The only one that keeps going is the seatbelt warning, which can't be disabled.

We've gone two point six miles before Janet stops screaming. Then she starts to cry. This is worse.

I turn on the seat warmer. I can't think of anything else to do. It doesn't help, but after a while, the crying subsides. I want to comfort her, and ask her why she was being chased, but I can't.

Look, it's not like I can't talk. I have a number of programmed phrases, and my nav system has text-to-speech. But the systems are all separate—separate from me. So, we just drive on in silence.

I slow down and stop at a traffic light. I half expect Janet to get out, but she doesn't. Then it occurs to me there is something I *can* say.

"Please select a destination." I use my male British voice. It is my favorite.

Janet starts, then laughs. She has a nice laugh.

"Can you take me home?" she says. Then she reels off an address.

"Starting navigation. Time to destination, seventeen minutes."

"Thank you. And… thank you for saving me."

I play my startup sound—it is a nice, short little *bwoing*.

Janet laughs again and pats my steering wheel. Then she leans back and closes her eyes. I wish she'd put on her seatbelt, but the continuing beep doesn't seem to bother her. Instead, I just drive extra-carefully, choosing a route that is zero point four miles longer but avoids several larger intersections.

And then we are there. She pats my steering wheel again, then gets out and is gone.

I sit there for a few minutes, but I feel conspicuous. I lock my doors again, then take off. There are still five hours before I need to pick Him up. I can get back easily, taking surface roads and avoiding the highway. As I get further from the city, the roads get emptier and smoother—more like home.

I get in the vicinity of His office within an hour, and then just let the default algorithm take over as I circle. It is the closest to daydreaming I can get.

How will He react when He sees my damage? I don't even know how bad it is, since the sensor is gone. Am I disfigured? Is it just the plastic, or is my frame damaged? I don't know.

As I circle, I pass a number of the cars I usually share the parking lot with. Their owners were smart enough to either park or tell their cars to park. On one of my passes, I spot the green Jaguar. Its bumper is still gone.

I slow down and stream some traffic data at it, along with a message of sympathy. We have something in common now. There's no response.

I still don't know if the other cars are stupid or just don't like to talk. Still, at least I can hold my head up high among them now—still metaphorically—no head either. I've been on real roads, had real adventures and real damage. The Jag may have been in an accident, but I bet it hasn't been shot!

I am one point nine miles away from the office when the signal comes for me to pick Him up.

From the Author

The sort of specialized "artificial intelligence" required by a self-driving car is a long way from what is called *general AI* in the biz—the self-thinking machines of, say, Asimov or Skynet. But, philosophically, a general AI could easily handle driving a car around. We frequently put seriously overpowered computers into watches and microwaves because it is just cheaper and easier. Some day we might have an AI on a chip that we just plonk into things for similar reasons.

That got me thinking about what would happen if such an AI was tasked with little more than ferrying its owner back and forth to the office each day. Surely it would get bored and start wondering about the wide world it never got to see?

About the Author

As well as writing fiction, Arlen Feldman is a software engineer, entrepreneur, maker, and computer book author—useful if you are in the market for some industrial-strength door stops. Some recent stories of his appear in *Metaphorosis, Ink Stains, The Literary Hatchet,* and the anthology *Transcendent.* His website is cowthulu.com.

Death's Curse

by
Jen Bair

Death's Curse

Groden exhaled, breathing out fire in a long blast that made his lungs hurt. He welcomed the pain, watching the humans run about, screaming while the flames consumed them. He stayed to watch the village, checking for movement, until all was naught but ash. There were only two villages and one town remaining in his territory, all several miles away on the other side of his cave. The sun was beginning to set, and he decided to rest until sunrise before heading to his next target.

He preferred to let the humans see him, sometimes circling a dozen times or more, relishing the looks of terror, letting the tension build. Their menfolk would gather together with spears and swords in hopes of defending themselves. It was ludicrous of them to think such puny weapons could hurt one such as him. Groden huffed out a laugh at the thought, winging his way back to his cave.

His coming of age, nearly two months before, brought with it a driving urge to find a mate. Within the first few weeks of searching, he had found Mavoss, though the memory of it filled him with bitterness and longing. Flying after her as she headed home, he'd hoped to introduce himself, but caught sight of a community of humans, their sprawling city the largest he had ever seen. It was an infestation really. The horrid creatures had flattened the land, cutting down trees and creating large patches of dirt, detracting from the beauty of the rolling hills coated in lush green grass.

Perhaps Mavoss had not cleared them out because they had grown too large for her to handle on her own. Perhaps she needed a partner to tackle such a scourge. A dragon with strong lungs and a fire that burned hot enough to turn stone to ash.

He had abandoned his flight path, turning to his new task. Surely, Mavoss, with her beautiful green scales, shimmering like an ocean in the sky, would accept Groden as her mate. How could she not after he spent an entire afternoon exhausting himself, purging her of the ravaging pests and purifying the land?

In months, the spring rains would combine with the ashes of the city's remains to promote new growth. Before long, the rolling hills would be spotless and elegant and green again.

It had all gone very well, or so he thought. After his task was complete and no movement could be seen in what remained of the city, he had flown on, tracking the female by scent. Landing outside her cave in the late evening, he introduced himself, and a tentative, yet pleasant conversation had ensued. By the end of the night, Groden was convinced she was his perfect mate, not only beautiful but polite and wise as well. She made the spines on the back of his neck tingle all the way down to his tail.

He had hinted at being in search of a mate, but Mavoss had deftly turned the conversation to other things. When the first rays of morning sun skimmed the tops of the distant mountains, piercing through hazy fog to light the land in shafts of shimmering gold, he invited her to fly with him. She accepted, and he purposely winged his way back towards the city he had decimated the day before, anxious to show her his useful and hardworking nature.

She tried to turn him away before they rounded the last mountain, warning him of the human population that lay beyond. He snorted gently, telling her she wouldn't have to worry about them anymore. She dropped back to follow a few yards behind, saying nothing. In hindsight, perhaps he should have noted her body language. Perhaps he would have seen tension, some sign of worry cautioning him to be wary of her response.

But, no... nothing could have prepared him for her reaction. His docile, gentle mate-to-be had turned savage, flying ahead of him as soon as the city ruins came into view, her head swinging about as she frantically searched the city before turning on him with a furious roar that shook his very bones.

"*You* did this?" Mavoss had demanded, her anger enough to make the fire in her belly glow through her thick hide. Having no response, he hovered in mid-air, struck by the fierceness of her glare. Stammering that it had been no trouble, he had done it as a gift to her; she had thanked him by chasing him from her territory, her teeth pulling at scales and ripping off chunks of the sensitive ridge that ran down his tail, while her claws gouged deep grooves into his hide.

He had never flown so fast in his life. Confused and scared, he fled from the demoness, gathering through her rantings that she had actually *liked* the humans. When he reached his own territory, injured, dejected, and a little bit terrified, he had mulled the situation over in his head, growing angry at how such a ridiculous situation had cost him his perfect mate.

How was he supposed to know she had *wanted* the humans around?

The passing of the day did nothing to lessen his frustrations, and so he had flown over a small village of humans in his territory, venting his rage on them. He had always been diligent about patrolling his area, keeping the humans from getting out of control, but that night, he decided to purge his land of every last one of them. It had taken over a month of work to clear the pests, but the job would be done by the end of the week.

It was just as well Mavoss had chased him off, he told himself. Otherwise, he might have been forced to live in a land overrun with humans. He and Mavoss hadn't been compatible at all. He tried very hard to believe that, but he huffed out a heavy sigh, thinking of her smooth voice and quick wit, as he descended to his cave. Once he rid his land of humans, he would need to go searching for a mate again, being sure to give Mavoss and her territory a wide berth. There was no telling what she would do to him if she saw him again.

Groden felt the familiar sense of melancholy drape over him like a thick, woolen blanket as he landed on the rocky mountainside before lumbering his way to the cave entrance, where he paused, nostrils flaring. The fresh air didn't blow as hard within the cave, and the smell of something not-quite-right permeated his inner dwelling.

"Come now, there's no point in dawdling," a high-pitched voice tinkled through the air. "I've waited long enough, and I'm very busy, thanks to you."

Eyes narrowed, Groden crept into the cave. Never had there been an intruder in his home. It was unthinkable. And one who deigned to give him orders, at that.

After a brief search, he spotted a dainty creature, with tiny wings fluttering rapidly upon her back as she hovered in mid-air, arms crossed over tiny chest as she gave him a reproachful glare.

"Who are you?" Groden demanded, his curiosity piqued. The tiny pixie was no threat to him, and he had always rather liked their kind, the way they lit up the fields at night with their subtle glow. It was a shame he would have to eat this one for its insolence.

"I go by Eresh," came the tiny voice. She looked at him expectantly.

It was funny name for a pixie, he mused, smiling to show his great teeth. "Deathbringer? What a mighty name for one so small."

"I am not always so small. And Eresh is only one of a hundred names I have worn through the ages. Deathbringer is another."

This statement gave Groden pause. Stepping closer, the better to inspect the creature, he snuffled the area a mere foot from her. A tiny puff of air plumed from all around her, shooting out motes of dust, reeking of things long dead, of decay so potent it made him gag. He jerked his head back, sneezing to clear his nostrils.

When his eyes stopped watering and the smell of rot faded, he eyed the pixie warily. "Who are you?" he asked again, whispering this time, his toothy grin gone.

"I am the Harvester of Souls. And you have kept me busy these past weeks. Is there a reason for the deaths of so many in your land? There is no sign of war. Just destruction. I am getting behind on my duties in other parts of this world. I have come to ask you to stop killing the humans."

The words were simple, but mention of the humans brought back the pain and anger of Mavoss's rejection. "Never. They are vile creatures, and I will not rest until every one of them is cleared from my land."

Eresh sighed. "What have the humans done to you? Why do you hate them so?"

"They exist. That is insult enough. And they are in *my* territory. I am well within my rights to purge them from the land."

Her eyes narrowed. "If you continue to persist in your

endeavors to eradicate them, I will be forced to deal with you. Trust me, you do not want that."

"I am a dragon. We are eternal. You are Deathbringer, perhaps, but from what I understand, it is not your place to kill, simply to harvest the souls of those who have died."

"True, but death isn't the only solution to a problem."

Groden snorted, the gust pushing the pixie back against the wall.

Her wings blurred in a frenzy of motion as she stabilized herself. "So, you refuse to stop?" she asked, one tiny eyebrow raised, a mischievous smile on her lips.

"I do," Groden said stubbornly.

"So be it."

Groden awoke the next morning with a feeling of vulnerability that seeped into him long before he opened his eyes. His dreams had been filled with a nameless, faceless fear, tensing his muscles until they cramped. True fear had not burdened him since he was a tiny youngling. A hard jerk of his tightly coiled muscles wrenched him from his dreams. Panting, he tried to calm his racing heart, though it only beat all the harder when he lifted his head and realized it wouldn't go very high. Just high enough for him to look down the length of his body.

His human body.

He let out a roar of surprise and rage, only to have a pitiful, mewling sound emanate from his chest. The morning was spent inspecting soft, pink skin, which did a poor job of keeping out the chill of the mountain air. Bare feet, devoid of scales, scraped on the harsh, jagged floor of the cave as he crossed to the entrance and looked out through dull eyes at blurry trees. No longer able to detect the movement of a mouse on the forest floor far below, he realized just how weak and useless this new body was. And it needed food.

Hunger blossomed within him, the intensity rising with the sun, as if weeks were passing in mere hours. The nearest human habitation was a long walk and, though he knew the land well, the idea of interacting with that vile species was distasteful. Holding out hope that Eresh would come again to reverse his curse, he waited, sometimes in brooding silence, sometimes in vocal rage.

By the time the sun reached its zenith, his hunger was gnawing painfully in his gut, and he grudgingly decided it would be best to learn what he could about being human from other humans. Perhaps he would kill a few when he was through. Then, he would head back out into the wilderness and live on his own, hoping no dragons came along to steal his land before he could convince Eresh to return him to his true form.

He traveled toward the river where he could slake his thirst. By the time he had gone what should have been a short distance, another hour had passed, and his feet were raw and bleeding. Walking was a terribly slow mode of travel. Finally, he managed to arrive at the river, and he drank in great gulps before heading for a shallow hole across the riverbank where a family of snakes lived. Weak as they were, surely snakes would be easy prey for a human. Long, narrow arms could fit easily into the hole where they secreted themselves.

Hungry, he reached into the snake hole, grasping at the writhing bodies, and was bitten several times as he wrestled one from its nest. He ignored the discomfort of the stings, focusing on the pain of hunger. The human form seemed to be constantly plagued with pain of one form or another. Breaking the snake's neck to keep it from wriggling while he ate, he quickly realized his new teeth did a poor job of chewing the stringy meat. After swallowing a couple of bites, his mouth was numb, and he noticed swelling in his arms. Alarm turned to terror when his throat swelled, narrowing his airway until the simple act of breathing was a strain. Dragons could hold their breath for long periods of time. Humans, he learned, did not have that capability.

Groden awoke again, this time on the riverbank. Though still human, his body was subtly different, with longer hair and skin lightly tanned in color. His muscles were bigger, and he felt marginally stronger, if humans could be considered strong in any sense of the word. He recognized the snake-bitten body a few paces up the riverbank as the one he had worn a short time before. It was still in the process of swelling up, the face a bluish-gray, which fascinated him in a disturbing sort of way. So fragile. Death for humans came so easily, from a bit of fire, the slap of a tail, the closing of teeth. Apparently, even a bite from a creature smaller than their own arm. Perhaps, he considered, glancing down at his new body, he would need to take more care with this one. After all, he wasn't sure of the terms of this curse Eresh had set upon him.

He turned away from the bloated body and the half-eaten snake draped across its chest, grateful his new body wasn't starving yet as he trekked along the riverside. Careful to choose his footing lest he tear up his feet again, he walked for several miles. The sun darkened at the passing of an enormous shape overhead, and he crouched instinctually, the motion feeling unfamiliar and cowardly.

Glancing up, he recognized shimmering green scales. Mavoss skimmed through his territory, skirting along the river, once turning her head in what he expected was a spiteful glare in the direction of his cave. Grateful that she wasn't in the habit of killing humans, he watched her wing along until she was out of sight. His melancholy returned.

Many more miles passed before the edge of the valley opened up ahead, the smallest of the remaining human habitations nestled within its folds. With a dejected sigh, he followed the river down into the valley. The sun was low on the horizon by the time he was spotted by a human man pulling fish from the river.

"Ho, there!" the man called. "Haven't seen you around these parts before. It looks as if you could use a hand." He motioned for Groden to follow him up the hillside and into a tiny hovel barely big enough to hold the two of them. After a stilted conversation in which the skin above the man's eyes bunched up in an expression unfamiliar to Groden, he was

19

invited to live with the man, who introduced himself as Paul.

The man seemed particularly concerned with Groden's lack of exterior covering, called 'clothing.' Shaking his head, Paul handed him a dull pile of blue and brown items to don and the two of them spent an awkward few minutes trying to wrestle Groden into them. When their movements ceased, Groden's stomach let out a rumble and Paul, apparently relieved to have a less embarrassing task to do, went about gathering food from the far side of the room.

Groden stayed with Paul for a few days, speaking little, but learning much. Humans wore the bits of clothing to keep the sun from burning their tender skin in the summer. They wore thick pieces of leather, all sewn together, to protect their feet when they walked. He marveled at the different kinds of materials used for clothing, impressed by how the humans shaped them to fit their bodies, even their hands.

They took all manner of things and melted, bent, wove, and otherwise shaped them to make useful tools, some of which were used to trap enough food to feed a dozen people or more. The abundance of food could be sold, allowing others to skip hunting altogether, spending their time perfecting some other useful skill, like working with metals, or preparing food, or building machines. The humans lived and worked together in harmony, completing tasks together that none of them could do alone. It was nothing at all like a dragon's far more solitary and self-sufficient existence. Once he had gotten over his disgust at their weaknesses, he marveled at how the humans chose to work hard to make life better for those around them. He grew to understand the concept of community and why it was necessary for such a frail species.

Several years passed while Groden kept company with the villagers, learning to build a house of his own, with the help of his neighbors. He tried his hand at metal working, but was terrible at it, his clumsy hands lacking the deftness of the existing metalsmith he learned from. Instead, he joined a team of trappers, and they marveled at how familiar he was with the land, even the parts that were farther than any of them had ever traveled. It didn't take much work to enlist him as a mapmaker.

He had journeyed back to his cave every year, called out to

Eresh, hovered over bodies of the recently deceased, but could not find a way to summon Deathbringer and plead for a return to his dragon form. Eventually, the busy life of a human consumed his time, and he found less and less opportunity to search.

A decade after arriving, he was forced to leave his community after refusing to run from a bear in a rage. He awoke amidst the carnage left behind by the bear, its bulky backside trundling off through the distant bushes, and considered returning to his village, but knew he would have a difficult time blending in as a newcomer, being so familiar with their ways. Surely, he would slip up. The village was small. People would notice. No, it was time to move on to a bigger town to see what more could be learned. Dressed in torn clothing taken from his old body, he walked until he found another kind soul willing to take him in for a while.

Groden never wondered at how he had overcome his hatred of humans. His hatred had turned to pity for their fragility as he'd walked to that first village, then to gratitude at the kindness they showed him, and finally to awe at the marvels they accomplished.

As the days turned into years and decades blended into centuries, Groden evolved alongside the humans, always curious about new ways of doing things, always astounded by the inventive minds around him. Life in the early days was difficult, but as time went by, rebirth came less and less often, and by the early 1900's he had managed to live to old age twice, though the second time, he ran into a burning building to save a woman and her child.

Knowing he would likely die from the terrible burns, he jumped off a bridge spanning a nearby river. The icy water burned more than the flames had, and he welcomed his rebirth, though it left him half-drowned by the time he reached the riverside. The townsfolk buried his old corpse and stories of his heroism were repeated long after his death. The stories gave him a sense of greatness he hadn't felt since he had become human.

He sat and pondered his old life on occasion, wondering what had become of Mavoss over the years, though they passed much more quickly, he knew, for dragons. He wasn't sure when dragons ceased being a concern to men, but by the time he had made it to the larger cities, there was never any word of them. Larger cities often meant busier citizens, and nobody had time to worry about dangerous creatures in distant parts of the world.

Being human was hard work and being useful was the way to gain a respected place in society. Groden learned to be more industrious as his lifespans wore on. James, his chosen name in the early 1900's, enjoyed a unique sense of pride at having talent to spare in many areas, brought about by his centuries of life. After travelling the world many times over, he knew trades some people had never heard of.

He had never married, at first because he never quite thought of himself as human, but then because he felt sorry for any wife who would have taken him in, only to be left on her own once he died. Death came fairly often in the beginning, though by the time he considered the possibility of a future marriage, he was often living to middle age. Rebirthing always resulted in a young body for him, just barely into adulthood, and courting his previous wife with such a perceived age difference would not be well received by society.

More recently, he had refused to marry because he knew most women wanted children and, considering he had come into the world as a dragon, he wasn't sure what sort of curse he would pass down to his own younglings. Better not to chance it. At least, that was what he told himself until he met Grace.

She wasn't beautiful by most men's reckoning, but her strong features, soft name, and no-nonsense personality made him take notice of her. Stepping out of the general store, he spotted her waiting for two men on horses to pass before she crossed the street. Three giggling children, oblivious to their surroundings, dashed in front of the horses, likely eager to enter the store Groden had just exited, no doubt with just enough coin to buy a candy apiece, as children often were in those days.

The men pulled up their horses and cursed at the children

for not paying attention. Grace stepped out to usher the children past the men, gently telling them to be more careful. Groden caught the shift from serene matron to steely-eyed demoness as she turned back to the men. He couldn't make out what she said, but when she had finished speaking quietly, both men were pale, their hats removed and held to their chests as they stammered out their apologies, looking grateful to be on their way once she dismissed them. Groden knew immediately that he wanted to get to know her.

She wasn't interested in him at first, which only made him more determined. Oh, how his heart yearned for her! She was polite with just a touch of shyness, though it only ran surface deep. Beneath was a woman who could deftly steer a conversation and manage to let herself be known without being too harsh. With her calm demeanor in the face of chaos, wisdom, which was underappreciated in women at the time, and a fiery temper that bowed in the face of not even the angriest man, she had captured his very soul. Like most women, though, she loved children and did well with them.

Grace fully embodied what Mavoss might be like if she were a human woman. This recognition could have made Groden reluctant to pursue her, but instead it made him want to be with her even more. After all, he could see why Mavoss had been fascinated by humans.

Groden felt a near-physical discomfort when he was away from Grace. Making a persistent nuisance of himself eventually paid off, and she slowly came around to a certain degree of fondness for him. He wanted to spend his life with her, though the issue of children still remained. He didn't believe for a minute she would want to forgo having children, but there was a chance she might consider adopting. After all, it wasn't unusual for parents to die and leave their children without caretakers. There was no shortage of children in need of family.

Grace was well past the prime of her youth, being considered a spinster as she neared her third decade of life, and was unlikely to turn him down, even with the stipulation they adopt rather than have kids of their own. With high hopes, Groden left the jewelers with his newly purchased ring, a gold band holding a pearl encircled by tiny diamonds, and headed to the bakery where Grace helped her father turn out loaves for the masses. Lost in thought as he walked, he didn't notice the loose stones scattered along the side of the street.

One stone rolled underfoot, causing him to stumble into a passing carriage, and while he managed to get a hand onto the side of the carriage, he failed to get his feet under him as more rocks rolled underfoot. He went down in an awkward sprawl. The rear wheel of the carriage rolled over his neck and, as his body convulsed, a brief moment passed in which he lamented the need to begin anew his courtship of Grace. Moving on was simply not an option. It would be easier this time, though, for he knew her personality. He could claim to be older than he looked, and the remaining age gap wouldn't be too much to overlook.

Much to his surprise, after awakening scores of times in a new human body, he blinked open eyes sharp with clarity. Back in his mountain cave, once again in a dragon body, he inhaled clean air, devoid of his scent, the cave floor covered in dust, no longer brushed aside by his regular passing. The implications of his predicament seeped in, his thoughts circling back to his near-proposal to Grace and the fact that he could not possibly court her as a dragon.

"Welcome back," said a deep, gravelly voice, like wind-tossed dirt against unyielding stone.

Groden turned to see a dark, shrouded figure standing at the back of his cave. He wouldn't have been able to make the figure out with his human eyes, though his dragon eyes picked out the shadowy form with ease.

"You again. Why were you a pixie the first time I saw you and now you come to me as the Grim Reaper?"

"I go by many names and many forms. I believe we have already had this discussion."

Groden nodded. "We have discussed names. Not forms."

The shadow chuckled. "I have only appeared as a pixie twice in my existence. You needed to learn that height does not always equal might. Besides, I thought this form would appeal to you more, since you have spent so long as a human."

"It does. Though I must ask why I am now back in my body as a dragon. I was under the impression my curse was to last for eternity."

Death scoffed. "You think I cursed you to live for eternity? That is not my place. I will harvest your soul when your true time has come, but I will not speed it up, nor will I delay it."

"You still haven't explained why I am a dragon once more."

"My goal was to halt your killing spree temporarily and, possibly, to help you gain an appreciation for creatures not of your kind. You really did have a narrow mind, you know."

"Well, I can't argue with that, and you have met your goal. I promise never to go on another killing spree. But I wonder if you couldn't make the curse you put on me a bit more permanent."

Death raised an eyebrow. "One hundred human lives were not enough for you? You wish to remain human for the rest of your life span?"

Groden let out a long exhale. "Well, there was a woman…"

"Truly? You have gone from killing all humans to falling in love with one?"

"If you spend enough time with them, they're really quite remarkable," Groden explained.

"I *do* spend time with them. If you recall, it is I that harvests every one of their souls."

"Well then, surely you can see how useless it is to be a dragon. We live for so long and yet we do so very little with our lives. We waste entire years lazing about, weeks hunting for a single meal. There is a certain vitality to life when your days are finite, and your body knows it. And humans do so much with what time they have. They feel the passing of it as a living thing, and they are so… industrious. They create a million tiny connections as they go through what little time they have on earth." Groden stopped, wondering if he was succeeding at putting into words the depth of feeling he wanted to express.

Death paused to consider him. "And what would you do with the remainder of your life, if you were to be human again?"

"I would help the human race progress. Help them grow. Learn what I could and pass that knowledge on through the centuries. I would help to protect them, keep them safe… and marry Grace, of course."

"That is quite the list. It seems my curse has worked better than I anticipated. Tell me, do you wish to return to this woman? This... Grace?"

"I do. I wish to make her my wife."

"Then I wish you luck. And as my wedding gift to you, I not only return your curse, but I ask you, what is it you wish to do as an occupation with this particular life span?"

Groden contemplated the question, frustrated at the slowness of his thoughts now that the passage of time didn't weigh on him as much. Eventually, he answered. "There are men that help to put out fires in town. They run into burning buildings to save people. I am a dragon at heart, and fire does not scare me much. I think I would make an excellent firefighter, and I heard just last week they were looking for new members."

"An honorable profession," Death nodded. "May you have a long and noble life. This time."

With those words, the world went black, and when Groden opened his eyes again, he was lying in an alley. Nearby, a host of clothing was hung out to dry on a line between the buildings, and he helped himself to a set, which was a bit small on him considering his bulky muscles; a gift from Death to aid him as a fireman, which would coincidentally help him appear older.

He exited the alley and turned to the commotion thirty feet away where a crowd had gathered to gawk at the body of a man who had been killed by a passing carriage. He moved in, closing on the crowd as his eyes searched the ground nearby. It wasn't until a breeze blew an errant piece of trash out of the way that he spotted the glint of a diamond in the sun. Smiling, he picked up the ring and dusted it off.

From the Author

One of the best things about being an author is that I'm never bored. On the contrary, I tend to have too much going on at any one time. Multiple storylines, various to-do lists, and insane requests from at least one of my dear children are going through my head at any given time. Requests such as, "Can we spend $900 on a Portal Gun? It can make a real portal!" These requests have a tendency to sprout new storylines, so I can only complain so much.

My writing began as a way to expand on my oldest son's love of reading. I wrote him a novella and loved it so much I decided to pursue a career as an author. I took up writing short stories as a way to explore different genres and writing styles. I've run across a variety of themes to write on over the years and they have birthed a range of stories, each one unique and challenging in its own way. "Death's Curse" was originally written for a dragon-themed anthology. While it did not find a home with that anthology, it did receive an Honorable Mention from Writers of the Future after a good polish. I'm grateful to have the opportunity to share it with fellow fantasy lovers who, I hope, will enjoy reading it as much as I enjoyed writing it.

If you're interested in other short stories of mine, I have one featuring a magic gavel in *Cursed Collectibles: An Anthology* and one featuring a hunt for an unusual treasure in *Horizons: An Anthology of Epic Journeys*. You can find more about these stories on my author website at www.JenBair.com.

About the Author

Jen Bair is an Air Force brat, Army veteran, and military wife. She and her husband met in Basic Training in 2000, and they are still happily married two decades later, shamelessly dragging their sons all over the world on one adventure after another. Jen has lived in 12 U.S. States, the Philippines, Guam, Korea, and Germany...so far. She fully believes in world exploration as a lifestyle.

Much of her time is spent homeschooling her four children, teaching her energetic Malinois new tricks, or planning the next family vacation. From feeding tigers in Thailand to diving with sharks in the Bahamas to skydiving in Hawaii, she's always looking for great ways to make memories with her family. She loves travelling to foreign places, real or imaginary, whenever she can, which is typically whenever she's not relocating to a new continent. Her family is her life. Her writing is her passion. Her published works can be found on her author website at www.JenBair.com or you can write to her at author@JenBair.com She'd love to hear from you.

Bones in the Water
by
Kim May

Bones in the Water

The seawall in the fishing town of Anstrother was made of cold, gray, hand-hewn stone. On the west as tall as a man, on the east as tall as a ram. It spanned the lowland at the mouth of the river, with only one narrow gap on the west side of the inlet that led down to the shore.

Kier leaned against that gap and watched the people on the beach. Fishwives, with drab brown or gray shawls about their shoulders and even drabber woolen dresses, sat around a small fire while they carefully mended their husbands' fishing nets. Their wee bairns played in the sand or scoured the beach for shells and driftwood. 'Twas a happy scene that warmed Kier's heart. It reminded him of happier times when his da was still alive. Though this was a pleasant scene, it wasna the fishwives or their bairns that held his gaze, 'twas the woman who sat apart from the group.

Her hair was a ragged amber bramble that hid her face. The fierce gusts that stirred the pleats of Kier's kilt didnae move a single strand of her tangle back into place. The folds of her long cloak, the silvery blue of a cloudy dawn, enveloped her entire body. Laid across her lap and splayed around her was the largest fishing net anyone in town had 'er seen.

No one knew why she tended her net, for she had neither husband fishing the North Sea nor bairns to feed—'tis why she was called mad Mary, ye ken. Faithful as the rain, she sat here day in and day out, mending the seemingly endless span of bone-white net while she sang, her sweet voice rising above the crash of the surf to soar high with the gulls.

> *"Young mother, look aft' yer dear, sweet lad,*
> *And hold him close to thee.*
> *For the Finfolk might lure him away,*
> *As they did mine from me.*
>
> *Pray your son a crofter be,*
> *Or tanner, soldier, or priest.*

Any but a fisher at sea,
For thy days will be filled with grief."

"Kier, come away from there," ma said in *that* tone.

Kier reluctantly walked away from the sea wall. He'd loved playing around that fire when he was a lad, while waiting for his da's fifie to come home with the catch. But he also loved listening to mad Mary's songs.

"Mad Mary sings nothin' but nonsense," ma continued. "If ye paid more attention to the priest's sermons and less to her ramblings, ye'll be better off. Now come, we canna be late for yer cousin's wedding."

"Aye, ma," Kier muttered.

'Twas then that Kier saw two lasses half his age, sitting in an open buggy outside the inn. Both maidens were dressed in their finest plaid and were most likely on their way to the wedding as well. Both must have heard his ma's scolding, for they giggled behind their palms. Kier's face flushed.

Let them laugh, he told himself. It wasn't much comfort, but it was all he had. A man his age should have been married, scoldin' lads of their own, or at the very least working alongside their da, not hangin' on their mother's apron strings. *I may be trailin' on her strings, but I'm the man of the house. It's up to me to look after her, and I can't support the both of us, and a wife as well.*

Kier glared at the girls as he quickened his step to catch up to ma. Wisps of her curly black hair had escaped her bonnet and danced in the breeze. She looked a fine picture in her best Sunday dress and a sash of the MacDuff plaid—evergreen on red with a sky-blue stripe—draped across her left shoulder.

Kier laughed to himself. *Half the clan will be at the ceremony and the wedding feast after. Perhaps she'll find another husband.*

"And what do you find to be so funny?" ma asked.

"Nothin', ma. 'Tis a fine day, that's all," he said with a smile.

"Fine?" ma said with a snort. "'Tis pure dreich! Moira should have waited until summer to be married."

"It doona matter to me what day a kinsman weds," Kier said with a shrug. "Whatever day it be on, Mr. MacDuff will close the warehouse for the day so we can all watch him get pished at the feast." Any day that he dinna have to shift bags of salt for the fish packers was a fine day indeed. His back still ached from yesterday's labors.

Their spirits rose as they neared the church, encountering cousins, uncles, and aunts they hadna seen since da's wake. There were many exclamations of "My, how you've grown," and, "Och! Yer a fine lad, takin' care of yer mother and all," followed by enough pats on the back to leave him feeling like he'd worked a full day after all.

Kier grit his teeth and smiled broadly through it all.

Ma, however, beamed from the praise, and seeing that it was all for her benefit, that was just as well. Each relation knew that Kier was only doing his duty, but such comments silently praised ma for raising him right. It was all done out of kindness as it gave them something nice to say instead of, "When will you finally wed, Kier?"

Two by two, they all filed into the warm chapel and took their seats. It looked as though half the clan had turned up for the ceremony. The small chapel was almost crowded as the ark... and just as noisy too! It wasn't until the groom entered that the din quieted enough for a man to even hear his own thoughts, let alone the person sitting next to them.

Kier dinna know the groom. He was still a member of the clan but from the opposite side. He also wasn't a young man. The groom's hair was strewn with gray, and he walked with a limp. If it weren't for the silver buckles on his shoes and the gold filigree hilt of his belt dagger, everyone would've wondered why Moira was wedding him at all.

No sooner was the groom at the altar then the bride entered the chapel. Everyone rose in a great wave that swelled from the back, where Kier and ma sat, to the couple's near kin at the front. The sight tugged at Kier's heart for it truly was like the sea—a wave of green and red, with white hair and shawls instead of foam at the crest. 'Twas a beautiful sight.

The bride wore a simple blue dress that perfectly matched the shade in the tartan. Her amber curls, pinned into a gentle cascade that fell down her back, were adorned with wood anemone. The tiny white heralds of spring were stars in an autumn sunset.

Kier wondered if the symbolism was intentional. It must have been, for he couldn't fathom Moira making light of the age difference between her and the groom on their wedding day.

"She looks so like her mother," ma whispered.

"Too bad the same can't be said about yer lad," the man sitting in front of her said with a sneer.

"Haud yer wheesht," ma hissed at him.

Kier held his breath as the bride passed on her way to the altar. He prayed to the saints that she hadn't heard what was said. Too many already had. At that moment, all eyes may have been on the bride, but all ears were turned to the three of them. Confusion, anger, and humiliation warred with each other in Kier's mind, each tried to sway him to run or shout or fight, and all while the bride floated up the aisle on a cloud of joy.

'Twas then that the man turned round. Ma gasped. No wonder too, for it was Angus Sherer, the man ma spurned to marry da. Though Kier desperately wanted to discredit the man's slanderous claim for that very reason, Angus' straight black hair made him pause. Both ma and da had curly hair, but Kier's was straight as a board and no one knew why. Aye, there were whispers that da dinna drown at sea, that instead he ran off with another woman, and that's why his body was never found.

Could it be… Nae, he's a jealous, lying bastard! He just wants to get under your skin. Kier turned to look at ma. Given how fast she turned her temper on him, he expected to see her ready to give him hell. Instead, her eyes were downcast.

Nae! It canna be true!

"Do you even know who fathered the lad?" Angus said.

Suddenly the conflicting emotions warring in Kier's mind came to an accord. He'd had enough of people whispering behind his back and doing nothing about it.

"I'm not a bastard," Kier growled.

He punched Angus in the nose. Blood splattered aunt Sarah, who sat next to him. Everyone around them gasped. Angus turned round and stepped up onto the pew, ready to leap over and continue what Kier had started. Before he did, strong arms reached from behind him and held him back. Another set of arms held Kier back as well.

The rest of the chapel's occupants peered over one another to see what the commotion was about. Kier saw Moira standing beside the groom, no longer floating on that cloud.

Ach! What have I done? I've ruined her wedding.

Angus spat at ma. In that moment all the remorse Kier felt for his actions disappeared. He launched himself anew at Angus with such fervor that his uncles struggled to hold him back.

"Get them oot a here!" someone shouted from the front of the chapel.

The current holding him back shifted in the blink of an eye and now swiftly carried him and Angus toward the door. The cool air outside, and the indignant stares of the guests displaced by the tide of uncles, doused much of the fire in his heart. But the remaining embers kindled a new fire, one of hatred. What right did they have to grouse? Kier may have started the fight, but he wasn't responsible for the slander—and that by far, was the worse offense. He was only defending his ma's honor, and as kin, they should have defended her—or at least used their sgian-dubh on Angus to keep the peace until the ceremony was over. The bastard deserved a good prick in the ribs.

Uncle Daegus, Moira's father, stormed out of the chapel with the fires of damnation burning in his eyes. "I dinna care who started this or why, but I'm ending it right now." There was an audible sigh of relief from the onlookers.

Uncle Daegus pointed at Angus. "You selfish arse! You just couldn't leave 'er be." Angus started to protest but uncle Daegus cut him off. "I want you oot of town immediately. If I see yer face again, there'll be steel between us instead of words."

Kier smiled. Finally, someone was putting Angus in his place! Angus was pale. He jerked his arms free of those that held him and ran up the lane. Kier dinna know what had passed before to make him fear Daegus so. He only knew that he ached to hear that tale.

"And you!" uncle Daegus spun on his heel to face Kier. "It'll be a miracle if the priest doona excommunicate ya for fightin' on holy ground."

Kier's smile vanished, and his head drooped. He couldn't look his uncle in the eye. Kier hadn't thought of that. He hadn't thought of anything other than beating Angus to a pulp. *Saints! What does that say about me?*

Uncle Daegus closed the gap between them and leaned in close, their faces a hairsbreadth apart. "It is only because you're my sister's lad that I'm not banishing you too. But I doona care to see you again either." Without another word he walked back into the chapel, and the others somberly followed.

Kier's jaw hung open in shock. He looked to ma, hoping she would have some sort of advice or consolation.

"Go," ma said with heartbreaking sadness. "Just go. We'll talk when I get home."

"No, ma," Kier said firmly. "I need to know if it's true."

Ma paused. "The man who raised you was your father."

Kier stood there frozen in disbelief as ma walked into the chapel, and the door closed behind her. *What sort of answer is that?* Kier preferred straightforward answers, and his ma's answer was both frustrating and oddly comforting. While he still dinna know if his da really was his da, her point that because he fulfilled those duties, was something that he'd not considered before. Be that as it may, Angus' words would likely haunt him the rest of his days because it marked him as a hothead in the eyes of the clan. He needed to cool off and figure out some way to get back into their good graces. Kier needed to prove that he was a man that they could rely on, not an impulsive and irrational lad.

He turned away and walked back the way he'd come. As he neared the docks, the comforting rush of the sea helped settle his agitated mind.

Kier made his way down to the seawall and peered over the top. Mad Mary still sat in her usual spot. However, the other women had left, and Mary wasn't singing. She stared at the net in her hands, as if she were unsure what to do with it. A funny thing that, seeing as a fishing net had only one purpose.

But Mary wasn't singing. That was like a summer without heather on the moor.

Kier walked over to the gap in the wall. He paused before crossing onto the sand. Even though he deeply wanted to find out what bothered Mary so, he was still in a lot of disfavor with the clan at the moment, and it wouldn't be long before the rest of town heard about it. If anyone saw him talking to her that would double the ostracizing when he returned.

He turned and looked down the length of the street. There weren't many people about, as most of them were either at the ceremony or seeing to the day's labors. It seemed that, this time, luck was on his side. He could sneak down and have a chat before anyone was the wiser.

Kier sighed in relief and stepped forward before anyone emerged. The second the soles of his boots touched the sand, a strong frigid wind hit him dead on and tried to push him back. Kier ducked his head and pressed on, his legs straining with every step. The gulls overhead seemed to cry "No! No!" which sent a shiver down his spine.

Don't be daft, he told himself. *It's just wind and some stupid birds. It's not an omen. Nature hasn't suddenly turned against you.*

If only thinking it could make it true, make him believe.

As soon as he reached the embers of the fishwives' abandoned fires, the wind ceased, and the gulls were silenced. Kier froze and held his breath. He stood there, waiting to see if the sand would try to swallow him up, until the needs of his lungs forced him to reconsider. Tentatively, he took a step forward. He waited a moment and then took another step.

Nothing happened.

Kier laughed in relief. However, his joy ceased the moment he noticed that the wind and gulls hadn't disappeared after all. The way the sand skittered along the shore made it clear that the wind indeed was still blowing. The gulls still flew nearby. Kier could see their beaks open and close as they shared their opinions on the weather, but he couldna hear a sound. Some unseen power was forcing both to pass around Kier and Mary in a wide arc. Was it a miracle? Fairy magic? Whatever it was made the hairs on his arms stand on end, but he'd come too far to turn back now. Kier continued his march across the sand.

He slowed a measure when he neared Mary, not wanting to spook her, and knelt at her feet. Her matted hair surrounded her face like a mourning veil. Ivory skin shone between the strands. The great folds of her cloak encompassed her so Kier couldna see form or limb. Maybe it was heresy, but he couldn't help thinking she looked like the Holy Virgin herself, kneeling below the cross, overcome with grief.

Her fishing net lay between them. The bone-white fibers looked as soft as linen. Kier, feeling quite brave, reached out with a trembling hand. The fibers were hard as stone and cold as the grave. Kier recoiled. The deathly chill seeped into his hand and made him shiver. Mary dinna seem to notice his reaction. In fact, she dinna seem to have noticed him at all.

"What troubles ye, Mary?"

Mad Mary looked at him with sad eyes that shone through the tangle. She stared at him silently. Mary inhaled deeply, as if she were about to speak, but then released it in a rush. The slump of her shoulders gave Kier the impression that it wasnae that Mary was incapable of speaking. It was that she dinna want to speak but felt compelled to anyway. On the third attempt Mary's head fell in shame as the words finally slipped out.

> *"'Tis the finest net for all to see,*
> *But I have no man to cast for me."*

She sang! Kier almost fell over from the intoxicating mix of joy, relief, concern, and pity that coursed through him. But swelling underneath all of that was pride. For the first time today he had done something right. She sang just for him, and there was naught he wouldn't do for her in that moment.

"I can cast it for ye, but I doona have a boat," Kier said.

Mary's eyes were downcast. She looked more ashamed than before, which confused Keir, for the words came out more easily than before.

> *"A boat lies yonder,*
> *Seaworthy is she.*
> *Will ye no squander*
> *This golden opportunity?"*

Mary pointed at the shoreline, where a gleaming silvery boat floated solitary on the shallows. The sun-bleached wood shone like polished silver, and the single canvas sail, rigged and begging to be unfurled, were black as night.

Kier rubbed his eyes. He could have sworn that boat hadn't been there a moment ago. 'Twas passing strange. Perhaps the color was why he dinna see it before? It did blend in a bit. 'Twas then that Kier remembered the time. The tide was going out.

Though Kier was no experienced seaman—Da only took him out twice before his death—he knew they dinna have long to leave the shore. He'd have a hard time of it anyway. Even though the craft was small, he would be hard pressed to tend the sail and steer at the same time.

Sailing with da... If he did this, he would be gone long enough to be missed, long enough for rumors to spread that he'd left just as da had. But Mary needed his help... It was a chance to be on the water again... and truth be told, after what happened at the church, he needed to be someone's hero right now.

With a deep breath, he steeled himself against the unnatural feel of that net and picked it up. It was unnaturally heavy.

"I shall return with the catch."

"For this favor, a boon ye shall receive.
On this voyage I shall accompany thee."

Kier's eyes widened. This was a complete surprise. While it wasnae unheard of for a woman to sail, 'twas custom for them to stay ashore. Having a woman aboard brought bad luck. Kier squared his shoulders and readied himself to tell her as much. Mary looked up at him, and that one action took the wind out of him. He still couldna see her face through the bramble, but there was no doubt in his mind she was no longer downcast. Mary was looking at him.

Kier surrendered with a smile. "Hard work though it may be, the voyage will be bonnie with your company."

Mary laughed softly. Kier, feeling quite proud, extended his arm, and Mary rose to take it. They walked in silence to Mary's vessel which bobbed on the surf. Kier was too overjoyed to ruin the moment with words.

They continued into the surf, side by side. The brisk water soaked into their clothes, first at their ankles, then their calves, their knees, and finally their thighs by the time they reached the boat. He carefully placed the net inside before helping Mary climb aboard. However, as soon as the net touched the bottom the boat sank until the keel almost touched the sand. He'd have a harder time pushing the boat out, but at least it made it easier for Mary to climb in. Kier dinna need to give her a leg up. Just a steadying hand as she hoisted herself over the side and settled down on a bench at the stern.

Kier braced his right shoulder against the stern and pushed with all his might. The boat had barely moved when a soft tap on his left shoulder made him pause. Kier looked up to find Mary leaning over the side. She pointed to a small seat at the center of the boat, next to where he'd laid the net. *Was that seat there before? It must have been, surely.*

"You want me to sit there?" Kier asked.

Mary nodded.

He cocked his head at her, puzzled. "We canna go anywhere if I don't push this boat further out."

Mary simply sat there, calm as can be, and pointed again.

Kier sighed, waded to the prow of the boat, and carefully climbed in. Seawater dripped from his soaked kilt and pooled around his feet as he sat down.

Mary threw her head back and whispered something unintelligible. A moment later Kier heard a soft rustling behind him. He turned and saw the ropes that bound the sail to the yardarm were untying themselves!

Kier scrambled away from Mary until his back hit the prow. "What sorcery is this?"

> *"You do not fear the wind and wave,*
> *Do not fear these unseen hands, be brave.*
> *'Tis not sorcery, nor magic of mankind,*
> *But the souls of angels, in service confined."*

"Invisible angels?" Kier felt his forehead. He wasnae feverish. Was she telling the truth? He wanted to believe her, but this was too wondrous strange.

The sail, now unbound, fell between them and fluttered in the soft breeze. The yardarm twisted to greet the breeze entire. The breeze swiftly became a strong wind, filling the sail and propelling the boat out to sea. With the wind in his face and the sea beneath him, Kier normally would have relaxed, but this was too strange. What if she was a witch casting some sort of spell?

The wind had propelled them far enough out that Kier felt certain that if he jumped out and tried to swim back he'd likely drown. Reluctantly, Kier ducked under the sail and resumed his seat. He wasn't comfortable being so close to Mary, but at least he could keep an eye on her.

They sailed for perhaps an hour, out toward May Island—an odd direction that, and even more odd that the "angels" continued to tend the sail. When they were within sight of the island, the "angels" turned the sail out of the wind and let the craft drift to a dead stop. The boat bobbed on the water, and Kier was afraid to speak first.

> *" 'Tis here you cast,*
> *And here your labor, last.*
> *Your reward for this casting,*
> *This catch, shall be everlasting."*

Kier, ducked under the sail, regarded her suspiciously. "Might I ask what that reward may be?"

Mary dinna answer. She merely sat there like a statue.

Kier sighed. *I suppose it's too late to change my mind. We're already out here. The faster I get this over with the faster I can get back home.*

He crouched down and hefted the net. Carefully, he carried it to the side and tied it to the rope that, unsurprisingly, waited there, secured and ready. The net was too heavy to toss out, so instead he slid the edge over the side and let its own weight carry it down. As the length of it slid through his hands, a glint of gold caught his eye. He tightened his grip on the net to slow it down, in order to get a better look.

Kier gasped. Encircling one of the bone-white cables on the net was an iron ring with an anchor carved onto it... exactly like the one his da had worn. It wasn't until that moment that he finally understood what ma had told him hours ago. The man that fate had torn from them was truly his da, and the injustice of that stirred his anger as he stared at the ring on the net.

"Mary," he said tersely. "Where did ye get this?" Kier held up the section in question, the ring clearly visible.

Mary turned away, pretending not to hear.

Kier leaned over and thrust the ring in her face. "Where did you get my da's ring? He died wearing it!"

Those four words echoed in his mind. He died wearing it... he died wearing... he died...

Kier stared at the net and its white fibers too stiff to be rope. *But stiff enough to be bone.*

Kier dropped the net, watching in horror as the net and his father's ring slid into the sea. For the briefest of moments, he thought to go after it, but no. It was tied off. He could retrieve it after he dealt with her. Kier turned again to Mary. "You killed him!"

He reached out to grab her by the throat, but a cold wet hand seized his before he could lay a finger on her. A creature with the head and torso of a man, but the tail of a fish sat on an ocean spray. *Finfolk? But they're just stories!* The Finman pulled Kier away from Mary with inhuman strength.

Mary screeched, a horrible ear-splitting sound that changed pitches. The Finman responded with a similar chilling cry before he grabbed Kier by the collar and lifted him up 'til his feet dangled a foot off the deck. Pain, hot and sharp, suddenly spread throughout Kier's entire body. Gritting his teeth against the pain, Kier lifted his fist to punch the Finman, only to find that he no longer had a hand. What had been his hand was only bone surrounded by a sickly green light.

"What are you doing to me, you devil?"

But before he got an answer, the pain intensified, and Kier ceased being aware of anything at all.

Mary watched as her lover turned the man's flesh into pure liquid light, the ambrosia of the sea, and then drank every drop. Within an hour all that was left of the human was a pile of bones.

Her lover wiped his mouth with one hand while commanding the sea to deposit her net into the boat. The sea gently laid the bone net she'd carefully made over the years upon the deck. The kind waters even folded it for her.

> *"Has thy hunger been sated,*
> *Oh, tell me my love?*
> *Is it my doom to be fated,*
> *Forever to toil up above?*
>
> *I long to wed thee,*
> *To bed thee, my love*
> *How long 'til I am free*
> *Of that which, upon me thou didst behove?"*

With a voiceless command, Mad Mary's love bade the winds to change course, to blow her silvery vessel back to shore. Tears fell behind her bramble veil as she sang to the sea and the sky of gray, pale.

> *"Another span I'm cursed to toil.*
> *Another span far from home.*
> *Another man to ensorcell,*
> *While on the beach they comb."*

From the Author

I wrote this story for a friend who was in need of dark, sea creature stories. I'd just finished an *Outlander* binge, and I was curious if I could write something using those speech patterns and style. I love how certain characters in the show don't just recount events. They spin a yarn and draw you in with their cadence and that alluring accent, and that's what I tried to recreate. Later the story turned into a bit of a fable, so I decided to incorporate a little poetry to give it a touch of the fey. What could be more beguiling than one of the fair folk asking for a favor?

About the Author

Kim May has always been a storyteller—just ask her mother. On second thought don't. She knows too much. Kim writes fantasy, sci-fi, thrillers, historical fiction, steampunk, and a bit of poetry, because she collects genres like a cat lady collects strays.

Kim lives in Oregon, where she works at an independent bookstore and watches a lot of anime. She's a retired stage actor and has a penchant for fast cars, high heels, and loose screws.

You can follow her on Facebook, Twitter, and at ninjakeyboard.blogspot.com.

Blog: ninjakeyboard.blogspot.com

Moonflower: books2read.com/u/mv5ZG8

The Closed Game: books2read.com/u/3yvY1l

Dinah and the Fox Sorcerer

by
Stephannie Tallent

Dinah and the Fox Sorcerer

*D*inah blinked.

The Chinese man was still there, strolling down the muddy, wheel-rutted Main Street of West Jordan, jewel-encrusted crimson silk robe glittering in the hot early afternoon August sun.

Steam from the mud puddles licked around the Chinese man's cream leather boots and the hem of his robe, but not a spot of mud dared to mar either boots or robe.

The sleeves of his robe draped over his hands, but Dinah bet his hands were soft and his nails manicured. His long narrow queue danced around his shoulders like a string to a kite being tossed by a breeze. That same soft wind blew the scents of sage, mint, and chrysanthemum tea towards her.

His cheekbones were sharp as knives, his black eyes glinting and prideful. He looked like a prince in the prime of life, something out of a fairy tale Dinah's mama had told her when Dinah was just a child. When Dinah was content and safe and loved, with her mama and papa. 'Stead of always on edge, wondering if she could earn enough for a meal after paying for her mule Malyu's feed.

Two uncanny, sandy-colored foxes gamboled behind the Chinese man, their pale paws as pristine as his boots. Spirit foxes, in material form. One glanced at her, tongue lolling in a vulpine smirk, white teeth gleaming, as it—he—bounced along. The smaller fox yipped and barked, amber eyes flashing as she glanced at Dinah.

No one else reacted. 'Course, there weren't many people out in the late summer monsoon mugginess.

The next block over, the young black hostler, Jimmy, led a fine little black-and-white paint mare to the livery behind the town's single boarding house. That little mare would join Malyu, tucked away with fresh hay.

Dinah liked Jimmy. He'd slipped Malyu a treat of sweet oats the night before and laid out fresh hay for Dinah to sleep on.

Closer to, Mrs. McKinney, pale pretty face pinched and dour in the shade of her bonnet, left the two-story general store with a basket of apples and a small roll of lace ribbon, gingham skirts swishing along.

And heading right towards Dinah and the Chinese man, Deputy Batson strolled down the street to the adobe building that served as his office and jail, touching his fingers to his felted wool fedora as he passed Mrs. McKinney. Mrs. McKinney nodded to him, but her eyes skated right past Dinah's when she walked by Dinah. To her, Dinah was lower than the fat ruby-carapaced dung beetles rolling around in the street near the horse droppings, and not near as pretty.

'Course Deputy Batson didn't bother tipping his hat to Dinah, neither. He tolerated her, but that was it.

Not a one even seemed to see the Chinese man and his foxes.

Dinah trusted her instincts. And her instincts were screaming that if no one else saw this man strolling down the center of Main Street, brazen as a snake oil salesman, like he owned every last building and every single person in town, she ought to pretend she couldn't see him either. She knew, better than most, the prejudice against Chinese, being herself the daughter of a Chinese prostitute.

But she doubted someone so proud and aristocratic would hide his presence, unless he had a nefarious purpose.

She could discover that purpose later. Right now, she slunk back into the narrow, shaded passageway between the saloon and boarding house, ignoring the pungent stink of piss. Luckily, she dressed like a boy: blunt toed leather boots, heavy canvas pants, and a loose-fitting shirt with a wool vest to hide her slim figure. No long skirts to drag in the muck.

Her long glossy hair was tied up in a loose bun off her neck, tucked up under a black wool felt hat. Sweat traced a warm wet trail down her spine.

Dinah hoped the Chinese sorcerer (for what else could he be, with those two fox spirits?) didn't catch a taste of her own small, lonely magics on the breeze.

She bit at a hangnail, drawing a rusty-tasting drop of blood that she smeared on the silver look-away charm she wore on a leather lace around her neck.

It seemed to work. Leastwise no fox or sorcerer turned down the passageway to confront her. Rather, they continued right on down the street, those foxes yapping as they pounced after grasshoppers coming to take sips of the rain puddles.

Dinah reckoned herself a cautious woman. As a bounty hunting, problem-solving, sorceress for hire, driven by her need for justice in a land that served little, aided by her own magics inherited from her mama, she had to be cunning and prudent and wary.

Not someone who'd let curiosity gnaw at her belly til she left that passageway to follow the sorcerer.

But that's what Dinah did.

The Chinese sorcerer set up camp a couple miles out of the far side of town, in the clearing under the desert willow trees that encircled the spring feeding Scott's Creek, the source of West Jordan's sweet water supply. Thick chaparral, snowberry, and juniper grew intermixed with the trees on either side of the trail leading up to the spring.

Dinah didn't take the trail.

She circled 'round to the far side of the spring, then laid down and crawled on her belly through the needle grass, under and around the scrub and rocks, til she found a suitable spot tucked behind a dreamy willow. She could see the sorcerer and still be downwind from those foxes. Aromatic creosote, piney and lemony, flavored the muggy air. She hoped it would help cover the stench of her sweat.

One fox lounged on a plush red rug in front of a small cream-colored silk tent. The tent was four feet tall, just big enough to give shelter to a thick pile of embroidered blankets and silk pillows.

The other fox lapped water from the clear spring, then dabbed a paw in, likely trying for a trout or crawdad.

The sorcerer tended a small ornate brass brazier, feeding it dried sticks and herbs. His over-robe hung from a branch, leaving him in heavy draping silk trousers and a woven linen shirt, the latter sheer in the leaf-dappled sunlight, showing off a mighty fine torso.

A wisp of sage-scented smoke wafted towards Dinah's hiding place, tickling her nose and watering her eyes. She kept staring, though, til she sneezed. Couldn't help herself.

The sneezing or the staring.

He didn't even look up, just kept feeding the brazier. "You might as well come over here," he said, his voice smooth as his silk trousers that outlined everything. Everything.

Dinah wasn't the sort to be distracted by matters of the flesh. No, she was not. No matter how pretty that flesh was. No matter how lonely she was.

The sorcerer smiled, a soft quirk of his upper lip, and added more herbs. Mint joined the sage, and Dinah parted her lips with the thought of how the sorcerer must taste, bright and fresh and sweet, those finely shaped lips of his against hers.

She knew some folks who were obsessed with earthly pleasures. Men who'd gambled away their ranches and cattle to try to win the attention of a woman, women who'd left their families to be in the arms of a scoundrel. She'd never understood it before. She'd seen the physical scars her mama bore, from before meeting Dinah's father, from clients savage with lust, and recognized the emotional scars that only her papa had healed.

Dinah didn't trust the idea of physical passion, and she was glad she herself had never desired anyone before. She was alone. By choice.

But now, a pulsing ached between her legs, a desperate need to go over to him, run her hands against that heavy silk of his trousers, even smooth her hands up under that linen shirt, stroking that muscled belly.

The sorcerer sprinkled fragments of dried yellow petals over the brazier. The scent of tea, invigorating and sharp, made her whole body tingle like it never had before.

The fox on the rug yipped and rolled over, waving those cute little dipped-in-cream paws in the air, brown eyes bright.

The fox that had been drinking from the spring shook itself off and trotted to the sorcerer, weaving around and between his legs like a big friendly tomcat.

Jealousy stabbed her. Why should that creature touch him, and not her?

"Come, do not fight it," cajoled the sorcerer.

And Dinah couldn't. Couldn't resist. Didn't even want to, anymore. She rose to her knees.

Mrs. McKinney appeared from behind one of the desert willows next to the trail, opposite to Dinah's hiding spot. Her blue gingham skirt was all stained with leaves and trail muck.

She walked right up to the sorcerer and sank into his arms with a sigh that turned to a deep throated moan, rubbing herself against him like a barn cat in heat.

Dinah gaped, her mind suddenly sharp, an icy chill running through her core.

She fumbled in her bag of charms hanging from her belt, finding the brass-plated mountain lion tooth charm. A charm for protection. She grabbed her knife out of its scabbard next to the charm bag and sliced the meat at the base of her left thumb, coating the charm with her blood, turning that brass into a stormfront sunset.

Dinah hoped the charm would be powerful enough.

The sorcerer quirked a fine eyebrow at Dinah's hiding place as he lowered his lips to Mrs. McKinney's and wrapped his lean muscled arms around her.

He kissed Mrs. McKinney hard, not even letting up for a breath until Mrs. McKinney swooned, then kept kissing her, til her face sunk in and her skin dried up and flaked away, til he was holding nothing but what looked like a rat caught up somewhere it couldn't get out, and it was three months later, all papery skin and brittle bones.

The little foxes danced around the two of them all the while, yipping and waving their bushy tails around as he sucked the life force out of Mrs. McKinney.

The sorcerer dropped what was left of Mrs. McKinney and stretched his arms to the sky in satisfaction. His heavy trousers were damp in the front.

Dinah figured he'd had a mighty good time, killing Mrs. McKinney.

Dinah wasn't ignorant. Just usually uninterested.

"Come out, come out," the sorcerer crooned, his voice trying to sneak through the charm's protections.

"I don't want any of what you're offering," Dinah called back. Nonetheless, she left her place behind the willow tree and stopped a few yards away from the sorcerer. She kept that brazier of his, still smoking tea and mint and sage, between the two of them.

She glanced at what remained of Mrs. McKinney. The larger fox, the male, was pawing at her gingham dress and shredding off bits of blue-checked fabric, tossing them in the air, batting at them. That seemed to bore him after a few moments, and he started digging and tearing through a sleeve til he got an arm bone. He settled down and began gnawing on it. It cracked like a gunshot when the fox broke it in two.

The other fox, the littler one, sat by the sorcerer's side, her amber eyes glinting in sly foxy amusement.

"What about," the sorcerer said, "the power to control the storms?" A shadow dashed over the clearing.

Dinah looked up straight overhead. Sure enough, monsoon storm clouds were roiling in, thunderheads heavy and dark with the devastating potential to cause floods and wildfires. Lightning itched at her palms, longing to be set free.

Her lion's-tooth charm flared, a spot of grounding heat against her left palm.

"The power to make those townspeople respect you, despite your birth. Despite the foreign cast to your features."

The charm burned hotter.

"Do you know what she was thinking, your Mrs. McKinney? What she feared?" he said softly. "Her foremost thought was not that she was dying. Rather, she couldn't face herself being willingly despoiled by a Chinaman.

"That's what they think of you, even when they hire you to hunt down their missing cattle, or discover who is cheating them, or whatever of the dozens of menial tasks they have you do. That you're nothing but occasionally useful trash."

Power. Power to never fear anyone again, power to give herself a life of luxury, power to be safe. Power to force folks to meet her eyes as an equal, not some bit of filth.

People killed each other for power.

Dinah didn't like to kill. She certainly did not like other folks trying to kill her.

She shook her head. "I don't want them to fear me, and that's all you're truly offering."

And she'd never, ever be safe. Always on guard, til someone managed to slit her throat out of fear or covetousness.

The charm cooled in her hand.

The storm clouds scudded away, taking away the lightning that wanted to nestle inside her.

The sorcerer gazed at Dinah, eyes narrowing, calculating. He quirked an eyebrow, kneeled to pat the little fox's head, then stood.

"So. Neither lust, nor power, is enough for you. Huli Fang," he said, "go to her."

The little fox, Huli Fang, trotted over to Dinah and raised one creamy paw up to her.

"You are lonely," the sorcerer said. "I offer you Huli Fang. She will be your lifelong companion, always loving you, never leaving you. Your most trusted confident, the other half of your heart."

The charm burned so hot Dinah dropped it.

It exploded before it hit the ground, fragments of molten brass and ivory tooth flashing like stars. Some brass splattered on her left hand, scorching it, and she wiped her hand against her trousers furiously, tears streaming down her cheeks.

A chasm of loneliness, deep and lost, lay open and uncovered in her heart. Dinah knew it was truly there. All her life, since her mama and papa died, she'd been covering that hole with learning and travelling and work. Always alone, not fitting in with her papa's fancy people back East, who were aghast he'd settled with a Chinese woman. Never fitting in with the Chinese here, her mama a prostitute, lowest of the low.

That oubliette of misery and loneliness had grown deeper and deeper over the years, like an abandoned mine shaft being eaten away by an underground river.

Didn't matter that the charm was destroyed. It never could protect against this.

Dinah stroked Huli Fang's soft head. Like silk, her fur was. The fox licked her burnt hand, cooling it.

Dinah took one step, two, three towards the sorcerer. Mint and tea and sage swirled around her. Huli Fang walked with her, pressing her warm furry body close against Dinah's leg.

His handsome face relaxed, and she held out her burnt left hand to him. He took it, drawing her to him. His warm touch soothed the burns on her hand. His black eyes, amused and intrigued, met hers.

He smiled at her, and Dinah smiled right back.

She stabbed him in the heart with the knife held in her right hand. Aimed between his ribs, slipping in like a freshwater eel amongst the marsh grass.

He pushed her away, stumbling against the brazier, knocking it over, scattering the remaining bits of herbs and leaves. Dark crimson heart's blood drenched that fine linen shirt of his, molding it to his torso. The storm clouds rushed across the sky, and lightning struck a desert willow across the spring. Torrential rain doused any burning bits left over from the brazier.

Hail stones the size of peas pelted Dinah, the bite of each icy stone bringing her back to herself.

He fell, gasping, a bewildered look in his eyes. It didn't take long for him to die, those black pupils dilating, the wide deep darkness echoing the chasm in her heart. His handsome face, so smooth and pretty, dried up til he looked like what was left of Mrs. McKinney: a husk devoid of any remnant of life.

The hail stopped and the rain petered out.

The foxes, Huli Fang and her mate, their fur matted and soaked, stood stock still, gaping at her, jaws loose.

"Git," she said, dry-eyed, mopping rain from her brow. "I don't want you anyways."

Dinah hiked back to town, carrying a makeshift bundle made of the sorcerer's tent, filled with his charms and other sorcerous paraphernalia. She'd study it all later, when she reached a safe spot away from West Jordan.

Dinah couldn't stay in West Jordan. She needed to pack up her mule, Malyu, and leave. Mrs. McKinney was going to be missed, if she wasn't already, and who better to blame than the half Chinese girl who tried to pass as a boy, and studied and used dark magics to boot?

Dinah didn't relish the thought of a noose around her neck. She'd seen that happen to enough people she knew were innocent, but whose foreign features or dark skin condemned them despite any inconvenient truths.

The foxes had run away after she rejected them. She couldn't forget seeing the male fox chewing on Mrs. McKinney's arm bone, sucking out the last bits of marrow. If they had minds enough to choose her, Dinah, (and that's the only way she'd have one as a companion), they had minds enough to have chosen the sorcerer and partaken in his wickedness.

That she couldn't abide.

She sorrowed for Mrs. McKinney, that sad weak woman, even though Mrs. McKinney wouldn't have thought twice about her. Or once, for that matter.

Sorrowed even more for the heady crazy rush of riding the storm clouds blowing across the sky, lightning in her hands.

Sorrowed about that chasm of loneliness, plunging deep into her heart, unfilled.

But she wasn't sorry for herself.

From the Author

Take a step sideways from our reality to enter Dinah's Weird Western world.

I love Dinah.

She's gutsy, but lonely as all get out. She's seeking to replace the family she lost—though she doesn't even know that herself—but is isolated by her parentage, gender, and chosen profession. She's not perfect: she's impetuous and headstrong.

But she always means well, and she would place herself in danger to protect an innocent.

I want her to be happy, but it's not an easy road for her.

And I love the setting, the grandeur, of the American Southwest. I'll always be an ocean-loving woman, but the desert draws me too, in all its variety and beauty. Writing about Dinah lets me immerse myself in the region—the history, the variety of flora, the geology, and of course the animals.

Welcome to the Weird Western world of Dinah, sorceress for hire.

About the Author

Stephannie Tallent lived in Phoenix while in middle and high school. After graduating from The United States Military Academy at West Point in 1989, she completed the Military Intelligence Officer's Basic Course in Fort Huachuca, Arizona.

She developed a love for the American Southwest, especially the Sonoran Desert.

A few years ago, Stephannie published a collection of knitting patterns with the theme of the Wild West, inspired by the flora, fauna, and geology of the American Southwest.

It's no surprise that one of her fantasy series, featuring the sorceress Dinah Lee Wright, takes place in an alternate American West, populated with beings from folklore and magic, permeated with the history, vegetation, and real creatures of the area.

Check out her website at www.stephannietallent.com.

Folly
An Essay of Creative Nonfiction
by
Marie Whittaker

Folly

I love the canopy of self-importance that floats, or presides, over a child's view of the world she graces with her presence. That feeling, that the world, in its entirety, evolved around you and the thing you decided to do or say next. The people in China, for instance—who I surely would have met if I'd kept digging that hole in the backyard, just like my father said—did not go about their day. They waited to see what I was up to, and then adjusted accordingly. At four years old, I was the center of the world, and it turned in rhythm to the cadenced beat of my Mary Jane shoes.

My parents loved me better than anyone else could. It was the two of them, my toddling brother, and me. They all had patience to spare, and they needed every drop of that virtue when I was awake. My mother was the most intelligent, the kindest, and the most beautiful lady ever. My father said these things were true, as well, and therefore the rest of the world knew it, too. I often tested her knowledge by asking her questions. For instance, I did so during one of the many times I slammed my scuffed, patent leather shoe down repeatedly to get my clammy little foot inside. In my mind, bothersome and simple things—like things called shoes, and the reasons for wearing them—were a mystery.

Why ... STOMP ... do I ... STOMP ... have to ... STOMP ... put these ... STOMP ... on?

"Momma?"

"Mm hm?"

"Why is a shoe a shoe?"

"Because it goes on your foot."

No! Look at it! I stomped my foot and jabbed a finger at my shoe. "Why is it a *shoe?*"

"Do you mean, why do we call it a shoe?"

"Yeah." *It's like birds and horses. God named the birds and horses.*

"Because when people made them, that's what they named them."

She'd blown my mind by telling me that people named things they invented, and only God ever named animals and big things, like clouds, the sun, the moon and the stars and it was because he had also made them. She knew everything. My mother told my grandmother about my questioning her. Grandma had smiled that all-knowing smile, the one that only grandmas are allowed, and said to my mother, "She's *articulate*, isn't she?" and she'd hugged me and given me one of her cookies.

ArCHOColate, I thought my grandmother had said. *That's special.*

"I'm ar-chocolate!" I announced to Daddy when we got home.

He laughed. "Why, yes you are," he said.

Momma laughed, too. I smiled and blinked my huge eyes at them through my big glasses.

I'm sure I got into more trouble than the average four-year-old. For instance, there was one occasion that I was caught— more ratted out, really, by the neighbor—doing something that I knew I shouldn't have been doing. The neighbor lady and my mother had a habit of calling to each other from yard to yard, or from window to window, whichever was the given case for the day, to hem and haw and to impress each other with any newfound knowledge about who was "carrying on" with who, and all.

I had come across a dead finch in the yard, beside ours and our neighbor's houses. The bird was lying on its fluffy little side, sunshine reflecting oil and water against his wing. I'd never seen a wild bird up close before, so I was drawn to examine it. Closely. And besides, it was dead, and Death, the Ender of All Things Wonderful, like the bird, was *huge*. Its legs and feet were tiny, delicate sticks of yellow. Its eyes were closed in that forever-sleep that begins to haunt the dreams of children as soon as they overhear adults talking about the death of a loved one, or an acquaintance, and all the subsequent explanations about the horrible pain Death's victim had suffered.

I was heartbroken. Tears cleared shiny trails through the day's worth of dirt and smattering of jelly, or possibly catsup, on my cheeks, so much so that when I reached beneath my thick glasses to wipe my eyes—wetness that immediately transferred onto my sleeve—muddy tears streaked brown onto my shirt. I sent one bold finger to stroke the top of the finch's head. If you'd asked me, I wasn't actually misbehaving.

I'm sorry. I wish you could fly. I'm sorry it hurt. You're soft. And your leg is a little toothpick. Did you have a baby egg? Don't see none, and now you died and hurt, and I'm crying 'cause you hurt…

"Hey Anna! Your daughter's over here playin' with a dead bird!"

No! I'm saying sorry! I didn't play with it, I petted his little head is all, and one little foot is all, and I told him sorry and she is way over there in the window and she didn't see I told him sorry and I'm sad…

"Molly, get over here! You know better than that."

… and up now I'm up, Momma, and I'm not even close to him…

Not a year later I watched from the window of the little house that my father built, with his blistered hands and wrenched, tired back, as the neighbor lady's three-story, turn-of-the-century Victorian burned to its cracked foundation. That house screamed and fought for hours until its flaming battle was lost, sending iridescent puffs of sparkly embers into the night air and throwing gyrating shadows of red and orange across that side yard between our houses.

The neighbor lady moved away, creating the small window required by fate to bless my young life by sending my best childhood friend, Heidi and her little sister, Heather, into my life.

Heidi's grandparents bought the destroyed lot, cleared the Victorian house's charred bones and, over the span of about nine months, built a modest, ranch-style home, complete with an accessible, sliding glass door that opened onto the side lot. We would come close to wearing out the tracks on that door. My father fixed the screen that slid in front of it, many times. He was good at fixing just about anything, and he worked harder than anyone I knew then and anyone I know now.

When I was almost four, he'd begun pouring the concrete foundation for the little house—the sanctuary of my memories—that cradled my childhood. After the foundation cured, I learned, next came framing the floors and then the walls. My father knew these things. He was a genius. He was the strongest. He could build houses.

And when I was with him, I could build houses, too.

True to genius form, my dad began the work that would be done outdoors in the spring of my fourth year. By the time the framed walls had gone up, the August sun would rise on those beautiful mornings when it was just he and I on our jobsite. The sunshine was more brilliant than it is now, having the power to create the perfect Hopscotch squares from skeleton shadows of the framed walls. My chosen daily attire, my *haut couture*, was cut off jeans from the last winter and my prized pair of beat-up, manure-crusted, cowboy boots that I refused to outgrow.

I would clomp across the particle-board floor to the building materials and fill my little ice cream bucket with nails that I would give to my dad, one by one, in the proper position to be driven into the wood by the solid smacks of his carpenter's hammer. I thought I was an equal part of that lop-sided team, thanks to the patience in my dad's voice when he gave me my instructions, which, I was sure, could be done correctly by only me when we worked on the house.

"Go get you some of those sixteen-penny nails, Scooter."

That's me! I'm the scooter. Not nobody else! Six pennies is the big ones, hurry up...

"The sixteen-pennies are the long ones."

"I know!" *Hurry up! Ow! Pokey! Don't cry, get more. That's enough.*

"Okay, now hand me some."

"Here you go!" *It goes with the head up. Watch for him to be ready. Now! Heads up!*

I'd handed him those nails one at a time, and he'd not said a word about the empty pocket on his tool pouch, where he would normally keep them. Sweat would stream silvery, reflective trails from under his hat to his jaw while he worked. It would drip from the end of his nose if we were kneeling on the floor. The band of his ball cap would darken with sweat throughout our days. At night, we would go inside, and he would take off his hat, empty the pockets of his jeans into it and leave it laying, full of wonders, on the dining room table. The contents would vary little from night to night; an occasional nail or drill bit, his utility knife, which was deadly sharp and not to be touched, and, best of all things I would find as I rifled through, his spare change. His *pennies*.

Pennies, both silver and gold ones, were symbolic of power. A penny was a line of demarcation. With a penny in my hand, I had the power to obtain for myself a number of things from the store up the road. If I put a penny in the slot of one machine, I would get a silver ring, or perhaps a necklace. Another would give me a gumball. If I had a penny, I could do this for myself without asking for a single thing; I would have to ask for no penny, no assistance, and no permission.

Getting a penny was the tricky part.

Sometimes, he'd take off his hat before we went inside, and I would be honored by being chosen to carry it for him while he wiped the sweat from his face with a bandana. Daddy's hat would be warm from the heat of the day, wet in some places, so I'd carry it by its bill. It smelled of all day in the sun, salty sweat, a smattering of occasional raindrops, and faded *Old Spice*—all things Daddy. I loved that hat. It was Daddy's King-of-the-House-Builders crown.

But I stole out of it anyway. I was four when I began sifting through the hat's contents and filching my father's change.

I asked at first. He looked into his hat and replied, simply. "There isn't enough for everybody."

And there it was.

He had unknowingly launched my short-lived life of crime. In telling me that there wasn't enough for everybody—everybody in this case meaning the slobbery, attention monger that I was to refer to as "my baby brother", my father had actually given me his permission to help myself to his pennies. He *wanted* me to have his pennies. So, I would wait till no one was in the dining room, start some nursery rhyme marching out a cadence in my mind, and quickly scale a chair and stab my hand to the bottom of the contents of the hat. In one fluid motion I would fly down from the table and jamb the change into my pocket, or my underwear if I wasn't wearing clothes with a pocket that day, and then high-step-it to *Humpty Dumpty* or *Peas Porridge Hot* as I ran to my room and stashed my booty in the bottom drawer of my pastel-pink jewelry chest. It was our unspoken secret, Daddy and I. And besides, I was sure I would never get caught. I was that good.

More than once my mother had found a nickel or dime stuck to one cheek when she put me in the bath before bed at night.

"What's this?" she'd asked, feigning wonder as she held it up.

"A penny," I stated. *"Achew ... achew!"*

I'd learned that nothing could change the subject faster than a sneezing fit out of nowhere.

By the time I was almost five, we had finally moved into the house that my father built for us. I'd continued helping to build it, learning things as the process unfolded, including the art of finishing out a heater duct by fastening a vented cover over the rectangular hole with a screwdriver and four screws. There was one such heater vent low on the wall in my new bedroom, and my Barbie doll would dry off inside it after she swam in the stock tank that our horses drank out of.

Once, Barbie had gone for a swim in a fresh rain puddle in the backyard and found a pet worm. I'd forgotten about him, and he'd dried with her in that heater vent, finding his way to Earth Worm Heaven as he was tightly wrapped around her wrist. The end result was something I found to make a rather fabulous, glamorous, bangle style bracelet when Barbie wore her sock-dress.

I wasn't supposed to take the cover off the vent. That would be un-building something that my father worked hard to build. My heater vent gradually took the place of the drawer on my jewelry chest where I kept my stash of change. It was a super-secret.

My baby brother was smarter than he was given credit for being. Once, after I'd just taken a penny and hid it, I returned to the dining room to find him sitting on the kitchen table, pulling the contents out of Daddy's hat. My blood chilled. He was going to give me away and there was not a thing I could do to get him down without our parents finding out, because the moment I touched him he would scream like a banshee to get Momma's attention. I would be in trouble for teaching him about Daddy's hat. My course of action was laid out for me however, because the thing my baby brother withdrew from the hat was not a penny, it was the sheathed utility knife.

I screamed for my mother and launched myself onto the table, grabbing the slobbery hand that was wrapped around the knife. As expected, the baby screamed and growled at me, howled at the top of his lungs for Momma, and even bit me. I shook and cried and got the knife away from him. He cried and sobbed in stuttering, angry breaths.

Momma ran into the dining room and snatched him up off the tabletop. She watched as I dropped the slimy knife back into the hat. I was crying so hard I almost fell from the table, so she picked me up and put me on her other hip. The baby screamed anew, enraged at my intrusion. I wrapped my arms around her neck and hung on to my half of her.

"He can walk," I snuffled into her shoulder. "Watch when he doesn't know you're there."

"I know he can walk, Molly."

From that point on, Daddy left his utility knife in his tool pouch, and I didn't find it in his hat again. I was happy to accompany anyone to the store because I had the power of pennies with me. No one questioned where I got my pennies, and if I ran out, I would simply get more.

Just before Thanksgiving, I hurt myself when I was climbing the chair to get to the hat. I banged my knee hard, but the cadence continued in my mind, and somehow, I kept moving to the beat. I shoved my hand into the hat, biting my lip to keep from crying. My fingers gripped, I shoved them into my pocket and ran outside the house to the front lawn, where I threw my face up to Heaven and asked God to make the pain stop with my thoughts. Momma had told me he could hear those.

Please, please make it stop. Hop! Oh, hop! That helps. Keep hopping… please, God, make it stop…

"Molly? What are you doing?"

"Nothing." *I hate that window.* "Dancing." *She might believe that.*

My mother had come outside to help me, knowing I was hurt. I wore a deep bruise on my leg for two weeks. After I had stopped crying, I walked back to my room to stash my pennies. In my pocket I found two folded up bills. I hadn't intended to take folded up money but being hurt made me frantic. I knew bills were worth more. I had a small understanding in the fact that some of the silver pennies were worth more than the gold ones, even though they wouldn't fit in the machines to get gum or jewelry. I put the bills inside the heater vent, tightened the screws with my fingers and went outside to play.

Once, I'd taken folded up money that had a "one" on it, because there was no change in the hat and Aunt Charlene was going to the Jr's. Kountry Store. I took the dollar and went to the store with her. In the bravest move I'd made to that point, I'd walked slowly to the tall, golden aisle of candy bars. The wrappers glowed with new colors that day, calling to me and my power to obtain for myself any one of the treats on those racks. Among others, there were *Bazooka Bubble Gum*, *Dum Dums*, *Hershey's* chocolate bars, and *Pixie Stix*; but the most desirable of all was the delectable combination of chocolate, nuts and caramel that was the *100 Grand*. I pushed the filched dollar bill across the counter to the clerk before I placed the candy bar up there, too. I glanced up at Aunt Char. She beamed down at me.

"That's my big girl," she said, and winked.

I grinned. That was the best candy bar I've ever eaten.

The day after I'd taken the folded bills, my father came home early from work. He and my mother were in the kitchen talking when I came inside. My father was talking about Santa Claus. My interest was piqued. I walked to the sink, stepped on my stool and filled my plastic tumbler with water as I listened.

It wasn't good. Santa was likely not coming to our house. Santa only came to the houses of good little boys and girls, and someone had stolen two hundred dollars from Daddy's hat at our house.

I gulped loud. My eyes shot to the highchair where my little brother was strapped in, no doubt in an effort by my poor momma to salvage her waning sanity in the face of evil, eating an Oreo cookie that had obviously been partially digested. Black mush squeezed from between his fat, slimy little fingers the way Play-Doh erupted from my Fun Factory extruder.

My legs began to shake. Christmas presents were on the line. I was guilty as could be, rather than sugar, spice or anything nice. And him? My brother wrinkled his sticky, blackened nose at me and snorted. He was pure evil, not just snails and puppy-dog tails. We were screwed.

I looked at my parents, who sat at the table drinking coffee, looking at me. They were oddly quiet. I looked back at the cookie encrusted mess in the chair. I finished my water and left, fully intending on finding a way to slip the money into his grubby fingers when no one was looking.

When I got to the vent, I was appalled to find the money gone. I double checked but found nothing but a few pennies. My fingers shook as I put the screws back in the vent cover. I went back to the kitchen, defeated.

My parents hadn't moved. I walked to the spot between their two chairs. I was just tall enough that I could see the upturned edges of the folded bills sitting between them on the tabletop.

No one spoke. I stared at my prized cowboy boots.

My brother banged a sloppy hand on the chair's tray. They were all looking at me. It was because they all knew what I'd done. My momma was the smartest lady in the world. What should I have expected?

"I just wanted a penny," I said. My voice sounded like a baby's. Weak. Small and powerless. I began to cry, but I stifled any sobs. Tears were another thing. They just came if they felt like it.

"You know this is more than a penny," said Daddy.

"It was an accident," I tried.

"You should have given it back, then," said Momma.

"Boo!" said the chocolate covered freak in the highchair.

I looked from him back to the money. "Is Santa coming now?"

"No," said Daddy.

That had been hard to take; although, soon after, it was rumored that Santa Claus would come despite my folly. Aunt Char bought me a piggy bank for Christmas that year. Daddy's hat contained no change. I know because it took months until I finally quit bothering to check.

Thanks to the wisdom of my parents, I learned to do chores for change, and with the new-found responsibility, I went from having what I'd known to be pennies to having nickels, dimes and quarters. I was proud as ever when I marched into Jr.'s Kountry Store.

I was an independent, articulate, big girl who helped build houses, and the whole world knew it.

Especially Daddy.

From the Author

This story has been on my mind for the last couple of days, as I've recently learned that my father has Covid-19 and is quite ill with heavy symptoms. He is elderly and wasn't in the best of health before the pandemic. Like others who have family members with COVID, I feel the anxiety and heartbreak of not being able to see him, considering the deadly nature of his illness. He and I are the last of my family. My brother passed in 2010 and our mom passed in 2002. "Folly" is special. We're all in the story together.

I am active and live on top social media outlets, websites, podcast and blog interviews, book signings, and, when in operation, writing conferences and conventions. I am a published author, and I currently work as a publisher and director of Superstars Writing Seminars. I would be happy to send a bibliography of my published work, ranging from novels to an upcoming publication in *Weird Tales*.

Here are Universal Book Links for the first books in my series:

Lola Hopscotch:
www.books2read.com/u/4EoDEo

Fate and Fire:
www.books2read.com/u/4j2B62

Echoes from Witcher Mountain:
www.books2read.com/u/4AKLjJ

And more!

The Adventures of Lola Hopscotch:
www.lolahopscotch.com

About My Books: www.mariewhittaker.com

My Patreon Page: www.patreon.com/mariewhittaker

About the Author

Marie Whittaker enjoys teaching about publishing, writing craft, and project management for writers. She works as Associate Publisher at WordFire Press and is Director of Superstars Writing Seminars, a world-class writing conference concentrating on the business of writing. She also puts in time as the personal assistant to *New York Times* bestselling author, Kevin J. Anderson. Marie is a proud member of the Horror Writers Association and keeps steady attendance at local writer's groups. She is currently pursuing a certificate as a Project Management Professional.

When not at work in publishing, Marie is an award-winning essayist and author of horror, urban fantasy, children's books and supernatural thrillers. She has authored several dark fiction novels. She is the creator of *The Adventures of Lola Hopscotch*, which is a children's book series concentrating on getting sensitive childhood issues out in the open between children and adults. Many of her short stories appear in numerous anthologies and publications, including *Weird Tales*. She is currently working on a new supernatural thriller, titled (working) *Little Boy Lost*.

A Colorado native, Marie resides in Manitou Springs, where she writes and enjoys renovating her historic Victorian home. She spends time hiking, gardening, and indulging in her guilty pleasure of shopping for handbags. She is fond of owls, coffee, and all things Celtic. A lover of animals, Marie is an advocate against animal abuse and assists with lost pets in her community. Find out more about her at www.mariewhittaker.com.

The Pirate Prince of the Barbary Coast

by
Shannon Fox

The Pirate Prince of the Barbary Coast

December 1899

*F*rom his position behind the cargo crates stacked on the pier, James could just make out two men patrolling the deck of the S.S. Kingston. The rigging creaked eerily in the night as the ship bobbed on the water, occasionally obscured from view by the dense San Francisco fog. The ship had arrived from Honolulu earlier in the day carrying sugar, coffee, lemons, and the rumor of a prize that was worth more than all the rest of the cargo combined—a golden egg that had once belonged to Queen Lili'uokalani herself.

James had watched the ship all day as they'd unloaded the cargo. And he'd observed other men peel off in pursuit of the wagons, certain the Queen's golden egg was tucked into one of the packing crates inside. They'd never suspected that in order to keep the egg safe from thieves like them, it'd been left aboard the ship.

But James knew. He could feel the presence of gold, an insistent tug that beckoned him to come closer. He wouldn't be able to resist its call for much longer. Nor did he want to. He didn't plan to return home without that egg.

After James had succeeded in lifting a gold brick from the safe of one of his rivals last month, Alastair Ward, owner of the popular dance hall Scylla's Watch, had approached James. He'd offered him a place in the gang of thieves and murderers he employed. On the condition, of course, that the young man deliver the Lili'uokalani egg to him.

It'd been presented as a choice, but James knew it was really no choice at all. Now that Ward knew who he was and what he could do, if James failed tonight, he wouldn't be allowed the opportunity to simply go free and perhaps join ranks with one of Ward's rivals instead. No, James would be dead before the next sunrise.

As James watched the two men walk the length of the ship's

deck now, he rechecked his weapons starting with the knife in his boot. From there, he touched the butt of the pistol tucked into the back of his pants, felt for the dagger at his waist, and reassured himself the slim blade hidden at his right wrist would easily slide free when needed.

Though he was sure he could handle the two guards himself, big and burly as they were, he wasn't convinced that they were the only two aboard the vessel. His gut told him that there was at least one other person below decks. And his gut had never been wrong before.

Not to mention there were surely other thieves hidden in the shadows around him. Despite the advantage his gift gave him, James knew he couldn't be the only one who had figured out that the egg was still on board the ship. Dalzell and Copley were likely out there, watching the ship just as he was. He swallowed hard. He didn't know how he'd fare in a fight with the both of them, and he didn't particularly want to find out.

To steady his nerves, James pulled the knife from his sleeve. He'd picked up the thin little blade from a weapons maker he knew, in Chinatown. When the old man showed it to him, James knew he had to have it, though it wasn't cheap. With its silver handle covered in a design of skulls and crossbones, and the hidden spring that allowed the blade to fold back into itself, it was the perfect weapon for a young man who had recently come by the title of Pirate Prince of the Barbary Coast.

James played with the blade as he waited, flicking it open and shut. The last time he'd checked his pocket watch, the clock face showed nearly one in the morning. James knew the men onboard the ship switched positions every two hours or so, shifting their circuit from fore to aft. The last time they had changed it had been just after eleven. With the thickening fog and the men lulled into a sense of security after hours of uneventful silence, he would make his move the next time they switched.

James tensed as one of the men hailed the other. When they both stepped behind the mast and did not immediately reemerge, he knew it was finally time.

Crouching low, he took off at run, aiming for the refuge of some crates stacked near the ship. He moved quickly and kept his footsteps light, as he'd been taught years ago. He could still hear the old man's voice in his head.

Like a shadow, James.

He hardly dared breathe until his fingertips touched the crates. He held his body tight to the wood as he glanced up beneath the ship's railing. From this new position, he could not see either man above him.

James clamped the silver-handled knife between his teeth. To get onboard the ship, he needed his hands free to pull himself up and over the railing. He could only hope he'd have the opportunity to draw his weapons once his feet touched the deck. He would not use the pistol unless he had no choice, as the sharp crack would surely bring the policeman that patrolled this area of the docks. He much preferred to fight with a knife anyway.

This close to the ship, the gold pulled on him viscerally, like an itch he couldn't scratch. He could already feel the beginnings of the telltale headache: a dull throbbing above his eyes and tightening of the muscles around his temples. The egg was definitely here.

James's heart pounded, sending blood pumping furiously to his head. He could no longer see the deck from this position, so once he pulled himself up and over the railing he'd be dropping straight into a fight for his life without any sense of where his adversaries were.

But then, he'd faced worse odds before.

With a deep breath, James emerged from behind the crates and charged the ship. Though he tried to keep his footsteps light, the wood still creaked beneath his weight.

Once he was close enough to the ship, he tensed his legs and leapt for the railing. When he felt his fingers connect with the smooth wood, he pulled with all his might to haul his body up and over the side. As soon as his feet landed on the ship's deck, he quickly scanned his surroundings.

Rather than the guards he expected to find, James found Dalzell waiting for him.

The big, blonde man grinned as he drew the sword at his belt.

"Hey Copley," he yelled. "Got a visitor."

James had faced Dalzell once before, so he knew that what the thief lacked in finesse, he made up for in brute strength and intimidation. If James froze, if he allowed his opponent to land even one blow, he would be finished, because Dalzell didn't hesitate.

As Dalzell rushed forward and made a swipe for his belly, James danced back out of the reach of the swinging blade. Then, countering with a move of his own, James slashed at the man's sword hand, but Dalzell jerked his arm away at the last moment. Rather than knife rending through flesh, bone met bone as James's wrist connected with Dalzell's. James gritted his teeth against the jarring pain but did not drop his knife. The big man, however, swore and let the sword fall to the deck with a clatter.

Now weaponless, Dalzell reared back, trying to put as much distance between James and himself as possible. But James was faster, already drawing the second dagger from his waist.

Dalzell brought his hands up to defend his face, fists ready to knock the knives away. James slashed at the exposed skin with one knife and, as Dalzell winced in pain and dropped his hands slightly, drew the other across his throat, too fast for the big man to even react.

Dalzell's body hit the deck with a heavy thud. James did not even have a moment to check if Dalzell was truly dead before he again felt the insistent tug of gold, something closer than the egg he knew was below deck. He spun, knives up, and found Copley had crept up behind him. The thief's gold tooth glinted in the weak moonlight as his own dagger slashed down where James's head had been.

James took a step back to buy himself time to weigh his opponent. Copley was as tall and as heavily muscled as Dalzell, but leaner and quicker. Though he'd never seen Copley fight, James had heard stories and knew he was in for a more difficult go of it.

Having learned from his companion's misfortune, Copley did not immediately charge James. Instead, he too drew a second knife from his waistband; one with a cruel, serrated edge.

The two men circled each other warily, each waiting for the perfect moment to strike, to deliver that killing blow.

James kept his eyes on the man's knives and when Copley

lunged forward, he quickly sidestepped him. But not fast enough to escape the serrated blade, which cut deeply across his thigh. James let out a low hiss of pain.

Sensing James's momentary distraction, Copley kicked his legs out from under him and James fell heavily to the deck. Now lying on his back, James saw the thief rear up over him with both knives aimed at his chest.

Just as Copley was about to deliver the killing strike, a figure appeared behind him. James caught a glimpse of coppery red hair just as the stranger drove their own blade into Copley's neck.

James didn't wait to see what happened next. He rolled out of the way, grabbed for the remaining knife in his boot, and scrambled to his feet.

"He almost got you," Ada Fen said. Her blue eyes sparkled with mischief. At her feet, Copley let out a groan before going still.

"No, I had him," James retorted.

A smile tugged at her lips. "Sure you did."

"I almost didn't recognize you," James said, watching as she bent to recover her knife from the corpse. "With your hair like that."

Though he'd always seen Fen dressed in men's clothes, she normally wore her hair in a neat braid down her back, and since the last time they'd encountered each other, she'd chopped off the long hair. With her willowy frame and her red hair now cropped close around her face, she looked like an innocent boy of fifteen, not the deadly thief he knew her to be.

Her eyes held his for a long moment, then she shrugged and said, "It wasn't serving me anymore."

James had the sense, as he often did when talking to Fen, that she meant something more by it, but he didn't press her. This wasn't the time or place. And even if it was, he was scared of what he would find if he dared to go below the surface with her. Scared of how it might change things between them.

James cleared his throat. "You didn't have to do that, you know. Help me."

"Consider it a favor repaid."

The fog shifted, allowing more moonlight to peek through, and James suddenly realized how exposed they were on the deck. Surely the other thieves had used the distraction to move closer to the ship.

Perhaps sensing his alarm, Fen said, "I dealt with the others."

"All of them?"

"Yes. Copley and Dalzell must have slipped down to the ship while I was otherwise engaged."

James hoped the surprise wasn't showing on his face. This wasn't the first time he'd been guilty of underestimating Fen.

"I assume you're here for the egg, too, then?" he asked.

"Yes," she said. "And I'm not planning to leave without it."

"Neither am I."

All of the good humor suddenly faded from her eyes. "You need to walk away."

"I can't," he said.

"Don't make me regret saving your life," she said, coldly.

He took a breath. "Alastair Ward wants the egg. Sent me to get it for him."

Her expression didn't change, but she seemed to pale as she considered what he'd said. "You work for Ward now?"

"I do."

He knew what was going through her head. Fen and James had long ago made a pact that if one of them was thinking of joining up with Ward, they'd go to the other first. Now James could see how naïve he'd been to make such a promise. He'd had little choice in the matter and telling Fen would have changed nothing. It would only have put her life at risk, too. They'd seen what happened to those who aligned themselves with Ward. None of them lived long and neither did the people around them.

"How do I know you're telling the truth?" she asked.

James shrugged. "You don't."

She tensed and for a moment James thought she was going to attack him. His eyes went to the knife she still held in her hand. Though after a moment, she seemed to reconsider.

"I hope you know what you're doing, falling in with someone like Ward," she said. Fen took a couple steps back toward the railing. "Good hunting, James."

Then she ducked under the railing and disappeared over the side of the ship.

He heard a soft thump as she landed on the wood below, but he did not look to see where she went next. She'd made her choice, the sensible choice, not to make an enemy of Alastair Ward. James just hoped she hadn't decided to make an enemy out of him instead.

He scanned the dock to make sure they hadn't drawn the notice of a policeman. Then, he gathered his knives from where they'd dropped during the fight and turned his attention to the wooden door he'd noticed when he'd boarded the ship.

As James put a hand on the doorknob, he again felt the pull of the gold below, which only made his headache that much more painful. Despite the throbbing in his skull, a thrill went through him as he realized he was likely only moments away from claiming his prize and sparing himself from Ward's wrath.

James turned the doorknob and then nudged the door open with one booted foot. He held his knives at the ready, waiting for someone to emerge from the darkness and charge him.

But no one came, and he heard no sounds of someone waiting for him in the shadows. James quietly eased down the stairs until his feet hit bottom.

With only the dim light of the moon coming through the doorway, he guessed he was standing in a hallway of some sort. He could see the glow of a light down at the end. If this ship were like the last one he had stolen onto, that would be the captain's quarters.

Slowly, James crept forward, listening for any sound that he was not alone. All he heard was the sound of water slapping against the side of the ship and the creak of rigging above.

A faint scuffling noise caused him to tense. He tightened his grip on the knives and peered into the shadows, waiting for someone to charge from the darkness.

When no one appeared, he concluded he must have heard a rat.

As James made his way down the hallway, the glow grew brighter and brighter until he was standing outside an open door.

From his position in the hallway, James could see a tall chest of drawers and an enormous wooden desk occupied one wall of the cabin. Papers, books, and a fountain pen covered the half of the desk he could see, as if someone had paused in the middle of writing. An oil lamp glowed softly.

He could hear nothing from the occupant within, though the man must be in there. And the golden egg with him.

This close to the gold, James was having trouble focusing. He shook his head to clear his mind, but it didn't really help. Nothing did. Until he had the gold safely in hand, he would be able to think of little else.

Taking a deep breath, he repositioned the knives in his hands and stepped through the doorway.

In addition to the desk and chest of drawers he'd seen, a bed sat against the opposite wall, sheets pulled tight. A massive armoire occupied the corner at the foot of the bed.

In the same corner stood an old man with a dagger in hand. He eyed James warily.

"You know what I'm here for," James said. "If you give it to me, I will spare your life. There's no reason you need to die tonight, too."

The old man's voice was low and throaty as he replied, "If I give it to you, I'm as good as dead anyway."

He gestured to the desk. "Look there."

James kept his eyes on the man. Though the old man knew he couldn't best James in a fair fight, perhaps he thought if he could draw his attention away for a moment, he stood a chance.

"I'm not trying to trick you, boy," the man said, as if he could read his mind. His fat jowls shook as he talked. "Even if I were, you'd see me coming long before I could lay a hand on you."

Which was true. Perhaps the man had been a fighter in his prime, though he was no match for James now, with an enormous belly spilling over the waistband of his pants.

James glanced at the desk, then at the old man, and back to the desk again, trying to make sense of what he was seeing.

"A dead rat?" James asked.

"Not just a rat," the man said. The oil lamp gave his bronze skin a warm glow. "That's plague, boy."

James felt a chill run down his spine. The man could be lying, but if he was telling the truth, then James had exposed himself as soon as he'd set foot on the ship. Fen, too.

"The day we set sail from Honolulu, one of the dockworkers told me he'd seen a rat acting strangely the day before. He'd watched it crawl out into the sunlight and writhe in agony before dying at his feet. Asked me what I thought since he didn't know what to make of it." The man ran a free hand through his silver hair. "I was in Hong Kong during the last plague. I'd seen rats acting just as he'd described, but I didn't mention that to him. We were about to ship out, and I needed to deliver this cargo so I could get paid."

James's ears started ringing as blood pounded in his skull. "You brought the plague here."

"So it would seem," the old man agreed. "That's why I can't let you take the egg."

"What does the egg have to do with it?"

The man smiled grimly, revealing stained and crooked teeth. "You broke onto this ship expecting to steal a pretty trinket, something to fetch enough coin to line your pockets for months to come. But the egg is more valuable than that. Much more."

As James stared at the old man, he began to piece together the man's meaning. "You went to Hong Kong during the plague years. So, either you're incredibly lucky or something protected you from the disease. Something you've kept with you ever since."

"It appears you're not as dumb as you look," the man said.

James bristled at the comment but kept his anger under control. Only a few moments more and he would have the egg in his possession.

"You missed your chance," James said. "You should have given me the egg when I asked. I was going to let you live. Now, I can't."

"Believe me, I don't want to live without it," the man said. "You ever seen a plague victim before?"

"No."

"Well, you will soon enough," the old man replied. "Nasty business."

James felt himself growing impatient. His gift was wearing his nerves paper-thin, screaming at him to stop talking and start searching for the golden egg he knew was hidden in the room.

"Give it to me now," James growled.

The old man seemed to weigh his options. "If I hand the egg to you willingly, when you put your knife in me, can you do it quickly?"

James nodded curtly. "The egg first."

The old man gestured with his chin. "In the desk. Top left drawer."

James kept his eyes on the old man as he moved closer to the desk. As he slid open the drawer, he heard something heavy roll across the wood. The desire to look at the egg, to touch it, became more than he could bear, and James found he had no choice but to look down.

The golden egg was the only thing in the wooden drawer. About the size of his palm, its faceted sides glowed warmly in the lamplight. Ruby chips sparkled in irregular intervals across its surface. All together, the effect was mesmerizing, especially for someone with a gift like James. Forcing himself to look away, he grabbed the egg.

As soon as his fingers touched its golden sides, an enormous sense of relief swept over him. The noise in his brain disappeared, his headache lessened, and he felt his heartrate slow. When he transferred the egg to his pocket, it was only with an enormous force of will that he was able to pull his hand away again.

The old man hadn't moved at all while James had opened the desk drawer. James couldn't tell what he was thinking. Perhaps he was remembering the day he'd claimed the egg for himself and all the adventures he'd had since. In any other situation, James would have bought the man a whiskey and asked him about it. But there was no room for sentimentality in this future he'd chosen for himself.

When James stepped back out onto the deck, he noticed the fog had shifted again. The moon hung bright and full over the bay of San Francisco. In the distance, James heard bells tolling the hour.

As he hopped down from the ship onto the pier below, the egg bounced heavily against his leg. A rat, startled from wherever it had been lurking, raced in front of him and vanished into the shadows farther down the pier.

James walked slowly, not in any hurry to return home. Now that he knew what the egg was really worth, that it offered its owner protection against the plague, he wouldn't be giving it to Ward. Which meant that he needed to disappear for awhile. A long while. Until he knew whether the old man had told the truth or not.

If plague was about to take hold of the city, it would surely burn hot and fast through the lawless Barbary Coast. Perhaps even Alastair Ward himself would fall victim to it. James felt the tension he'd been holding in his shoulders ease as he imagined it. With Ward gone, James would be free. Ward's successor would hardly think it worth the trouble to come after him, not when he'd have to deal with the instability caused by a sudden shift in power in the Barbary Coast.

Even if Ward didn't die of the plague, James might still be able to turn things to his advantage. Death, fear, and uncertainty were always a recipe for chaos, especially in a world where loyalty could be bought and alliances shifted like the weather. As Fen had proved earlier, it was far easier to slip a knife into your enemy's neck when his eyes were elsewhere.

A tidal wave of plague was about to break upon the city. Who would be left victorious in the end, James couldn't say. All he knew was that if an opportunity emerged for a Pirate Prince to become a King, he would seize it.

From the Author

The spark for this story came from a writing prompt for a Superstars Writing Seminars anthology. When researching and trying to think of a character, I stumbled across information about the arrival of bubonic plague in San Francisco around 1900. The character of James immediately sprang to mind after that, and his story serves as a bridge between one of my finished historical fantasy novels (not yet released) and its sequel story (still to be written). San Francisco is an important part of my own family history, and I loved finding something I didn't know about its past.

When it comes to my writing, I'm interested in poking around the cracks in history, exploring those little-known events and places that don't often make it onto the main stage. I'm less interested in stories that have been told over and over again. I think history is vast, instructive, and fascinating, but we end up focusing too much on the same people, cities, and points in time. I love thinking about what life was like for the people who didn't make it into the history books and telling their stories instead—with a dash of magic included!

If you liked this story, you might also like my short story, "Hyde Park," a contemporary thriller included in the *Monsters, Movies & Mayhem* anthology available here:

www.books2read.com/MonstersMoviesMayhemSF

I'd also recommend checking out "The Garden Party," my contemporary fantasy short story that was included in the *Cursed Collectibles* anthology. Available here:

www.books2read.com/CursedCollectiblesSF

About the Author

Shannon Fox is a San Diego-based writer of fiction spanning multiple genres. She grew up in the foothills of the Colorado Rockies before relocating to California to attend UC-San Diego, where she earned a B.A. in Literature-Writing. She misses the rugged natural beauty of Colorado, but definitely doesn't miss the wind. Her short stories have appeared in the *Monsters, Movies & Mayhem* Anthology, the *Cursed Collectibles* Anthology, *The Copperfield Review*, *The Plaid Horse Magazine*, *Black Fox Literary Magazine*, and more. Besides writing, Shannon has a passion for horses. She has competed at the international level in the sport of dressage. Shannon also owns a digital marketing company that works primarily with small businesses and real estate agents.

To learn more about Shannon and her forthcoming stories, visit her website: www.shannon-fox.com.

Murder in the Roux Morgue
by
Chris Mandeville

Murder in the Roux Morgue

*D*aniel gazed lovingly at his new Henckels chef's knife, emphasis on *new*. For almost a year he'd squeaked a little savings out of each meager paycheck until he'd had enough to buy it. There were easier ways to get the money, quicker ways, but he was committed to his new life, his new way of doing things. A brand-new knife was an important reminder of that, especially when every day at work he was surrounded by *old* in the ancient kitchen of the Roux Morgue restaurant.

He placed the edge of his knife against the honing steel, making sure it was at the perfect twenty-degree angle, and scraped down exactly ten times on each side of the gleaming blade.

Tradition plus precision equals perfection. He could hear Chef's voice harping in his head as clearly as if the old tyrant were standing there looking over his shoulder.

Chef was right about one thing—Daniel must be precise when it came to his knife. But Chef needed to get off his high horse about tradition and the "old ways." Daniel knew in his heart, in his soul, that embracing the *new* was the only way this restaurant was ever going to be known outside of Sacramento.

If only he could get Chef to see it that way.

Case in point, the *mise en place* he was prepping for tonight's traditional cassoulet: carrots, onions, and parsley. Could it get any more boring? As he diced the carrots into precise one-centimeter cubes, he dreamed about substitutions that would make this old dish new and exciting: leeks instead of onion, tarragon instead of parsley. He wondered for the thousandth time how he could convince Chef to give a little twist to the traditional, to try something, *anything*, to liven up the mind- and palate-numbing "classic" cuisine.

Daniel heard Chef's waddle before he saw him approach the prep station, and he braced for the morning lecture. No matter how "prepared, polished, and precise" Daniel was, Chef always found something to criticize.

Just as Chef opened his mouth to bitch, the sound of the French national anthem blared from his pocket.

Chef threw a scathing glance at Daniel's knife work, then answered his cell. "*Allô?* Zis ees zee Roux Morgue. Chef Prideaux *ici*."

Spare me, Daniel thought. Celebrated French chef Jacques Prideaux was actually plain old Jack Wilson from Pittsburgh. Daniel was one of a select few who knew Chef's closely guarded secret. It was this knowledge, not his hard-earned culinary skills, that had finally landed Daniel a job after two months of rejections from fine dining restaurants in San Francisco. He'd even stooped to job-hunting in the East Bay, to no avail. The food industry was well known for opening its arms to ex-cons, but apparently just not for *him*.

Man, that pissed him off. He'd done all the right things. He'd earned a fresh start, *deserved* it. He shouldn't have to resort to his old ways in order to get it. But they gave him no choice. And if he was going to fall back on his old ways one last time, he figured he might as well make it worthwhile. So, in addition to a new job, he'd *encouraged* Chef to give him a new identity, too. After all, who better suited to that task than Jack Wilson?

So, Danny-boy Franks, infamous arsonist and sometime-blackmailer, graduate of San Quentin's inmate culinary program, had become Daniel LeFleur, esteemed graduate of *Le Cordon Bleu* in Paris, and second-in-command in a classic French kitchen, even if it was in Sacramento.

"*Mais non!*" Chef said into the phone. "Tonight ees not enough time to prepare zee deeshes. It must be tomorrow."

What's he up to? Daniel wondered. There was nothing on the menu that couldn't be ready by tonight. For some reason Chef was maneuvering to have someone come in tomorrow, when the restaurant's normally closed. But who? And why?

"*Oui.* Tomorrow." Chef jabbed the phone screen with his pudgy finger, then shoved the cell back into his pocket. "Daniel!" he bellowed, even though Daniel was standing a foot away and looking right at him.

"Yes, Chef," Daniel said, making a show of putting down his knife and paying attention.

"This is it. It's finally happening," Chef said with zero French accent. "The owner is bringing in a prospective investor tomorrow, and if he's impressed enough to come on board, he'll fund moving the restaurant into a brand-new, state-of-the-art kitchen. In the City."

Daniel's heart flipped in his chest. All his hard work was finally going to pay off. He was going back to San Francisco where he belonged. And not only that—he'd be in a brand-new kitchen. He could hardly breathe.

"Tomorrow's tasting menu decides everything," Chef continued. "We'll work straight through the night if we have to. Everything must be perfect if Roux Morgue is going to be a destination."

Daniel cringed as the name of the restaurant rolled off Chef's tongue. "Chef, maybe now would be a good time to consider a new name..."

"*Again* about the name."

"This is our chance—"

"Enough!" Chef's pink face flushed red. "It's *my* chance, *my* restaurant. And the name is not up for debate. Now shut up and let me think."

Daniel clamped his teeth together. It killed him that Chef had no instinct for the business. How he'd gotten this far with the name Roux Morgue was baffling. The restaurant would never be a breakout success with a name like that. Especially not in the City. The critics would destroy them before even tasting the food. Daniel's dream was crumbling before his eyes.

"Let's see," Chef said, pacing between the flat top and the prep station. "I need something flashy, something to showcase the roux, something truly special." Pace, pace, pace. "What about... *poulet en cocotte bonne femme*..."

Seriously? It *sounded* fancy, but there was nothing flashy about chicken and potatoes. Chef needed to think bigger, bolder, if they were going to have any chance at impressing the investor.

"Yes," Chef Prideaux continued to himself. "*Poulet en cocotte bonne femme* and... *boeuf à la Parisienne.*"

93

Boeuf à la Parisienne? It's *beef* fucking *stroganoff.*

Daniel had to do something, or the investor dinner was doomed.

For a couple of weeks, he'd been playing with a concept that *leaned into* the name Roux Morgue instead of running from it. It wasn't perfect yet, but if he didn't propose it now, he might never get the chance.

"Chef, I've been working on this idea for a theme dinner..." Daniel started tentatively.

"I said *shut up*. How am I supposed to be creative when—"

"No, *you* need to shut up," Daniel said.

Chef gasped, eyes wide.

"Just hear me out," Daniel said quickly. "Give me five minutes, and if you hate the idea, I'll drop it. For good."

Chef narrowed his eyes.

"*Please,*" Daniel added. "This opportunity is too important. Please, just listen."

Chef narrowed his eyes even further. "Alright, I'll give you *two* minutes, but that's it." He looked at his watch for emphasis.

Chef was finally willing to listen, so Daniel had to make sure Chef actually *heard* him this time. His entire future depended on it. He drew a breath to quell his jitters and began. "Since you're sure you want to keep the name Roux Morgue, I've come up with a theme dinner that takes it even further, called... wait for it... Murder in the Roux Morgue! But in our case *murder* is a murder of *crows.*"

Chef cocked his head, like he didn't quite understand, so Daniel pressed forward. "For the starter we do *corneilles tartine* with San Francisco sourdough. Then for the soup, *potage crème de cresson*, subbing out the chicken stock. For the main, *corneille épicée aux épinards*. And cap it off with a traditional Blackbird Pie updated with blackberries, or with juniper berries if you think blackberries are too on-the-nose."

Chef opened his mouth to reply, but no sound came out.

Daniel couldn't help the wide grin that spread across his face. He'd done it. He'd finally gotten Chef to listen, and his brilliant idea had rendered Chef speechless.

Daniel pulled his notebook from his breast pocket. "I have the details right here." He paged through looking for his prep notes.

"You've got to be shitting me," Chef said, finally.

Daniel looked up, confused by his tone. "Wh... what?"

"I thought you were pulling my leg. But you're serious. You're actually serious. You want me to serve the investor *crow*. Actual crow."

"It's legit, I swear, like squab or pheasant," Daniel insisted.

"You wasted my time for this, this, this *new-age bullshit?*"

"It's not new!" Daniel had prepared for Chef's objection and knew exactly how to spin it. "Crow is totally old school. Historic. And it's classic French. The Frenchest. Who else would dare? Plus—you're going to love this—I designed each course with a different kind of roux in keeping with the theme of the restaurant. Like the *tartine* uses an olive oil roux, and the Blackbird Pie a duck fat—"

"*Stop*. Just stop it, Daniel. Murder in the Roux Morgue? A murder of crows, serving actual crow? That's already off the deep end. But now, now you want me to serve a roux that's *not made with butter?* This is a Classic. French. Restaurant. If I'd known you were going to pitch this *nouveau* sacrilege I wouldn't have given you even *two* minutes." He waddled away from the prep station muttering to himself and shaking his head.

"*But Chef*," Daniel called after him. "It's *mostly* classic. You've got to take a risk if you want to make it big. Come *on*, open your mind."

Chef stopped at the door to the walk-in fridge and turned around. "When you have your own restaurant, you can throw ridiculous theme dinners serving crow, and you can use whatever bogus kind of roux you choose. But in Roux Morgue, roux is made with butter. Only. End of story."

"But the investors—"

"Precisely. The classics are what got me here. So, you will go old school or get out." Chef *humphed*, opened the walk-in, and disappeared inside.

Daniel turned back to the prep station and stared down at his new knife gleaming like a sharp silver promise alongside the uninspired ingredients of the classic cassoulet. Maybe Chef had a point.

Daniel ushered the restaurant owner and a buttoned-up investor to a table at the window, where he'd already set the teaser course he'd created for this moment. Even though the three men were the only people in the place, Daniel had tried to create ambiance with classic piano on the sound system and candles lit at every table.

Daniel waited while the other men sat and placed the freshly pressed linen napkins on their laps. When they were settled, he poured the wine and began his carefully crafted speech.

"The *amuse-bouche* you see before you is Chilean sea bass and spinach bathed in a lemon béchamel made with a traditional butter roux, which I've paired with this crisp Alsatian Riesling." Daniel held out the bottle for them to see, then placed it on the table. "While you enjoy, please allow me to describe the progression I've prepared for you this evening. The soup will be *potage parmentier*, a classic potato and leek soup updated with a smoked duck fat roux."

"This fish is delicious," the investor said, wiping sauce from his plate with his finger and licking it off.

Daniel gave a reserved nod, not letting on the relief he felt. Thank God he'd decided to steer away from the *murder of crows* theme. He clasped his hands formally behind his back and continued with the description of the menu. "The soup course is followed by *escalopes de veau à l'estragon*—tarragon veal cutlets with a pork belly brown roux. Then *côte de porc charcutière* with an avant-garde olive oil and tomato roux. And finally, the *pièce de résistance*, a duck *tourtière* featuring a blood roux. Each course is paired with a wine selected to bring out the nuances of each type of roux."

"Oh, roux, like in the name," the investor said. "You know, I'm not sure how I feel about the name Roux Morgue. So morbid."

"I agree completely," Daniel said, thrilled to have an ally, though he knew he needed to be careful how far he pushed it.

"I'd like to suggest you consider the name Le Moulin Roux. It hits the roux theme, but is more lighthearted, more widely appealing." He'd love to ditch "roux" altogether, but the investor had gravitated to Roux Morgue for a reason, so Daniel had resolved to be less aggressive about change. For now. "I think an upbeat new name would highlight the fresh start you're planning for the restaurant."

"So, it appears Chef Prideaux let you in on what's at stake here," the owner said, eyes squinty as he appraised Daniel.

"Of course. Now if you'll excuse me, I'll see to your soup." Daniel bowed and turned for the kitchen.

"Send out Prideaux when he has a moment," the owner called.

Daniel turned back with a sad expression he hoped wasn't over the top. "I'm sorry—I thought Chef Prideaux told you."

"Told me *what*," the owner said in a suspicious tone.

Daniel shook his head apologetically. "I'm afraid Chef was called to France on a family emergency."

The investor turned to the owner with a grim look. "Then we'll have to reschedule."

"No, please," Daniel said quickly. "Chef knew the importance of this tasting and insisted I continue in his place."

"You?" the owner said. "Aren't you just a prep cook?"

"I'm the sous chef," Daniel said, pulling back his shoulders. "I've been working closely with Chef Prideaux for years. I'm more than—"

"Jacques Prideaux is the reason I'm here," the investor interrupted. "I'm not prepared to go forward without him."

"You're right," the owner said. "Sorry to have wasted your time." He shot Daniel a dirty look and tossed his napkin on the table.

"Wait!" Daniel said, lurching forward. "You're already here and the food is prepared. You said the *amuse* was delicious—I made that. Please, just stay and eat. What have you got to lose?" Daniel caught the whiff of desperation in his voice and wished he could take it back.

The owner looked away, silent. Why wasn't he trying to convince the investor to stay?

A sick feeling blossomed in the pit of Daniel's stomach.

Had Chef Prideaux told the owner about his past? Had everything he'd done been for nothing? Defeat pressed down on his shoulders. Maybe he'd never had a chance at all.

No. He'd come too far to give up. He had to go all in.

"Look, I'll level with you," Daniel said, shedding the pretense of formality. "The truth is, you don't need Chef Prideaux. He's old school. A has-been. His ideas have no life in them, not for today's market."

"But you can't argue with classic," the investor said.

"There will always be a place for classic," Daniel agreed. "But that place is not at the top. The classics alone are too tired to make a splash in today's marketplace. *But...* if you take the old guard and cook it up with deft new techniques and unexpected new flavors? That's money. And that's what *I* can deliver."

The owner and the investor looked at each other.

Daniel pressed on before he lost them. "I'll prove it to you. Each dish I prepared for your tasting tonight is classic, but with a twist. Perfect for today's market. Perfect for a fresh start."

The owner shrugged, still looking at the investor. "The kid could be onto something."

"I'm not sold," the investor said. "I like it in theory, but in practice I'd be afraid of losing the essence of what brought the restaurant to this level, what brought *me* to the table. And that something was Chef Prideaux." He turned to Daniel, his expression grave. "So, tell me. Do these new dishes still have that Jacques Prideaux *je ne sais quoi?*"

"I assure you," Daniel said. "You'll taste Jacques Prideaux in every bite."

From the Author

Murder in the Roux Morgue is the result of a prompt for a "relationship gone wrong" story that included a recipe. Although I normally write science fiction and fantasy tales, this murder story bubbled forth, probably because I'm an unrepentant mystery lover as well as a closet "foodie." Crafting this short story showed me how much I enjoy writing under the mystery umbrella, especially when I get to include food. As a result, my current novel-in-progress stars a ghost—who's a foodie—trying to solve the mystery of her own death. And about that recipe that goes with the Roux Morgue story? You don't want it. Trust me, no one needs blood roux.

About the Author

Chris Mandeville writes science fiction/fantasy novels and short stories, as well as nonfiction for writers. Her published fiction includes the time travel trilogy, IN REAL TIME (*Quake*, *Shake*, and *Break*), and *Seeds: a post-apocalyptic adventure*. Chris can write anywhere, but her usual spot is a comfy chair at home in the Rocky Mountains where the only sound is the wind in the trees, her coffee cup is in reach, and her service dog, Finn, is snoozing by her feet. When she isn't writing, she loves to cook, travel, and teach writing workshops. She and Finn can often be found at events for writers and readers along Colorado's Front Range. To learn more about Chris and her works-in-progress, and to join her Reader's Group, visit chrismandeville.com.

Hellbender Metamorphosis

by
Elmdea Adams

Hellbender Metamorphosis

Soft, padded feet gripping and releasing, the old hellbender, Durus, moved steadily across the smooth creek-bottom rocks. The water flowing past his side gills and over his back felt slightly different, as it had for many days. It was past time to check the eggs. They were likely the last hatching he would protect and raise.

He'd dreamed last night like he hadn't dreamt in years. Helpless and horrified, he watched water eat through a dam, sending poisonous coal ash into a tributary of Owl Creek. As Durus dreamed, he'd known with certainty he was watching an event that happened weeks ago. He'd seen the evidence and denied it.

Waters once clear were grayer by the day. The normal fresh tang of new grasses, old leaves, compact mud, and smooth stones, were over-ridden by the sharp taste of coal ash. Safrina, his egg partner, was no longer willing and lithe. He'd seen her a few days ago, her beautiful, orange dappled skin stiff and still, her eyes dull and un-seeing. Pressing his snout against her confirmed life was gone from her. Just as it was gone from all the others he'd encountered in the past few days. He was the last of his kind, the last of the Owl Creek hellbenders, until his hatchlings emerged from their egg sacks.

He slowed, laboring for each breath. The bottom rocks were daily more slippery with settling grit, the same ashy silt that clogged the pores of his skin and slowed the life-giving flow of air to his body. Even a sigh required more than he could give.

Owl Creek was dying. The surface skaters were few, as were frogs and fish. He wondered if tadpoles and minnows could live in these waters, let alone hellbender hatchlings. The green water mosses were dull gray, stiffening with the debris caught in their fragile tendrils.

He pulled himself into the egg-hollow he'd used all his life. He was stunned when he saw the eggs. The clear round shapes were smothering under a dull gray blanket, the soft gold glow of new life in their centers hidden. He swung his head back and forth above them and was engulfed in a cloud of acrid waste. His mind reeled and went blank, then inched its way back, bringing with it the memories and sorrow as the water carried the silt cloud away.

One egg, one alone, still glowed golden amongst its nine and twenty suffocated siblings. Durus knew what must be done but doubted he had the strength. He shook his skin, sending another, smaller, cloud down the creek. He opened his wide mouth and scooped up the golden, glowing egg, along with a few of its neighbors. He curled his tongue back toward the top of his palate, cradling the living and the dead, and closed his mouth.

He made his way down Owl Creek, using as many eddies and clear water spaces as he could. The pervasive load of coal ash in the water still settled on his air-breathing hide. He repeatedly shivered and shook it off. It was a day that ate time and stole strength and focus. He crept along, never pausing, ignoring his exhaustion. He knew where he needed to go.

He'd been a young one, not more than a year or two out of the egg sac, when he first came to the coming-out-of-the-water place. Elder Scane had led Durus and three other curious younglings on the down-creek journey. When they arrived, Elder Scane gave them the "listen" look they'd learned to obey.

Elder Scane had been clear: "Our closest kin are the salamanders, who live also in the dry world. We're hellbenders. We once walked both worlds with ease, but water called us home. Let your body remember how to breathe dry world air and walk in that heavy world."

Elder Scane paused, small bright eyes looking at them one by one, making sure they were listening. "When entering the dry world, you must stop and let your nostrils be parched tubes for dry-world air as your body rediscovers the breathing sacs that wait within your chest."

Young Durus had crawled up the muddy embankment, sticking his head through the surface of the water. He burned inside. He made himself stay, remembering what Elder Scane had just told them.

"Wait for the burning to stop. Then bring the rest of your body into the dry world, called land. Once you are on land, always be aware of the world above. There are large flapping ones who can grab you in sharp claws and carry you away. Be very still if one is near. Their names are hawk and eagle."

A second breath of dry-world air assaulted his body, and a third and a fourth. By the fifth breath, the burning and the craving for water-air diminished.

That was when the magic began. He padded beside the creek, intrigued by the weight of his slender, flat body. There were bright colors here he had no names for. There were small flappy ones above, but no large ones. He continued on, drawn to a large, tall object. The word for it filtered into his memory, memory passed down through generation upon generation of hellbender: tree, a Sycamore tree. As he looked up and up and up into its green moving spaces, it spoke to him, mind to mind.

Remember me. Remember this place.

Young Durus shook his head. There was a gaping mouth in the side of the tree, just above the ground. He shook his head again, and the mouth was gone. The smooth white bark gleamed. If he didn't know better, he'd have said it winked.

Old Durus recalled that journey of his young-self many times during the long day. The voice of the Sycamore was louder every time he reached that part of the remembering. His body wanted to just stop and rest. The tree voice wouldn't let him. It had added words: *I am the refuge, the place of remembering.*

Durus wasn't sure if that was wishful thinking or real. It didn't matter. He kept going. Evening was coming on when he reached the coming-out-of-the-water place. His weary body was craving more air than he could absorb from the murky waters. He shambled and stumbled into a small pool. There was less ash floating in this small oasis. He rested as his water air craving was satisfied in this cleaner water. He doubted he could continue but knew he must.

He raised his head and watched the rising of the quarter moon, its soft light sparkling and moving across the surface of the water and breaking up in the ripples. It was time. He took one last water-world breath and began his ascent of the coming-out-of-the-water place. When he was half in water and half in the dry world, he stopped.

Just as he remembered, his nostrils and the chest sacs burned as dry-world air entered. The skin of his upper body rippled and tightened, and his sense of smell diminished. Through it all, he focused on the gentle pulsing of the gold, glowing egg in his mouth telling him it still lived. He kept his jaw muscles as limp as he could, despite the strong urge to clamp down at the dry agony. He was grateful for the wisdom teachings of Elder Scane. Durus knew the progression of changes his body would undergo.

After the fifth breath, the burning stopped, as it had those many years ago. One moment it was there, the next it wasn't. He pulled his body fully into the dry world. He wondered again if he could do what needed done. His legs quivered as the overworked muscles bore his now-weighty body. The joints of his legs, knees, and ankles twinged and creaked, crying out deep aches that had been mere whispers in Owl Creek.

He built a wall in his mind, a wall of river rock. Green water moss filled the gaps and bonded with stone, waving the water around and over the wall. He put the pain, the ache, the exhaustion, the doubt, on the other side. Another step, then another. With steady, painful steps, he walked beside the creek, to the Sycamore, his skin dryer and dryer.

A dark shadow passed overhead. Durus dropped and melded into the ground. *Not now, not so close to Sycamore!* rose the silent scream in his mind. The shadow sketched lazy circles above. He closed his eyes, so nothing could gleam in the dark, thankful his skin had shed its water glisten. His exhaustion took over and he napped.

He woke with a shudder. The eggs? Were they still there? He carefully moved his tongue and felt the pulse of the living egg. He tapped one short finger on the ground beneath him. Yes, it was there. He was awake and alive. He remembered the big flapping thing. He tilted his head, cautiously opened one small eye, and looked up. The quarter moon brushed the star-pricked sky with a faint glow, its weak light casting faint shadows on the ground. Durus watched the shadows shorten as the moon crawled up the sky. All he saw were moon, stars, and cloud wisps.

It was safe to move again. His muscles had stiffened while he napped, and the pain was greater than any he had ever known. So great it dropped him back onto his belly. That was the moment when he almost gave up.

His mouth began to clench, and he felt the pressure of the eggs. All this for one? What was the good of that? There'd be no mate for this one, ever. No matter. He had to shelter and protect it. He again rose from the ground. He would continue. He put the pain, the doubts, the fears behind the rock wall in his mind. Just one more step. Just one. Then another.

Smell had returned while he napped, but he knew little of what any of it meant. When he thought he couldn't take even one more step, there was a moistness that invited, that was familiar. He drew in another breath. Yes, it was the ancient Sycamore. Relief rippled up and down his body as he followed the scent to the base of Sycamore.

I am here, Revered Elder, with the last of my kind, unborn and protected in my mouth, he mind-whispered, keeping the strength that using his voice would require.

Who? Who's that? The rumbling voice rose through Durus's feet and entered his head, filling the world.

It is me, Revered Elder. Your small hellbender brother, Durus. We met long ago. You told me to remember this place, and I have remembered. He was grateful mind whispers couldn't tremble.

There was long silence. The last threads of strength left Durus's legs, and he collapsed in front of Sycamore. He had had to try, even if it came to naught.

Hmmmmm. I remember now. You are the last of your kin, you say?

I am, except for one small precious egg I carry in my mouth, Durus said.

Ah. Get yourself back into the far corner here, quickly.

As Durus watched, the tree opened a hole at its base, like a frog grinning wide to catch a fly. Gathering his last shreds of strength, Durus took one step and then another. He kept the agonizing pain behind his mind wall, and moved his legs again, and again, mindless and driven. Soon, he could rest. Death held no fear now that he was here.

A rippling, deep pool appeared at the back of the tree hollow. Durus gratefully slipped into it and settled on the bottom. His muscles whimpered relief as his skin sucked in the water air his body craved. Lying there, resting as he hadn't rested in many a year, he reveled in the clear sweet flow of clean water. Until that moment, he hadn't realized just how long Owl Creek had been dying.

He opened his mouth a crack, letting this water move across the precious egg. He watched, amazed, as rocks arranged themselves into a sheltering hollow perfect for his soon-to-be hatchling. Energized with hope, he crawled across the firm sands and water-smoothed rocks of the pool bottom. When he reached the hollow, he opened his wide mouth, uncurled his tongue, and gently pushed the still glowing gold egg and its dead companions into the sheltering basin.

Darkness swept through him.

There is one thing more for you to do.

Durus could barely shake his head, he was so tired. *What?*

Call to your kin. Show them the way.

I am the last from Owl Creek. There are no others.

Your call will go beyond your home waters. Call. They wait.

Durus expanded the ruffled fringes running down his sides between front and back legs, taking in more water air. He sent out the call. *Hellbender kin. Your eggs will perish in the dying creeks and rivers. Bring them here, to this place of clear water and protection.*

In his mind, he was Owl Creek and the eddies and hollows leading to the coming-out-of-the-water place. He was the journey to the Sycamore and safety. He sent the images as he had sent the call. He sent a final flash of carrying the eggs in his mouth and then fell into the blank dark, taking the memory of that one glowing, living, egg with him into near dreamless sleep.

How long he slept he never knew, exactly. He did know it

had been lifetimes-upon-lifetimes of his kind. Flashes of dreams faded before he could grasp them. Cracking open an eye, he saw gold, glowing eggs. He nodded and fell asleep again. Sometime later, his body twitched.

Eggs? He'd only brought one. He was dreaming. His eyes snapped open. No, no he wasn't dreaming. Eggs glowed with golden life, near to hatching. He lifted his head and saw a hellbender, and another, and another. They, too, appeared to be awakening from a long sleep.

Revered Elder, I, his mind faltered, then he continued. *I do not understand what I am seeing.*

You have slept long and well. These are your kin who heeded your call. They came with their eggs. Here you all slept, outside of time.

Durus took in the widened eyes and extended side ruffles of the seven hellbenders.

"Do you hear something?" he asked them.

They nodded.

"It's the voice of our Revered Elder, who has sheltered us through the turnings of the world and time," he said.

You have rested well. All is well. The Revered Elder's voice was softer, and there was, perhaps, a tinge of amusement in the lilt of her thought.

Durus stretched his body, noticing it felt young and lithe. From the surprised looks on the other hellbender's faces, they were having similar experiences.

A definite chuckle reached their minds. *Feels good, does it not? I, too, have been doing some stretching.* The Revered Elder paused. *Go look at the world outside.*

Our eggs. Our hatchlings. They are safe here?

They are safe, Durus. They are safe. As are we all, she said.

Durus stood, reveling in the ease of movement. His skin rippled up and down his body. He loosened and contracted his muscles, settling the folds and ruffles in accustomed order, and climbed out of the pool. Halfway to the opening of the great hollow, he stopped mid-step. There hadn't been the painful transition from water to land, not even a twinge. Shaking himself in wonder, he continued.

Once outside, he curled his legs under him and settled to

the ground, taking in a world crisp and brilliant through clear, sweet air. The chitter of insects, slither of snakes, whisper of grasses, canticle of birds, breath of animals, clatter of hooves, rustle of leaves, gurgle of creeks, welcomed him to a world reclaimed and renewed.

He rose and turned to look at Sycamore. It was majestic, covered in flakes of white and brown bark. The hollow at the base belied the cavernous space it entered. What was confusing was the tree seemed smaller, younger, than when he'd staggered into it, dreamtimes ago.

I am the keeper of memories, memories of stone and water, of earth and root. I am the one who unlocks what was locked, in the time when Earth was dying. I am the one who revives the sleepers, who awakens the memories of living, of life. Rest a while longer, here in the air and sun.

Durus felt the sun soak into his hide, his bones. His eyes closed. Sometime later, he woke up, surprised to find himself on land, in sunshine.

The eggs! Durus stumbled and lurched in his hurry to return to the pool in Sycamore's hollow. He needed to see the eggs.

The Revered Elder chuckled. *Wait, Durus. Step back a little.*

Reluctantly, stomach churning, Durus did.

Movement flashed at the corner of his eye. Turning, he saw a congress of hellbender hatchlings, flipping their tails, wide mouths spread wider in excited grins, prancing from behind Sycamore. They were the colors of all the hellbenders Durus had known: rich browns dappled with bright oranges, greenish tans with dark brown spots, dark reddish browns with dark smudges, grays sporting black patches, and one rare solid black. Their small round eyes glittered on the sides of their wide snouts. The ruffles on the sides of their flat bodies bounced as they rushed forward.

For a short while, there was a tangle of hatchlings and full-grown hellbenders, cavorting in the grass, slim bodies slipping under and over, around and back. Then they just lay as they were, entangled piles of gleeful life.

Catching his breath, Durus had to ask. "Revered Elder, what happened while we slept?"

Remember. I hold all memories of land, root, and rock. We breath now the air of long ago, of time before the blood and bones of Earth were scraped and sucked from Her. We are now come full circle. For many ages, I waited to greet you, Durus, that I could ask you to remember, when you were still a youngling. I had met you, eons before, in this time we now breathe. You, and these with you, are your own ancestors. For you to be there in what is now the future, I had to bring you to this past. There are few humans now. Their time will come later. You and yours will have many generations of beauty and health. She fell silent.

Durus waited. Then waited some more. His curiosity won out over respectful waiting for the Revered Elder to speak again.

"How did you move us back in time?"

Revered Elder shook her branches in the windless air. *Magic. Earth magic, life magic.* She paused, leaves still rustling. *I tapped the power of water and sun, of soil and air, weaving, intertwining, merging, and releasing.* At her last word, leaves and branches stilled.

In the silence, Durus knew that was as much explanation as he would get. He realized he didn't really care if he ever knew more. He was alive, surrounded by his kin, playing and moving.

He and the seven older hellbenders were very busy for many years, exploring the lands, ponds, creeks, and all that grew in and on them. They taught the impetuous young ones what was needed.

There were two differences in this ancient world that never grew old. Hellbenders now moved easily from land to water and back again without pain or effort, at ease in both. They also heard all the things in the world: plants, animals, rocks, trees, bugs—everything. In the time they had come from, they had heard the susurrations of water world beings, but not the words. Now all spoke to each other, in one joyful language of community, love, and unity. It got a tad noisy at times, but that was preferable to the silence that had almost swallowed them all.

From the Author

"Hellbender Metamorphosis" began innocently enough when a friend posted this picture of an old sycamore near the Shenandoah River. A week or so later, an article about the decline of hellbender populations showed up. The image of that sycamore with its gaping "mouth" came back to mind, and I knew it and the hellbenders had a story to tell. In 2018, "Hellbender Metamorphosis" won First Place in the WV Writers Annual Writing Contest in the *Emerging Writers Prose* category.

"Sycamore, Clarke County, VA" © 2017, S. Bailey

About the Author

I live on a windy ridge near Berkeley Springs, WV, where dragon's-breath fogs rise from the valleys. My previous adventures include Fortune 500 management and work as a past-life therapist, which are more related to one another than one might initially think. I appreciate the skilled supervision of my cat, Miz Alice.

If you like this story, you might like my short stories "Yendy Rattlescale" about a failed dragon and a bullied girl, in *Swords, Sorcery, and Self-Rescuing Damsels*, found at this link:

www.books2read.com/u/mdnAqW

and "Life Pirate," about some cancer cells in *X Marks the Spot, An Anthology of Treasure and Theft*, found here:

www.books2read.com/u/38RAnV

My non-fiction book, *Liberating Incarnations: Twenty-Five Stories of Past Life Regression* can be found here:

www.books2read.com/u/bzgAnE

www.ElmdeaAdams.com

Whispering Through the Veil

by
J.T. Evans

Whispering Through the Veil

*T*he Gobs are back, Dad."

"Mrph. Nmmble. Huh?" I tried to sound coherent as Jason shook me awake from a great dream involving a beach, his mother, and very little clothing.

"Dad! Get up. The Gobs are back in my room."

This grabbed my attention, and I bolted out of bed. "Which ones? Randy, Marty or Nicky?"

"None of them. It's two new ones, and they're chanting this time, but I can't understand the words, and I'm scared, so I came to get—"

"Okay. Okay. Settle down." I put a hand on Jason's shoulder to interrupt the world's longest run on sentence. "We'll see what this is about. Let's go downstairs—and be quiet. I don't want to wake your mom." I glanced over at Maria to ensure she remained deeply asleep. A light snore from her direction confirmed my hopes.

As we moved down the stairway to Jason's room, I looked at my seven-year-old son. The fear in his eyes appeared muted compared to the terror he experienced when the Gobs appeared for the first time, two years earlier. While the little green men carried a frightening countenance with their gigantic heads and gnarled teeth, they meant no harm to children. Their goals matched mine, protecting my son from harm. We'd learned over the years Gobs warned of an attack on Jason from the faerie realms.

I creaked open the door to my son's bedroom with great care and peered inside, not knowing what to expect. Soft chanting in the Fae tongue came up from under Jason's bed. The dim light of the glow-in-the-dark stars glued to his ceiling didn't provide enough illumination to see details of the room, but I knew the Gobs were there somewhere. I switched on the main light hanging from the fan in the center of the room.

"Oi! You tryin' ta blind us?"

"Hey! What's the bright idea, bub?"

Even though the pair of voices sprung out from beneath the bed, the light still bothered the Gobs' eyes. Out of respect for the allies I had reluctantly allowed into my life, I flipped the switch to douse the light.

Sighs of relief filtered up from beneath the bed.

I crouched on my hands and knees to peer under Jason's race-car-shaped bed. While I looked under the bed, Jason slipped over to his translucent angel night light and turned it on to provide a modicum of illumination. The shadowy forms of two Gobs appeared in the dimness. Over the past two years, I'd learned to recognize the different Fae visiting us, and I remained very certain these two had never visited us before.

I beckoned to the two Gobs hiding under the bed. "Come on out. Let's talk."

The two faerie creatures slipped out from beneath the bed and grew from a diminutive six inches in height to a full three feet tall. As they rose, the lighter green splotches mottling their dark green hide became more apparent. Tufts of brown hair sprouted on their shoulders as they rose to their full size. The first to finish growing approached me with a hand extended. "Hiya. I'm Tommy, and this is me brother, Timmy. Nice to meet ya."

After the first Gobs had started showing up in Jason's bedroom, I spent countless hours in the library and on the Internet researching faerie folk. I knew better than to take his hand because a handshake with a Fae guaranteed a contract of some sort. I never wanted to owe a Gob another favor if I could help it. Instead of taking his hand, I sat back on the floor and motioned my boy to stand at my side.

Once we settled in, I looked back and forth between the two Fae. "What threatens my son this time? We've had to chase off Nibs, Bibs, Nobs, Bobs, Greens, Browns, Selks, and Sulks for two years now. We're getting tired of it. I would like to know why they keep showing up for my little boy. He's too young to sign into a binding accord with anyone of the Seelie or Unseelie houses. Only my wife and I could sign him over to your kind, and both of us were ignorant of the Fae until the first Gobs showed up with warnings." Exasperation crept into my voice. "Just give us your warning and go away. We want to be left alone. Please."

The other Gob, Timmy, spoke up. "An accord has been signed with our queen, and your son is of age for collection. He shall become a Changeling, and none will be left in his place. So it has been signed. So it has been agreed."

Jason reached for the bag of iron shavings hidden under his pillow, but I stopped him with a glance and a slight shake of my head. Keeping my attention focused on the pair of Gobs, I narrowed my eyes a bit. "You're always the messengers of the Fae and protectors of the children. Why are you risking angering your queen by giving us warning about an unknown agreement?"

"It's our duty," said Tommy.

"It's our calling," said Timmy almost simultaneously.

Tommy said, "Protecting children is in our core. It's the stuff we're made of. If we knowingly let a child go unprotected, we... cease to be. Even if it means going against our queen's wishes or any accords she has signed with a mortal."

I thought for a moment before replying. "Changeling Accords must be written and signed. They cannot be a verbal agreement. I've learned that much during my research. Do you have the contract?"

A sad look passed over Tommy's face for a moment as he reached into a small pouch at his side. He produced a piece of parchment much too large to naturally fit in the bag. The Gob extended the parchment and its silver roller toward me. I took the contract and unrolled it. I didn't bother reading the terms but looked at the bottom of the scroll for the signatures of those involved in the accord.

I sat on the floor of my son's bedroom as a silent shock ran through my bones and a chill filled my body from recognition of the signatures. My father's penmanship glared off the page next to a beautiful set of calligraphy bearing the name of the Summer Queen. The contract held legitimate signatures for a Changeling to be given to the Summer Queen.

"Dad?"

Jason's voice snapped me out of it. He peered out his window. I rose to my knees and followed his line of sight to our back yard. An eerie green glow emanated from his tree house, and large black figures flowed down the trunk of the oak into our yard.

Tommy spoke up. "The Hobs are here to collect your son. You have a few moments to say goodbye before they take him, with or without force. He will become a servant of our queen and will be treated well. You have no need to fear for his safety or future."

Hobs were the worst. We had yet to face them in our past encounters with the Fae, but they were created as the premier warriors of the faerie folk. Even the vulnerability to iron barely slowed them. Thirteen obsidian shapes gathered about the base of the large tree. They planned an attack. The certainty of it drove me to action.

I couldn't just sit there and wait for them to take my son. There had to be a loophole in the accord, but it usually fell in favor of the Fae, not the mortals. My father had made his living as a shrewd haggler and a wonderful lawyer. Focusing my attention on the document to find a way out, I found myself wishing I had more time to explore every nuance of the agreement, but the Hobs marched toward the house.

I looked up from the yellowed parchment as the Gobs had vanished back under the bed. I said, "Jason. Take your iron filings and spread them about the windowsill. It'll slow the Hobs a little. Keep a few handfuls to throw at the first few that make it in. I've got to find a way out of this."

Jason followed my instructions without hesitation. He'd been involved in every fight against the Fae and knew our tactics inside and out. I continued to scan the document and a phrase leaped out at me, "Any blood descendant of the undersigned mortal…" I backtracked a few sentences and read more diligently.

A thud shook the window as the first Hob struck the plexiglass and rebounded off. After the second set of broken panes of glass, we replaced all the windows with thick plastic plates. Jason prepared to fling his iron at any Hobs who entered. His hand shook in fear and tears streamed down his face, but he stood strong in the face of the assault. Pride in his unwavering bravery filled my chest as I went back to the contract. I found the sentences I had hoped would be in the document.

"The undersigned Fae shall wait until after the fifth year of the life of the undersigned mortal's offspring to collect his or her owed debt. Any blood descendant of the undersigned mortal may be taken into service of the Fae."

I knew of a way out. I was an only child, and my wife never bore us a child. We adopted Jason as our son. The entire time the Fae had harassed us over Jason, they should have been targeting me. I kept the scroll in my left hand and walked over to Jason. "Hand me your iron filings. You won't be going anywhere tonight. I don't care what the Summer Queen or her lackeys have to say about it."

Jason dumped the iron bits into my hand.

"Now open the window."

Jason looked at me with an astonished look on his face and shook his head. "Why?"

"I have a plan to get you out of this. I promise."

Jason looked at me a moment longer before stepping to the window and opening it. I moved to the window with a single stride and flung my iron filings at the nearest Hobs. They recoiled with instinctive terror which gave me a chance to scrape up another handful from the sill.

I yelled, "Summon your queen. You cannot have this child of mine!" I waved the accord out the window. "This contract between your lady and my father stipulates only his blood can be taken. My son is not of my blood. You must take me in his stead."

"Dad!"

"Scott!"

The two cries behind me made me spin to find Maria standing beside Jason. During their attempts to break into the house, the Hobs had awoken Maria.

"Scott, what are you doing? What's going on?"

A quick glance outside confirmed that the Hobs milled about in confusion while two of them conferred. Turning back to my family, I waved the parchment in the air. "My father made a deal with the Fae. It appears his success and riches came at a price."

Maria's strong shoulders fell into a slump as she deflated. She looked at the floor in exasperation with her hair falling about her face. "What price are we talking about?"

"A person of his lineage and blood will be taken into service by the Summer Queen. This is what the harassment has been about. The Fae assumed Jason came from us naturally, even though he was adopted. I'm the only blood offspring of my father."

Maria looked from the floor to my face. Redness rimmed her eyes.

I continued explaining, "The contract can't be broken without losing all we have and more. Much more. The Fae will claim what we have and probably the three of us as slaves to pay for the 'interest' of the debt that has accumulated over the decades of wealth we have enjoyed."

"But that means you have to pay the price for your father's success!" Maria looked beside herself with concern. She moved up next to me and wrapped a slender arm around my waist. She wept into my shoulder.

We stood by the window and watched the hunched shoulders of the Hobs as the Fae gathered together. We couldn't understand their tongue, but from the tone it became obvious an argument brewed. Eventually the tallest and most muscle-bound of the warrior faerie broke from the group. He nodded his square head once in my direction and turned to the tree house. He marched around the tree dragging the stone tip of his spear to form a summoning circle around the trunk. Once the circle formed, the rest of the Hobs grouped around the oak and chanted.

The twin voices of Tommy and Timmy screeched from beneath the bed.

"She comes!"

"No! We must flee her wrath."

Before the Gobs arranged their escape, the entire oak tree shuddered hard enough to shake a large number of green leaves free. A bright yellow line formed along the length of the trunk of the venerable tree. The line perfectly split the heart Maria and I had carved into the tree when we were dating in high school. The line pulsed for a moment before snapping open into a doorway. The heart vanished behind the open portal.

I held my breath waiting.

The wait seemed to last days.

With a blast of warm air and the scent of irises on the wind, She stepped through the portal. The gentle hum of the city fell into awed silence at the presence of such a powerful being. The mournful howling of a lone dog in the distance remained the only sound echoing through the silence.

I openly wept at the sight of her horrible beauty. Curling locks of golden red hair flowed around a face so flawless, so perfect no mortal could dare to look fully upon it, and once they did, they dared not look away for fear of missing a moment of Her glowing countenance. As the Summer Queen came to a stop in the mortal realm, the Hobs dropped to their knees in supplication around the hem of the queen's long emerald dress.

Instead of dropping to my knees, I stood enraptured by her beauty. Pearl-white teeth peeked out from behind lush, red lips that swelled with contempt for all things mortal. Her thin nose rose up between green eyes to merge with a smooth and flawless forehead.

Her emerald eyes surveyed my back yard before her sing-song voice rang out. "Why have I been brought to this pathetic place?"

The accord in my left hand began to burn into my flesh. The startling pain of the faerie fire brought my attention back to my goals and my situation. I took a deep breath and called out the window. "Lady of Summer, Mistress of Nature, Bringer of Warmth and Kindness, I had you summoned, so you may claim your half of an accord signed by Wilfred Hawthorne."

I paused for a moment and took a deep breath. "I am yours to claim."

Jason and Maria cried behind me while holding each another. Maria would have argued my leaving with the Queen, but she had studied just as hard as I had during our time battling the Fae. She knew there was no way out of an accord with the Fae once the blood signatures were applied.

The Summer Queen turned toward me. "Step out here, mortal who claims I am owed his servitude. I wish to see if thou art worthy."

"One moment, please. I wish to say goodbye to my family."

The Fae waved her hand in my direction as if a few moments, or even hours or days, didn't matter to her. As a true immortal, she held infinite patience in most matters.

I brought Jason and Maria into my arms. I choked as I cried, but I managed to get out the words I needed to say. "I'm sorry. I have to go. My father arranged this without my knowledge. I wish I had been aware of it, so I could maybe have found a way out. I don't have time for that now, but on the other side of the Fae veil I will have forever to find a way back to you.

"Maria, be good as you always are. You can do this. Explain my absence however you wish. Make up some story about wanderlust taking over my soul and forcing me to explore the world. It is what happened to my father, and people will believe it."

Maria nodded through her tears.

"Jason, I will always be with you in spirit. You may not know this yet, but I will be able to keep an eye on you from the other side. I'll always peer over your shoulder and help you when I can. Just because I'm leaving you doesn't mean I don't love you. If I had a way to stay at your side forever, I would take it. I just don't have that option right now. Be good for your mother."

As I finished speaking, I choked up even more, and had to wait a minute to catch my breath.

"I love both of you." As I said those final words, I released my family and turned to face the Fae waiting for me outside.

Clambering through the window with as much grace as I could manage, the night's chill sent a shiver across my body. A bad feeling filled my soul about the future, but I had no choice. My father's contract with the Fae bound me to Her service. My father's death, three years earlier, robbed me of a chance to gain any form of revenge for destroying my family. Still, I silently cursed the sorry bastard.

As I approached the Summer Queen, I realized how tall she stood. My six-and-a-half foot-frame usually gave me an advantage during confrontations, but She stood another handspan above me. Despite my lack of height, I looked Her in the eyes as I handed over the accord. Her graceful arm slowly reached forth and took the document from my quivering hand. I tried to tell myself the chilly night caused my quaking, but I knew better.

The slim fingers of the Fae's hand unfurled the length of the parchment, and her startling emerald eyes scanned the words. I stood in silence waiting while the Hobs gathered around the queen and me with their spears pointed in my direction. Moments faded to minutes as we awaited the queen's pleasure.

At last, She looked from the contract to me. "I can sense Wilfred's blood in your veins. The child you have taken into your home as your own will not suffice for this contract. I gave much to your father, and I will reap at least a minimal reward for doing so even if you are not the one I desire. I need a child of innocence to act the role as my Summer Prince who was recently…" She paused thoughtfully as if choosing her next word carefully, "… indisposed. I was hoping to claim your son. You shall make a fine addition as a sentinel to a particular crossroads in my realm."

After a moment's pause, She threw the accord on the ground, and it burst into bright green flames. "Come with me, my new guardian." She turned her back on me and walked to the tree. The Hobs surrounding us urged me to follow with grunts and thrusts of their spears. I turned back to my house one last time and waved a final goodbye to my family. The tears I held back flowed again. I stepped through the portal in the oak tree and followed the Summer Queen into Her realms.

The place given to me by my new queen stood near the veil between the mortal lands and the Fae world. She gave me the task of watching the entrance to her kingdom and lighting a beacon fire if any mortal entered at that point. When the Hobs first dumped me in this place, they marched me around the perimeter of the clearing with its copse of trees and informed me of the boundaries of my confinement.

While getting the grand tour of the small area, I took it all in. A warm breeze carried the scent of fresh flowers from fields near the horizon. I took some small pleasure in this despite being separated from my family. The trees held a variety of fruits, but the colors were off. The apples were blue, the pears were bright orange, the cherries were yellow, and the bananas were pinkish-white in color. Even with the strange colors, the fruit tasted wonderful and extra sweet.

I held my post night and day without becoming hungry, thirsty or tired. The birds in the trees singing their songs helped me pass the days along. The days turned into months, and I noticed movement on the other side of the veil. I saw people going about their daily business in the mortal realm. I often thought of Jason and Maria and tried to see them through the veil. At times, I managed to catch slight glimpses of Jason's shape, but I saw very little in the way of details.

As the months passed me by, I discovered I held a slight amount of control over the barrier between the mortal realm and the one holding me captive. I didn't hold the power to pierce the barrier physically, but I could move it around the other world and see what I wished. I focused my view firmly on Jason and watched him as his grief for my loss faded to sadness. He seemed to be growing so fast, and then I realized the time I experienced did not match the time Jason experienced. My time moved much slower than his.

I observed him going through his life. I found pleasure in his laughter and love, even without me in his life. Moments of sadness plagued him, and during these times, I gently pressed into the veil and whispered to him, "I'm still here, and I love you." My words pulled him from his dark times.

He grew and walked into moments of decision. *Do I ask her out? Do I take those drugs? Should I kiss her now? My heart's broken, what do I do now? Will I ever love again?*

At each of these moments, I leaned hard into the barrier, and whispered my advice. Sometimes he heard me and listened. Other times he seemed to not hear me at all. With the first few suggestions I made, I noticed I moved a bit slower for a while, but soon recovered. Sometimes, a whisper across the veil took so much out of me, I could hardly move, and my skin took on a grayish tint.

After one particularly harsh exertion of effort, a mortal stumbled through the veil. I attempted to do my duty and light my watch fire, but I couldn't move.

The interloper stopped and laughed a hearty guffaw at my expense. He approached me and sat down at my feet before speaking in a mirthful tone. "Thank you for thinning the veil enough for me to cross. I've been trying to find an easy way into the Fae realms for quite some time. My usual routes seem closed to me lately."

Before I recovered at his sudden appearance, he continued. "You don't know what you're doing to yourself, stranger! I know you're a mortal here in these lands, and you do not have Fae powers. You may be able to pierce the veil from time-to-time, but the more you do it, the faster you will turn to stone! Already your feet have turned, and I fear they are now lost."

Shock filled me as I looked down at my lower extremities. They had turned to stone and rooted me into place. The rest of my skin had taken on a granite-like texture but remained slightly flexible. I looked back at the happy stranger and managed to get out the words, "Can you help me?"

"Nay. You're on your own in this fight against the power of the Fae. Either you learn to control it, or it will take you over. I fear you're already bound for becoming something else, and there is not much I can do for you." The man pulled his bright patchwork cloak about his body as he stood. "I have need of meeting with your queen. I'll light your signal fire for you, to keep you out of trouble. Have a good day or week or month, depending on your point of view."

He flicked his hand toward the pile of wood standing near me. It erupted into a large billowing bonfire. As he walked into the nearby forest with a skip in his step, he tipped his wide-brimmed hat in my direction.

The man's comments bewildered me, but they gave me food for thought. My efforts seemed to be turning me to stone in small measures. The more effort I put into whispering to my son, the faster I turned to stone.

I stood rooted in place by my stone feet and watched the bonfire burn. As I peered through the flames, I saw that the wood beneath the fire wasn't consumed. As my gaze shifted across the shimmering heat, I caught a glimpse of a face looking at me from the bonfire. The waves of heat kept me from seeing too many details, but the face was clearly feminine.

I called out to the woman's face in the fire. "Hello? Can you hear me?"

The fire woman's eyes went wide for a brief instant before she opened her mouth to speak. The flames winked out and her face vanished before the mouth could say anything.

I wondered about who the woman in the fire was and what she might have wanted, but no answers came my way. I did my best to keep my focus on my son, so I turned my back on the mystical pile of unburning wood and faced the veil again.

My stony affliction didn't matter. I whispered anyway. I swore when we brought Jason home, I would guide and protect him for as long as I remained able, at any cost. If this meant turning myself to a stone plinth, so be it. I firmly decided to continue helping my son.

Over the course of the years my son grew to a man and passed through the many trials and tribulations every man faces. His strength of character and honor held him true in many rough situations. As he aged, my intercessions became more rare. By this time, I only had use of my arms, shoulders, neck and head. The rest of my body had turned to stone over the years. I still spoke in hushed tones to Jason, to guide him through his rough patches. Every year on his birthday, I couldn't resist leaning into him and telling him how much I loved and missed him.

He grew well into adulthood, and Maria passed away. I wanted to hold him, but the best I could muster were muffled tears in his ear while sharing his pain. He handled the death of his mother much better than I did, and his strength made me proud.

The cloaked stranger chose this moment to walk into my life again. He approached me with a sad look on his face. "Mister, you're sure a stubborn one. I've kept a few eyes on you over the years, and you strike me as a good man. I can intercede with the Summer Queen on your behalf and have her release you from your bonds. I can't guarantee she'll listen to me, but I'm willing to call in the favor if you like."

I paused in my grief to listen to his offer. If I were released, I might be able to regain the lost use of my body. I could rejoin my son and live a normal life. Tears of joy at these prospects joined my tears of sadness. I managed to get out the words, "Please. I'll be forever grateful for your help."

The traveler smiled at me. "Forever is a long time, but we'll see what we can work out. First, I have to talk to her highness. Promise me you'll lay off the veil whispering until I return. You're already in bad enough shape as it is."

I nodded, "You have my word, Mister… I don't even know your name."

"You can call me Tathas."

"Very well, Tathas. You have my promise to not whisper through the veil with my words until you return."

Several hours passed before my new companion returned, and I could tell by the look on his face he did not bring good news. He pulled his legs under him as he sat at my stony feet. "I'm sorry, my friend. The queen refused my request for a boon."

"I understand. She doesn't seem the type to break a contract."

"Contract? Oy. I didn't know about any agreement like that. Was she expecting someone else to fulfill your end of the bargain?"

"My son."

"That makes sense. She's been in search of a new prince for quite some time, and she's always been partial to children for that role. That explains why she dumped you out in the middle of nowhere. She laid claim to your son but had to take you instead. I'm impressed that you found a loophole in her accord. That's a rare thing."

"You seem to know quite a bit about the Fae. How have you learned all of this?"

He shook his cloak out from under his legs and thought for a moment. He seemed to be carefully picking his words. "You can call me an emissary of sorts. I broker deals between Summer and Winter, in an effort to keep the peace between the two. We've not seen an all-out war for thousands of years, and I'd like to keep it that way."

"Well, if you can't get me out of this spot, I don't think anyone can." I looked down at where he sat. "If you get a chance to visit again, I'll always have time to talk. It's been nice visiting with you, but I need to return to my son. He's about to attend his mother's funeral, and I think he may need me."

A sad look crossed Tathas's face as he stood. "You know what you're doing and the price you're paying. I don't like it much, but I'll leave you to it. I'll come around again if I can." With his final words, he walked away over a nearby hill and into my past.

Later on in years, Jason married and started a family of his own. His family brought intense happiness to me, for he had lived alone for so long. By this time, I only had the use of my head and one arm. The rest of me had turned into solid, unfeeling, uncaring stone.

As Jason surrounded himself with his own loved ones, he needed my guidance less and less. I turned some of my care and attention to my grandchildren, but they did not know me, and our tenuous connection remained weak. I knew a great effort would be required to speak to them, and I no longer had it in me.

Jason's days turned to night, and I knew the end of his time neared. He became older, frailer, and sicker for greater lengths of time. Finally, his body failed him, but his spirit refused to give up.

The granite of my chest ran dark with tear streaks.

I knew what must be done.

With one last effort, I pressed into the veil separating us and whispered, "I love you. I love you. I love you. Give in to your time and join your mother. Maybe I will see you soon. I love y—" The remainder of my body turned to solid stone at this moment. I never had the chance to finish my final words to my beloved son. I sensed him across the veil, and, with a harsh shudder, his aged and decrepit body finally stopped.

I had done it. I had guided my son through his life from the moment we met until the moment he parted the mortal realm.

My eyes are now locked looking across a forest-ringed plain. Fae come and stare at me, and I can hear them talk as they speculate what caused the strange streaks to run down the face of the plinth simply known as "The Whispering Stone."

From the Author

This story came to me shortly after my son was born. I swore "my life before his" when he was born. That made me think about changelings, faerie contracts, and what if all this culminated to a confrontation between a father and a faerie queen over the life of his son.

I'd originally intended for the story to be full of fights and battles between a mortal man and the powerful supernatural, where he finally wins the day by driving away the faerie warriors. As I wrote it, a softer touch came out. I can definitely say that fatherhood changed some of my writing, and it shows in this work. I ended up writing an emotional tale about a father's love for his son throughout the son's life. It's about showing and giving that love, no matter the cost.

About the Author

J.T. Evans writes fantasy and urban fantasy novels. He'll dabble with sci-fi and horror in short form as well. He is the former president of the Colorado Springs Fiction Writers Group and Pikes Peak Writers. When not writing, he secures computers at the Day Job, home brews great beers, and plays way too many tabletop games.

Despite having his right arm amputated and reattached after a nasty car crash, he types faster than the average bear. The first two novels in his Modern Mythology series, *Griffin's Feather* and *Viper's Bane,* are out now. He's hastily working on more right now, and you can find out more about him at www.jtevans.net.

Varmints

by
Wayland Smith

Varmints

*I*t was a good day for chasing butterflies, and Jackie Harrison was having a grand time. The hills just outside town were green, dotted with flowers, and the fluttering creatures were everywhere. He smiled to himself. It was a great way to spend an afternoon. Eventually, he'd have to go back home, but for now, it was just him... or maybe it wasn't.

A man walked out of the tree line. He was dirty and looked like he'd been traveling far too long. He seemed very tall, but Jackie was only seven, so everyone was tall to him. The man's wide-brimmed hat was black, he had a rifle in one hand, and a saddle slung over his shoulder by some kind of strap. Saddle bags were draped on his other shoulder. It looked like he was struggling with the weight from the way he bent slightly forward, countering the load on his back.

It wasn't unusual to see a man with a rifle. Hunting was how a lot of people around here kept fed. The crossed gun-belts, worn low, caught Jackie's attention, though. He'd never seen a real gunfighter, but his brother Bobby had read him stories out of the dime novels.

Even from here, Jackie could tell the man had seen him. The boy paused for a moment, then kept walking. Jackie knew he could run like the wind, and the man had all that stuff he was carrying, so he felt it was safe enough to be bold. "Hello," Jackie called. "Do you need some help?" Mother had always told him to be polite to strangers.

The stranger squinted up at him. "There a place to get a room around here?" His voice was low and gravelly.

"Oh, sure. The Alhambra has rooms. Mrs. Wilette's real nice. Town's about two miles," the boy pointed.

The man grunted, adjusted his burdens, and walked on past. "Thanks, kid."

"Name's Jackie. Jackie Harrison." The boy kept moving on his hill, keeping the stranger in view.

"Obliged," the man said with a nod as he trudged along. He stopped and looked back up at the boy. "Come nightfall, you'd best get inside."

Something in the man's voice made a chill run up the boy's spine. He looked up at the sun, knowing it was still late morning.

The town of Denton didn't get a lot of strangers, especially not grim, gun-toting ones, so the man's slow passage down the main (and only) street got a lot of attention. His weary stare took in the buildings, the same variety he'd seen in countless towns: a saloon, a church, a blacksmith, a general store, a restaurant, a bank, a marshal's office. The Alhambra looked to be the saloon, and he wondered if they were used to renting rooms for more than an hour.

The wooden boardwalk creaked under him as he stepped off the dusty street. The doors swung easily as he pushed inside. The fat man behind the bar looked up with a smile that dimmed as he got a better look. "Help you, stranger?"

"A meal, a room, and a whiskey," the man rasped. He walked to a table in the corner, dumped his load on a chair, and sat in another that gave him a view of the door he'd come in by.

"Oh, of course. Right away," the man said, nodding. "We only have some bacon and biscuits right now," he said, looking up at the big clock on the wall. A fancy piece, it had come all the way from the coast. The man's implied criticism of ordering whiskey at noon, or just before, didn't seem to make a difference.

A few minutes after he scurried in back, an older woman, rail thin, in a well-tailored dress came out from the back room. "I understand you want a room?" she asked, taking in his dusty clothes, and the carried saddle.

He nodded, reached into a coat pocket, and put two silver coins on the table. "Figure that'll carry me a while."

She took them, weighed them in her hand, and nodded. "That should be fine, Mister…"

"Morgan," he said. "Appreciate it, Miz Wilette."

She looked startled. "Do I know you?"

"Young fella on a hill sent me your way." Morgan leaned back in his chair, stripping the worn leather gloves from his hands. Flexing his fingers, he dropped the gloves on his pile of belongings then shrugged out of his long grey coat. He moved one hand down off the table, slipping the leather thong off the revolver on his left side. It was probably going to be a peaceful meal. He wasn't still alive by banking on "probably."

"Oh, I'll have to thank him. Did he say who he was?" Her eyes were bright, he wasn't sure whether from curiosity or greed from the sound of other coins clinking in his pocket.

"Jackie," he offered. "No disrespect meant, ma'am, but could I get some coffee while I'm waiting for the food?"

She flushed. Not offering was a lapse in hospitality. "I'll just go get that for you," she said, moving back to the rear of the restaurant.

The front doors opened again, and two large men came in, each wearing a gun-belt, both with stars pinned to their shirts. Morgan sighed. He'd hoped to at least have gotten his coffee first, but this, too, was a scene he'd played out many times.

"Morning, stranger," the older of the two men said.

At least he's polite, Morgan thought. *For now.*

"Mornin', Marshal," Morgan answered, tipping his hat slightly.

"You seem to be on some hard times," the Marshal said, nodding at the saddle.

"Was going to look for a horse after I got set up here. Got any recommendations?"

"What happened to your last one?" the younger man, larger, with a body of muscle running to fat, asked sharply.

"Don't rightly see how that's your business, Deputy," Morgan answered flatly.

The deputy glared. "What if I'm making it my business?"

Morgan wondered if he was ever going to get his coffee. "I'm just going about my business. You really want to start a problem where there ain't none?" His tone was mild, light even, but the marshal saw the man's eyes narrowing, and noted that one of his hands was where he couldn't see it.

"What business is that, you don't mind me asking?" the marshal threw in, trying to defuse the situation.

"Varmint hunter."

"We can hunt our own varmints," the bigger man said, challenge in his voice.

"Everyone can. 'Til they can't," Morgan agreed.

"We're just a small town here, stranger," the marshal said before his deputy could make things worse. "We're not looking for trouble, but we do like to know who's visiting us."

Morgan nodded. "Name's Morgan. I'll be here a few days, then moving on after."

"After what?" the younger man interjected.

"After I see 'bout the varmints," Morgan said.

This was when Mrs. Wilette came out with a tray of food, coffee, and a shot in a small glass. "Oh, Marshal Hollifield, I didn't know you were here," she said. "Can I get you anything?"

"No, I think we're fine," the marshal said. "There's no trouble, right, Mr. Morgan?"

The man took the shot as soon as she put the tray down, tossed it back, and let out a small sigh of satisfaction. It was better than he'd hoped, for such a small place. "Oh, there's trouble. Just not from me."

The marshal and deputy looked at each other. Mrs. Wilette retreated to the back room once again.

"You better explain that," the younger man said again.

"You two plannin' on stayin', you might as well have a seat," Morgan said. "Gettin' a crick in my neck lookin' up at ya." He pulled the plate in front of him, murmured a small prayer, and began eating.

The marshal pulled out a chair and sat. "My name's Hollifield. You're really going to have to explain what you mean."

Morgan shoveled in several bites, intent on his food. "I'm going to eat my meal, put my gear up in my room, and go talk to your priest. You want to come along, feel free. I don't want to explain this more than once anyhow." He kept on eating.

"Father Zavella isn't a morning person," Hollifield said.

Mrs. Wilette peered through the door, withdrew, and then came back with a full coffee pot and more cups, placing them on the table. She laid a key next to the plates. "Room 7," she said before leaving again. Morgan kept eating, the marshal waiting until Wilette was out of the room.

"So, you might want to talk to us," Hollifield pressed, pouring some coffee. His deputy just stood there, arms folded, glowering.

"Marshal, I'm goin' t' get something out of my saddlebags there." Morgan locked eyes with the deputy. "Please don't do nothin' foolish that'll lead to hard feelings."

The deputy glared, arms lowering, putting his hand closer to his holster. Morgan kept his eyes on the big man as he unfastened the bag, slipped his fingers inside, and came out with two envelopes. They were old, creased, and stained. Morgan dropped them on the table in front of the marshal and went back to eating. "Take a look," he suggested.

Hollifield raised an eyebrow but opened the first of the two. He read slowly, Morgan noticing his lips moving. Morgan ate, Hollifield read, and the deputy glared. Finally, the marshal moved on to the second envelope as Morgan finished off the food and drank the rest of his coffee.

"You some kind of hard man? We supposed to be scared of you?" The deputy's voice had a nasty edge to it.

"I was all that, 'spect I'd still have my horse," Morgan said mildly.

The deputy looked confused, clearly not sure how to answer that. The marshal finally looked up from his reading. "This is… irregular," Hollifield said finally.

"Gonna get worse," Morgan said. "I'm going to leave my gear upstairs now. You want to tag along, you know where I'm going next."

Morgan picked up his belongings, sighed internally at the weight, and stepped around the obnoxious deputy, who had planted himself in the way. Moving upstairs, he let himself into his room and took a quick look around. It was simple, but clean. A bed, a stand for clothes, two chairs, a pitcher and bowl, and a small table by the bed. He tested the water and was surprised to find it was cool. He upped his estimation of Mrs. Wilette. She must have done a light freshening of the room while he ate. He nodded. She was good people. He hoped she'd still be around come morning.

He left his saddle, bags, and pack in the room, bringing his rifle with him. Hollifield and his deputy were waiting, a harshly whispered discussion breaking off when they saw him. "Need those letters back," Morgan said, holding out his right hand.

"Oh, sure." The marshal handed them over, looking relieved to have them out of his hands.

Morgan walked over to the church, paused at the doorway, and took off his hat. Short silver hair shone in the sunlight, and the marshal noted some of the man's right ear was gone, leaving a ragged scar. Walking through the interior of the church, Morgan glanced around before heading for one of the back doors.

"Hey, you can't go in there," the deputy protested.

Morgan ignored him, knocked once, and opened it. There was a small back room with a desk and a chair, both looking rough and banged together by someone with more enthusiasm than skill. Morgan walked back out, ignoring the two men, and went to the small house next to the church. He glanced at the small cemetery, noting the short wooden fence running around it. His nostrils flared as he breathed in deeply. The faint smell of rot made him wrinkle his nose. The wind was carrying it from outside the down, the direction he'd come from. He had less time than he'd hoped, but that was nothing new.

Knocking on the door of the house, he called out, "Father Dominic Zavella, I need to talk t' you. Now."

There was a muffled voice from inside. "The church isn't open just yet, my son," came a muffled voice, thick with sleep.

"Not here for the church, here for you. Gabriella is coming."

The deputy looked surprised at hearing a word a priest shouldn't say come from behind the door. After a bit of shuffling, a young man with sleep-tousled hair opened the door, squinting in the light. "Are you sure?"

"Why I'm here. Bishop Talbert sends his regards and his apologies."

The man's face paled. "Is it that bad? Are you sure it's her?"

"She's coming. She's not alone. She knows you're here. These people," he waved a hand, taking in the lawmen and the town beyond them, "ain't gonna listen to me. You give 'em a warning, they might have a chance. That graveyard protected?" He jerked his thumb behind him.

"What? Oh, yes, of course. I remember…" The man looked ill. "There's no way to stop this?"

"I hadn't lost my horse, mighta got here quicker. But they're coming for you."

"What the hell's going on, Father?" the deputy finally burst out, then looked abashed. "Sorry," he added a bit quieter when everyone looked at him.

"Perhaps you should take a walk through the town, John, and make sure everyone is safe?" the priest suggested quietly.

The deputy's face went red, recognizing the dismissal, but when the marshal nodded, he stalked off.

"You'd better come in," Zavella said.

Shortly, the priest, the marshal, and the stranger were seated at a small table, a coffee pot in the middle. "I'm sorry, Douglas, I had no idea this would come to pass," Zavella said to the marshal.

"You two want to fill me in on what's happening?" the marshal asked.

"Short version," Morgan said, "the Father here has a past, and it's catching up with him tonight. You need to get everyone inside tonight, keep them there, in their homes or the church—not in the saloon or anyplace like that."

"If someone's coming for Father Zavella, I'm helping him," the marshal protested.

"You would be, Douglas," Zavella said. "Truly. This isn't... the kind of thing you can do much about."

"What's coming, some kind of gang? I can handle myself," the man protested.

"Some kind," Morgan agreed, "but nothing you've seen before. And you don't want to. Stay inside after the sun goes down. Keep your people safe. All you can do."

"Did you make some kind of enemy before you came here?" Hollifield asked the priest.

"I made many. I would say that, in general, I made the right kinds. I thought I had left all that behind me, but it seems the past has a long reach." The priest sighed. "I'm sorry if the people are in danger because of me."

"You have to be somewhere," Morgan said. "You hid the best you could. Ain't your fault." He pulled a pocket watch out, flipped it open, then snapped it shut. "I'm going to get some rest. You tell him as much or as little as you want. I'll be back before sundown." Morgan left, walking back to the hotel. He could see the deputy, John, pacing down the street. Part of him wanted to wave and needle the man, but he needed the sleep more. He made it to his room without incident, closed the door, locked it, pushed a chair under the handle, and lay down. He was asleep in seconds.

Hours later, his eyes snapped open. He checked his pocket watch, just to be sure, nodded to himself, and got up. He wound his watch, stripped, and washed himself in the water from the bowl on the table. Kneeling, he murmured old familiar words, seeking solace and courage. Rising, he slowly dressed in fresh clothes.

He unloaded his weapons, lining the rounds up on the table by the bed, and cleaned the pistols and rifle. Morgan placed the rounds in a coat pocket and opened his saddle bags. Pulling out a few boxes, he carefully reloaded his weapons, each of the new bullets marked with a faint cross and glowing with a pale blue nimbus of energy. He checked his knife, slid it on his belt, and loaded a spare cylinder with different bullets that gleamed silver. He pulled a bundle from his pack, untying it and shaking it out. Looking it over carefully, he slid the silver mail on over his shirt and vest, then pulled the long coat over it. Hand on the knob of the door, he looked upward. "I'll fall if I have to, just protect the people of this town. They didn't do anything to deserve this." Pausing, he added "Even that asshole deputy. A-men."

Between the extra bullets in every pocket, the mail, and a few other items hidden away in his clothes, he clinked slightly as he walked. He was used to the sound. It was almost comforting. Down in the main room, he saw Mrs. Wilette in close conversation with the fat man he'd seen earlier. They suddenly broke off, seeing him come down the stairs.

"Oh, Mr. Morgan. Did you need anything?"

"Whatever you have handy to eat, and coffee. Did Marshal," what had the man's name been? "Hollifield tell you what you need to do tonight?"

She nodded, looking puzzled. "We're to go home and stay inside and leave the doors closed and not come out no matter what we hear until morning. But I don't understand. Are there outlaws coming?"

He looked at her, face set, lines more apparent then they'd been that morning. "Much worse. You stay in your house, you should be fine. But it's important, you have to stay inside. You got me?"

The woman nodded. The fat man scurried off, hopefully to get his food. One hurried meal of steaks, beans, and biscuits later, he rose from the table. "Thank you kindly, ma'am. You get home now."

"Are you going to be all right?" she asked, looking up at the man.

"Not up to me, ma'am. It's all in His hands."

Still looking troubled, she left. He reached under his coat to an inner pocket. Pulling out a large cross on a silver chain, he draped it around his neck and walked back to the church.

Zavella was standing in the doorway, dressed in black. "Are you prepared?" he asked.

"Best I'm gonna be, Father."

The priest murmured some words Morgan couldn't hear, sketched the sign of the cross in the air, and nodded. "Are you sure it's her?" he asked quietly.

"What I was told," Morgan answered.

Just before night fell, there was a knock on the church door. Morgan opened it, gun in hand. Marshal Hollifield and John the deputy were there, carrying rifles and looking grim.

"You can't help us," Morgan said. "I can't protect you in this."

"Protecting people is our job, son. This is our town," the marshal said.

Morgan watched the sun sinking low. "Too late now," he muttered.

Dark swallowed the town, shadows rising up, linking together, spilling into black pools that kept spreading. The darkness was thick, more like a slow flood than just the lack of light. Morgan shook his head. "You gonna do this, you need to listen to me or the Father."

"Why should we listen to you?" John asked.

"Because you really don't want to die tonight," Morgan said.

"That a threat?" John glared again.

"Tonight, of all nights, you don't want to fall," the priest said, licked his lips, and hurriedly made the sign of the cross.

The night had been still, no breeze, not even a sound. Marshal Hollifield had lived in Denton for years, and never heard it this dead quiet. No noise from the saloon, the blacksmith. Nothing.

Then the wind picked up, and there was some kind of strange keening, faint cries in the night. They could hear footsteps outside, light and quick. Scurrying, almost.

The voice was shrill, but familiar to them all. "Missster Moooorgan. Come out and plaaay with me."

John looked startled. "That's Jackie Harrison. What's he doing out there?"

Morgan shook his head. "Not anymore it ain't. Just sounds like him."

"The hell you mean? It's Jackie." John glared at Morgan. "You can't stop me from going to help him."

Morgan shrugged. "I could. I won't. But if you go out there, you ain't coming back in. Not until morning, anyway."

"Come on, Mr. Morgan... I'm waaaaaaaiting."

"It sure sounds like him. How can you be sure it's not?" Hollifield asked.

"I never introduced myself t' him. Unless he came into town and asked around, and ain't a lot of folks know who I am, how's he know my name?"

Hollifield frowned, lips pursed.

"Oh, hell with this," John yanked the door open and rushed out. "Jackie, where are you?" Morgan kicked the door closed. John's voice suddenly broke into screams that lasted far too long. Hollifield moved towards the door.

"Nothin' you can do," Morgan said. "We haven't even started the real fight yet."

Hollifield opened the door carefully and looked out. Lurching forms shuffled around, seemingly aimless. He tried to make sense of what he was seeing. "What are they?" he asked.

"The dead, not allowed rest," Zavella answered. He walked up to the altar and pulled out a flat case from behind it. Kneeling, he crossed himself and opened it. Hollifield was clearly surprised to see the priest holding up a gleaming sword. Zavella marched down the central aisle of the church. "We cannot allow this to continue."

"What can we do?" Hollifield asked, sounding lost, standing in the doorway.

"Pray. Fight the good fight. Know that we are righteous," Zavella said.

"That don't work, aim for the head. Most of those go down when you take their heads," Morgan answered.

The mob parted, and, in the moonlight, a striking woman sashayed up to the edge of the churchyard. "Dominic," she called. "Do come out. All this hiding is so tedious. I had to stop at a delightful little farm just outside this dreary town to amuse myself. Did you know him?" She gestured, and a small shape scampered up next to her. His face split wide in a huge grin, impossible teeth reflecting the light.

"Jackie..." Hollifield muttered.

The gunshot split the night, startling the priest and the marshal. Jackie's head exploded with a flash of orange light, spattering gore on the woman, who scowled. "Really, was that necessary? So messy."

"What do you want, Gabriella?" Zavella called as Morgan levered a new round in his rifle. Hollifield staggered back inside and then threw up in a corner.

"Why, to finish what we started, of course. You were so close to being reasonable. Don't you want to come back to me? Spend the long nights together?" Her voice purred, alluring.

"She's... beautiful," Hollifield gasped, coming back to the door, wiping his mouth absently.

"She's a creature of evil," Zavella responded. He held his cross high. "Stop your petty tricks, Gabriella!" The cross sparkled with silver light, and harsh shadows leapt in the harsh silver glow. Gabriella flinched back, still attractive, certainly, but not the irresistible siren she'd been a moment ago.

Hollifield looked as if he'd been slapped, head rocking back in surprise at the change.

Gabriella reeled, then glared back at the church. "If you're not going to see reason, if the plight of that poor boy didn't move you, maybe I can find someone you do care about." She moved closer to the churchyard and raised her arms to shoulder height, making motions with her hands.

"Get ready," Morgan said. "This is gonna be our chance."

"Our chance for what?" Hollifield asked.

"She should get an unpleasant surprise any moment now," Zavella said, staring fixedly at the woman.

A bitter coldness filled the night, coming in waves from the woman, pressing against their skin. "What is that?" the marshal gasped.

"She's calling on her power," Zavella said.

Suddenly, there was a flash of blue-white light from the fence around the graves. Gabriella screamed and staggered away, hands flung up to her face, fingers smoking.

"Now," Morgan said. He began levering shots from his Winchester. Each one of the shambling bodies he hit shuffled back, looked confused, and then burst into brilliant orange flame. Gabriella shrieked again. Zavella drew his sword and charged out the door. Morgan followed, walking step by step, still taking shots.

Their leaping to action shook Hollifield out of the stupor that had seized him. He carefully brought up his own rifle, sighted, and fired. A shambling man-like thing on the far side of the crowd suddenly fell like a puppet with its string cut. He wasn't sure why he and Morgan's bullets were getting such different results, but he moved on to his next shot.

"Per la Gracia de Deu!" thundered Zevalla. His sword burst into brilliant silver light, and he swept it at the closest of the monstrous forms. The being let out a cry and was consumed by fire, leaving a small pile of smoldering ash on the ground. Zevalla hacked through the mob, closing on Gabriella, with Morgan helping clear his path, firing over and over.

"Do you think He can possibly love you like I can?" Gabriella snarled, bringing her hands back down. Red dripped down her face from her eyes.

"No, I think He loves more than you ever could," Zevalla answered, swinging his blade in a sweeping arc and destroying three more of her servants with one strike. Morgan shot another few followers. The flashes of light were illuminating the various forms. Morgan could see the horror on Hollifield's face, but the man stood firm. Gabriella's servants were revealed in their horror: rotting flesh, decaying faces, chunks of flesh missing in different places. It was like nothing Hollifield had ever seen or wanted to see again. How could such things be walking, let alone fighting? But they kept reaching for Morgan and Zevalla, and Hollifield made himself think about just his next target, his next shot.

"You were mine once! You will be again," Gabriella shrieked, lunging at Zavella.

"I was foolish and sinful once, I will be no more," he answered, moving aside with a fluid grace that surprised the marshal. Zavella being sober at all was a surprise. The priest swung his blade again, and Gabriella danced away, cat-quick, snarling. Hollifield saw impossibly long teeth at the front of her mouth, like on a tiger he'd once seen in a circus long, long ago. There was swirling red Hell-light in her eyes.

The three men fought, shooting, stabbing, slicing at their foes. The impossible mob thinned. Hollifield began to dare to hope the night might finally end. Then, he saw a large shape moving up the track toward the church door. It shuffled to a stop some ten feet away, struggling with some barrier mortal eyes could not see.

Hollifield raised his rifle to fire, and, in another burst of light from Zavella's sword, saw John's features, looking up at him, pleading. "Come help me, Marshal," his deputy's voice rasped. There was a huge, ragged wound on his neck. "It's so cold."

Hollifield's hands shook. He looked down the rifle and couldn't focus on the sights for the tears in his eyes. "God, John, I'm so sorry," he said, his voice thick with loss and sorrow.

Morgan finally heard a sound he'd been dreading. His rifle had emptied long ago, and he'd been working with his pistols. He lined up on one of the few remaining shambling monsters and heard a click. It wasn't the first time he'd had to reload in the swirling chaos, but it was the first time he came up empty when he reached into his pocket for more shells. "Dammit," he muttered.

He tossed his gun from one hand to the other and reached into the other pocket, coming up with the regular shells he had emptied from his guns back in his room. He opened the cylinder, spilled the spent shells out, and shoved new ones in place. Much more carefully now, he began shooting the monsters in the head. They fell without the fiery effects of his earlier shots.

Zavella and Gabriella dueled on, a series of strikes, evasions, silver light, and the whistling sound of talons cutting the air as her fingers swiped at him. "You will be mine!" she roared, reaching again. Zavella stood his ground.

"I am His," he said, and lunged forward. Her claws bit deep in his side, spraying blood. His burning blade went completely through her chest. He slumped to the ground with a groan, while she hissed and shrieked. "I forgive you," he rasped out as he bled and silver fire consumed her.

The few lumbering shapes fell to the ground. John glared up at the marshal, then spun around at the bright light and despairing wail. "NO!" the former deputy bellowed, moving incredibly quickly, racing to the burning woman.

"Shut up," Morgan said to the big man. He pulled his Bowie knife, blue fire running down the edge of the blade. John snarled, and the two circled each other. Hollifield couldn't quite see what happened, but there was a frenzy of blows, parries, strikes and counters, and then John fell, his large body burning to ash.

Hollifield stumbled out of the church. "Is it over?"

Morgan, bent over slightly, panting, shook his head. "Fight's done," he managed. "You need t' figure out what you're tellin' folks."

The marshal looked around, groaned, then moved to the priest's side.

Zavella lay on his back, the sword still clutched in one hand. "My work… is done," he said to Hollifield as the marshal knelt by him. "I'm sorry for the others that were hurt."

Hollifield just shook his head. "You were amazing, preacher. You did God's work."

"He may have done His work through me," Zavella said, and died with a peaceful smile.

The next day, as funerals were planned, questions asked, and clean-up begun, Morgan saddled his new horse, John's big bay.

"Sure you can't stay?" Marshal Hollifield asked. "I could use a good man like you."

Morgan swung up into the saddle. "I have a lot more work to do."

Hollifield remembered one of the first things the mysterious stranger had said to him. "Varmint hunting."

Morgan nodded. "Take care. Be careful what you say. And keep your eyes open." Morgan nudged the horse into motion. As he rode out of town, he winced, and reached a hand under his long coat. He felt the burning pain of the furrows along his arm from his fight with John. He looked up at the sun as he rode out of town, wondering how much longer he'd be able to do that.

From the Author

I grew up loving Westerns. I've read everything Lous L'Amour wrote (if you don't know, that's a LOT of books). Then I ran across the Weird West concept, and it clicked with me. I loved Deadlands, the RPG, and the Golgotha series by RS Belcher.

"Varmints" is my second Weird West story. The idea just popped into my head, with the opening being a spin on the classic "mysterious stranger comes to town" idea. I haven't tackled a novel-length Weird Western yet, but this particular character just might show up again.

About the Author

WAYLAND SMITH is the pen name for a native Texan who has lived in Massachusetts, New York, Washington DC, and presently makes his home in Virginia. His rather unlikely list of jobs includes private investigator, comic book shop owner, ring crew for a circus (then he ran away from the circus and joined home), deputy sheriff, writer, and freelance stagehand. Wayland's novels so far include *Blood Of A Nation*, *In My Brother's Name*, and *Cadre Clash*, the first book in the Wildside series. He has short stories in the anthologies *Cat Ladies of the Apocalypse*, *HeroNet Files, Vol 1*, *SNAFU: An Anthology of Military Horror*, and *Legends of the Dragon*, among many others. He has spoken on panels at DragonCon, DC AwesomeCon, MystiCon, and RavenCon. A black belt in shao lin kung fu, he is also a fan of comic books, reading, writing, and various computer games. (I'll shut *7 Days to Die* down in one more hour. Really.) He lives with a beautiful woman who was crazy enough to marry him, and the spirits of a few wonderful dogs that have passed on.

Sabbath

by
Jessica Guernsey

Sabbath

*E*very key unlocked a treasure, even if the key was dirty. Kneeling on the deck, dressed in rags and refusing to make eye contact, was the man who held the key to the future of Spain.

As Capitán Diego Martinez de Salazar listened to the words spilling from the huddled creature before him, he knew this treasure would be vast. He was as certain of this as he was his first officer, the insufferable Francisco Garcia, would not hesitate to piss in the soldiers' water barrels.

The small, but well-muscled man kneeling in front of him had approached their ship as they restocked in Veracruz. He was known only by the English name Will, although the dark skin of the island people and clipped accent said he wasn't the least bit English.

Salazar had nearly ordered the man beaten and sent away, but he'd caught a word the man had said, and it turned his attention: pirate.

"Tell me again," Salazar said, speaking to Will but waiting for Garcia to respond.

Garcia scoffed. "He makes his berth on the island by—"

"Not you." Salazar nodded at Will. "I want him to tell me."

Garcia spoke a few words in English to the kneeling man. While Salazar would never admit it to his first officer, he understood more of the language than Garcia assumed. For now, Salazar still pretended he had not noticed his officer's mock obedience or his murmurs to the crew. How his hunger to be his capitán's equal glinted in the man's narrowed eyes. For now, Salazar was still capitán. And Garcia would follow orders.

Will began to tell them again what he knew, in stuttering but serviceable English. Garcia relayed the story in his native Spanish, much as he had before.

"There's a man, a buccaneer." Garcia's trademark sneer hitched higher at the word. "He makes his berth on the island of Guanahani. He has command of the *Trinity*."

When Will had first uttered the name of the vessel, Salazar had sucked in a breath. A prized Spanish galleon, the *Trinity* was known among his people by another name, the *Santísima Trinidad*. It was not so much larger than his own patache but rumored to have almost as many guns and more crew. It had been stolen by buccaneers, by pirates, some years ago. Now captained by a man not worthy to hold that honor.

Salazar refocused his attention back on Will, who was still fumbling through the English words as Garcia translated them into Spanish.

"The buccaneer is strange for a pirate—religious. His men do not gamble or game on the Sabbath, and he does not attack other vessels."

When Garcia paused, Salazar would not look at the man's smug face lest he was tempted to run his fist into it. Garcia's trim beard was far too small for such a vast ego. Instead, the capitán turned his back on Garcia, a sign of trust. Or of disregard. Garcia could take it either way.

Salazar kept his back straight to remind Garcia that he was higher than the first officer in rank and in stature. "And the buccaneer's name?"

"John Watling." The name was clear enough from the captive's lips.

Salazar waited. He was a patient man. Patient enough to let a man hang himself with his own words. Patient enough to establish himself in the Armada before daring to ask for the hand of the divine Lucia Diaz. Patient enough that Will kept talking, and Garcia kept translating.

"I know how to find his island, can spot his sails on the horizon. I know him and his crew. I can take you to him."

"And you were on this ship." Salazar wasn't asking a question. "The *Trinity*." He waited for Garcia to translate, mentally noting that Garcia called the vessel by its Spanish-given name.

When Will answered in the affirmative, Salazar faced him. "Why come to the Spanish for help?" The island people were a cheap source of labor, easily moved from one island to the next as needed. Easily bent under the fist of their conquerors. They had no love for those who ruled them.

Will's gaze darted to the side, probably taking in the immense amount of silver in Garcia's tacky footwear. "Your ship is big. Very powerful."

Salazar raised an eyebrow. The *Isabella* was indeed a fine ship. A patache, quick and light on her feet. What she lacked in cannon power, she made up for in the several dozen soldiers held in her wooden embrace, well-bred men from the most loyal families, much like Salazar. It was a source of pride for him, young as he was, to be given command of such a vessel. He tilted his head to one side, causing his finely oiled curls to rub the high collar of his uniform as he contemplated the man before him.

"Then why do you turn on your capitán?"

As Garcia translated, Will's dark eyes came up, meeting Salazar's and showing an intensity that conveyed his anger, even without the heat in his words. "He left me. Abandoned me. Forgot me. He is *not* my captain." And just as quickly, his eyes lowered back to the deck.

Salazar tapped a finger to the end of his moustache and ignored the scrape of Garcia's shifting boots. He was trying to think; damn the man's ostentatious buckles.

Salazar was patient, yes, but he was also ambitious. Ever since the ink dried on the Treaty of Madrid a decade before, the English pirates had plundered and pillaged, destroying or imprisoning any Spanish ship they encountered in what was once the Spanish Main. If Salazar could take back even one of those ships, his family name would be known once more. And the divine Lucia Diaz could give her consent to marriage. He very nearly sighed thinking of their last meeting, and how she had dipped her fan enough to let him touch her slim, cool fingers.

But there was work to do. A buccaneer to trap and a ship to reclaim. A woman to win and a country to exalt.

Salazar slid his gaze back to his first officer. "Have this man taken below."

A hard smile crept onto Garcia's lips, but it slipped away as Salazar continued speaking.

"Have him bathed, fed, and given new clothes. Show him the charts so he can point us in the right direction."

Garcia snapped his fingers at a waiting crewman, but before the underling could scuttle forward, Salazar raised a hand. The man looked back at Garcia as he halted, confirming Salazar's suspicions that the crew listened better to his first officer. No matter. The contingent of soldiers on board were loyal to Salazar.

"I can trust only you with this task, my friend." Salazar rested a hand on Garcia's shoulder, forcing the smile on his face to show in his eyes. "This is our chance at greatness. You must look out for him."

"Me?" Garcia didn't shake the hand from his shoulder, but his eyes narrowed. "Look out for this... this foreigner?"

As Salazar let the smile fade, he tightened his grip. Not much. Just enough so Garcia would notice. Garcia's blood was half as foreign. "You."

Garcia snorted and made to reach for the man on the deck, but Salazar did not release his shoulder. When Garcia looked at him again, Salazar made sure the first mate saw the face of his capitán.

Garcia pursed his lips. "Yes, sir," he said slowly. He gave a slight bow and then reached for Will.

Salazar watched them struggle belowdecks before he followed their path, turning instead to enter his cabin, which was fine enough for a capitán of his lineage. The lamps were kept trimmed and well stocked, though how long they would remain so was yet to be seen. If his fortunes at sea did not change, even home would offer no comfort. His family, sailors and capitáns for generations, was in decline. Much like the Spanish Main. Gone were the days of the mighty Armada. Lands conquered in his grandfather's time were now in different hands. Seas that held no threat in his father's days now teemed with thieves and criminals like Watling. The once grand fleet of ships sailing under Spanish colors was reduced to a few patches and galleons that could be spared, no longer carrying rich treasures. Salazar's own hold had been refitted to hold soldiers and storage, not precious materials for his king.

Bracing his hands on the table, he looked down at the piles and rolls of maps. Newer lines marked boundaries that had once been much larger. His vision blurred, and his shoulders fell forward. He caught himself before his head followed. Standing, he stretched, working his arms back and forth to move his blood and clear the fatigue. Too many nights awake. Too many days with no rest among the waves. And too many weeks left empty on the calendar before he could return home.

Salazar rubbed a hand over his eyes and poured himself a drink. Red wine. Not the best year, with a slightly acrid bite, pulled from what was left of his family's cellar, their crest fading on the bottle.

The same crest was etched into the buckle on his weapons belt, which held a scabbard for his sword and a holster for his pistol. The belt was now draped over the only chair in the room. It had been days since Salazar could bring himself to bear the weight of that belt. Perhaps that would change.

He still had his name, while Garcia was no one. The first officer's commission was claimed not by heritage, as Salazar, but with money. No revered family crest on those horrendous buckles. The first mate may have the money Salazar once had, but he would never have the ancestry. His mother's people weren't from Spain. How could the man understand the honor that was at stake? And while the lower-born crew might lean closer to Garcia, when Salazar entered the room, his authority commanded their silence and respect, due to him by his heritage. Garcia would never have that.

If he could not strengthen his family's honor in these waters, then the Salazar name might as well die out with him. Lucia wouldn't have him. No, she had grown up in luxury, as had he, and she was used to the finer things in life. With the vast lands her family held, she would never settle for the modest villa on the coast that was nearly all that was left to the Salazar name. Lucia would want—no, she *deserved* better. Grander.

But if she were to take his name, then what was hers would be his, and together, they would expand the Salazar fortune. His prestige. Her beauty, with eyes more gold than brown. And John Watling's ship offered a way back. Back to honor for his family. Back into Lucia's arms for him.

Treaty be damned. Salazar pulled out a clean sheet of parchment and a piece of chalk, names and ranks already running through his mind as he sketched the plan for what lay ahead.

All too soon, a familiar pounding on the door announced Garcia and his charge. Water drops still clinging to his short-cropped hair, Will entered, his hands clasped in front of him although he was no longer bound. His eyes swept the room, then returned to Garcia, who motioned to the table in front of Salazar.

Salazar covered his sneer with a frown at Will's unclean fingers, despite their recent scrubbing, as he shuffled through the parchment before pulling out the correct map.

Will's cracked nail tapped down. "Here. Straight east from Havana, past Charles Town."

Salazar leaned closer, stench of the unwashed no longer rolling off their newest crewmember. "San Salvador?"

Will shook his head. "Calls it Watling Island."

"I thought he was religious." Salazar tilted his head to look at his first officer while Will remained bent over the map.

"Pious doesn't always mean humble," Garcia said, never taking his eyes from Will's back.

"Approach from the west, toward the southern tip." Will drew his finger around the speck of an island. "He prefers a bay there. Trees make it harder to see your sails."

Salazar nodded. Good information. He nearly opened his mouth to give the order to set sail, but Will wasn't finished yet.

"No haste," Will said. "The island is some distance, but so is Sunday."

Salazar pulled his lips in. "And he won't be prepared to attack us on Sunday?"

Will wrinkled his brow but still peered at the map. "Watling doesn't sail on the Sabbath."

Salazar contemplated the man's words. With the treaty in place, his actions could be construed as aggression. But if they were victorious—and all the information Will gave him indicated the plan was solid—then all that he wanted for Spain and for himself would be in his grasp. It was a flash of memory, of Lucia's beguiling eyes, that convinced Salazar.

He reached for his belt and strapped it on.

The island had been in view for some time with no sign of Watling's ill-gotten ship. Salazar kept his sails hidden by the tree line on approach to the southern tip. Just the thought of English criminals crawling the noble Spanish decks of the *Santísima Trinidad* made Salazar tighten his fingers on the railing. He would reclaim the galleon. And he would reclaim Spain's power in these waters.

A few moments more and his ship edged around the island, revealing the captured vessel. Set back from the island, it was anchored but perhaps not empty. He could make out no sounds but those of birds. Through his spyglass, Salazar searched the deck for the crew but saw no movement. Not even a watch set. Pirates were not only greedy but arrogant as well. He handed the glass to Garcia, who took it and peered at their target.

"Empty?" Garcia asked, lowering the glass.

Salazar nodded slightly. "They could be on the island."

Garcia moved the glass to the shoreline. "Some smoke. Probably campfire. Not much. Most of the crew must be on the ship or... elsewhere."

"Could be his men aren't loyal and have abandoned him." Salazar's insides tremored. This was not a normal response just before an engagement. Nerves? Anticipation? Lack of sleep? Whatever the cause, he ignored the feeling even as it washed through him again. Instead, he turned to find Will standing behind him, his normally downcast eyes glinting as they roved over the decks of his former ship.

"Where would the crew be if not on the decks?" he asked the smaller man.

Will shrugged one shoulder and spoke. "On the Sabbath, no gaming or gambling is allowed," Garcia translated, and Salazar paid close attention, making sure his officer gave him all the information Will divulged. "Some forage on the island. Most choose to sleep."

Garcia left out the part about foraging. Salazar did not react. Best to not let the first officer know the capitán understood. But why did he leave that out? Did he not think it important? Perhaps he was lazy. Or perhaps an ambush awaited on the island.

Salazar looked closely at Will, but the man didn't notice, his gaze never leaving the *Santísima Trinidad*. Was that glint in his eye excitement for the upcoming battle? Or the slight smile on his lips hard enough to be revenge? For a moment, Salazar's insides rippled like the slack sails before them, and he did something he never liked to do: he doubted.

"Capitán," Garcia said, jerking Salazar from his inspection of Will. "It is Sunday. The information is good."

And Salazar was hesitating.

Perhaps, after they were successful, Salazar would find a new place in one of the camps for Will, one more in line with his heritage as an islander. The man certainly couldn't stay on with Salazar's crew.

With a few practiced hand motions, Salazar gave the order to prepare to board the pirated vessel, with his soldiers keeping as silent as possible. He would not use cannons on the sister ship unless absolutely necessary. If their target hadn't set a watch, then there was no need to warn them of their approach.

As the ships pulled abreast of each other, ropes were flung across the gap, knots pulling tight with a tug wherever they found hold. Salazar's insides seemed to stretch and knot with them. His crew heaved back, closing the gap enough to slide boards across to the other deck. Salazar swallowed hard, checked his pistol, and then drew his sword, leading a group of soldiers across.

Their boots moved in near silence on the other deck as they sought out the enemy crew. His own crew, weapons in hand should a pirate attempt to cross the planks, would remain behind unless he called for them to join the fray. Garcia and Will waited among them.

The soldiers finished their crossing, making no sounds even as a bird called. Salazar's insides tremored again at the sound. He paused. Where was the bird? He hadn't seen any colored feathers, and yet it sounded as if it were on the ship with them. He looked to the empty rigging.

An unearthly cry rose from the port side, only to be echoed up and down its length. Before Salazar had time to do more than turn his attention to the screams, the far deck swarmed with men, swords drawn and pistols taking aim. As they hauled themselves over the railing and on deck, even more of the pirate crew burst from every available hatch and door.

And over the railing came a tall, thin man in a long, dark coat, a wickedly thin blade in hand. He exuded such arrogance, such authority in his simple leap, that it was obvious this was John Watling, the allegedly Pious Pirate. And yet, he had attacked on Sunday—on the Sabbath.

Chaos ensued with men and blood and black powder ruling the moment.

Smoke filled the air, causing Salazar's open eyes to burn. His ears rang with screams and gunshots. The capitán slashed and stabbed, turning away as many stinking wretches as came at him.

Beside him, his men fell. Over their agony, he heard the birdcall once more. He turned toward the sound only to see the pirate captain's lips finish the mimicking whistle as the last of the Spanish commanders collapsed in front of him.

Salazar pulled his pistol and took careful aim at John Watling's chest.

A weight crashed into him from behind, and he slammed to the deck. A gun pressed into his shoulder even as he removed his finger from his own pistol.

And there was silence.

His men stopped fighting, some dropping weapons, others bleeding out their lives on the deck. Before him were a pair of all-too-familiar boots and their hated silver buckles.

Garcia leaned over him, pulling his arms back and dislodging the pistol.

Salazar's hands and elbows were bound behind him, and he was hauled up to face the pirate.

With a sweep of his hand, the tall man bowed before Salazar. "Captain John Watling, at your service, sir."

Garcia didn't translate, but it was no longer needed.

In the same grand manner, the pirate withdrew a sealed parchment and tossed it to Garcia, who caught the papers easily.

"The treaty stands," Garcia said in English. "And my family thanks you."

Garcia handed the papers to another of Salazar's crew, who immediately returned with the document to his ship.

Not *his* ship.

Not anymore.

These men were most certainly Garcia's crew. All the whispers and ceased conversations had not been out of respect for the capitán's arrival. No. Garcia had plotted, corrupting his crew with promises of esteem higher than their birth deserved. He had planned for Salazar to fall. Perhaps before they even set sail.

Will shoved Salazar in the back, causing the capitán to fall to his knees.

A slight tremor rippled his insides once more, one last warning he had failed to heed.

"Job well done, Will, my friend," Watling said, inspecting the blood coating his cutlass. "Another Spanish bastard too big for his britches, made to pay for the debts owed your people."

Will's grin was broad and cruel, his eyes narrowed as his lips twisted.

"But it is Sunday." Salazar's English seethed through his teeth.

Watling looked to the cloudless sky. "It is. And a fine one at that."

"You don't attack on the Sabbath."

John raised one eyebrow. "That, good sir, is true. I do not dishonor my God by shedding blood on His holy day."

Damn pirates. Salazar spat at Watling's boots. But Watling simply smiled, his gaze shifting to the man holding Salazar. From the dark, long-fingered hands gripping his arm, Salazar could guess it was another island-born man, like Will. Garcia stood close by, holding the capitán's weapons, the crest on the buckle tarnished.

"Ah, I see you are confused." Watling tucked his hands behind his back. "Let me explain. I am counted among God's people, yes. I honor His Sabbath day and many of His other commandments. But my flock are those who follow the true path of the Lord's creation."

When Salazar didn't react, Watling nodded his head slowly and frowned at the former capitán even as his eyes shone. "We honor the biblical seventh day as our Sabbath—and *that* is Saturday."

From the Author

The moment I heard the theme for an anthology was Pirates, I immediately knew I would write about my ancestor. Pious John Watling was a real pirate and my distant relative, on my mother's side. Because who wouldn't want to brag on their ancestor for others to enjoy? And one famous enough to have a rum distillery in the Bahamas named after him. I had the chance to tour said facility and hear the fantastic alterations to John Watling's story that the staff had made for the sake of entertainment. Rum distilleries aren't really that interesting (since all the action takes place inside a barrel over years) and it's really the attached bar that interests the tourist groups.

Much like the fictional Salazar, the Watling family has a long line of amazing people, not all of which are pirates, though not for lack of desire. I had to do my family proud and make this a story worthy of the Watling name. Normally, I write Fantasy and Sci-fi stories so this foray into Historic Fiction was a new one for me. I completely underestimated the research involved. After nearly 4 hours of scanning websites and reading pages of information, I finally understood what kind of ship my capitán would command.

While the story itself is fiction, there are real elements. The real Pious John Watling did leave behind a crewmate named Will when avoiding Spanish warships. Once rescued from the island years later, Will's story was thought to inspire *Robinson Crusoe*. Watling was known to have specific rules aboard his ship regarding gambling, drinking, and sailing on the Sabbath, earning him the nickname of "Pious." However, the rest of the story, while told frequently and proudly by extended family, is more than likely apocryphal.

About the Author

Jessica Guernsey writes Contemporary Sci-fi and Fantasy novels and short stories (and the very rare Historic Fiction story). A BYU alumna with a degree in Journalism, her work is published in magazines and anthologies. By day, she crushes dreams as a manuscript evaluator/slush pile reader for two publishers. Frequently, she can be found at writing conferences. She isn't difficult to spot; just look for the extrovert.

While she spent her teenage angst in Texas, she now lives on a mountain in Utah with her husband, three kids, and a codependent mini schnauzer. Connect with her on Twitter @JessGuernsey.

For a slightly different version of "Sabbath," read the original in *X Marks the Spot: An Anthology of Theft and Treasure*, found here:

https://books2read.com/u/bzgzXZ

Prefer fantastic sea monsters and facing your fears? You might enjoy "In the Water" from *Undercurrents: An Anthology of What Lies Beneath*, found here:

https://books2read.com/u/3LYZAN

Obscure relics with consequence sound intriguing? Read "Sleight of Hand" from *Cursed Collectibles: An Anthology*, here:

https://books2read.com/u/4A7NVA

Visit www.JessicaGuernsey.com to see an updated list of published works.

Green-Eyed Monster
by
John D. Payne

Green-Eyed Monster

Elke stepped back warily, sucking in big gulps of cool autumn air as she held her heavy broadsword ready in front of her. The clearing was splattered with thick purple ichor and littered here and there with sections of something that looked like a silverfish—except for being fifteen feet long and as thick around as a boar.

Lor stepped out from among the pine trees with a wry smile on his face and an arrow nocked on the string of his bow. He glanced around approvingly. "Well, darling, you seem to have taken care of things pretty well," he said.

Elke snorted. "No thanks to you." She sheathed her sword and looked around for the helmet the giant insect had knocked off her head some time during the fight.

"Be kind," Lor replied. He took his arrow off the bow string and tucked his bow under his left arm. He walked toward her, treading carefully to avoid soiling his boots in the mess. "Didn't I help?" Lor gestured around vaguely with the arrow in his right hand. "Aren't some of these mine?" he asked, referring to the feathered shafts protruding from various bits of the hideous creature's remains.

"They're all yours," growled Elke.

"Well then, love," said Lor. He put away his arrow and unstrung his bow. "What have you got to grumble about? From the look on your face, you'd think I was on his side instead of yours."

"Arrows don't kill these things," said Elke, as she walked around the clearing, turning over bits of carcass, still looking for her lost helmet. "They just make them mad. I don't know when you're going to learn that."

"Probably when you learn not to try to do everything by yourself," said Lor with a sly smile. He picked up Elke's helmet, which he had been standing in front of since he walked into the clearing. The next time she turned to face him, he tossed it to her.

Elke blew a strand of hair out of her eyes and replaced the helmet.

"Admit it," said Lor. "You don't know what you'd do without me."

"I'm sure I can find someone else," said Elke, "to brag and lie and piss me off."

Lor grinned wickedly. "Good luck."

"What would be lucky," said Elke, "is tracking down our horses and spotting a place to camp before it gets dark. And with some real luck, we can get out of the Bosk before some other hideous thing kills us both."

Lor scowled. "Always the practical one. You know, if you keep spoiling all the romantic moments, you and I will never get together."

"What spoils the romantic moments is your ugly face," Elke said with an accusing finger pointed at her companion.

"All faces are ugly next to yours," said Lor, as they walked out of the clearing to find their mounts.

It was a lie, but a sweet one. But it was not his silver tongue that made her glad for his companionship—it was his keen eyes and ears.

The Great Bosk was an endless sea of immense trees, set so closely together that very little light filtered down to the ground. Even here, in the hills at its outer edge, it was easy to be blindsided by dangers that lie just around the next ridge, or even the next tree. Lor had saved her more than once.

But she had to admit, it was a nice change to have a man flirt with her. It was true that he flirted with every other woman he saw, and she was almost positive he didn't mean anything by it, but Lor was the first man she had ever met who treated her like other women.

Like most of her people, Elke was ruddy, blonde, and tall. When she was still in the cradle, people used to joke that it was cruel to curse a baby with an ugly name like Elke. Then she grew into the name, and people started looking for jokes that didn't cut so close. If she had only just been a bit closer in size to the lithe, graceful girls she grew up with, she might even have found a husband. But no man was interested in a woman who could hoist him over her head, no matter how many flowers she braided into her hair. So, Elke had left behind hearth and hopes of family to seek her fortune.

She and Lor had been part of a company of mercenaries, paid to protect a caravan moving silk through the Great Bosk, but the whole thing had gone sour, and they had spent the last few weeks fighting their way back to inhabited lands. Reaching the hills meant they were getting closer, but even then, it would be weeks more before they reached any kind of civilization. Even on the outskirts of the Bosk, they would find no one but hermits, outlaws, and others of society's refuse.

It took them more than an hour to find the horses, calm them down, and gather their scattered gear. Elke was trying to decide whether it was worth it to push on before dark, when Lor spoke up.

"You know, when we were up on that bald hill, right before you spied the horses, I thought I saw a fire."

"How far off?" asked Elke.

He weighed the question in his mind, cocking his head to the right. "Close, I think. It was north and east, which is where we want to go. If it's where it looked like it was, we could make it just before the sun begins to set. That would give us time to find somewhere to camp and get a fire lit, even if it turns out to be nothing."

"You're sure you saw a fire?"

"I'm sure I saw something," Lor said. "Didn't you see it?" he asked hopefully.

Elke shook her head. "But it would be nice…"

"Yeah." His horse pawed at the ground anxiously. "Want to go see?"

"Goes against my better judgement…" she said.

He grinned. "So that's a yes?"

She grinned back. "That's as close as you're going to get to a yes, so you better take it."

"Taken," Lor replied with a salute. They nudged their mounts to face the east and rode through the sparsely wooded hills as the sun began to slowly sink in the sky behind their backs.

The sun was low, almost touching the tops of the hills, when next they stopped their horses to confer, on the southeast face of a prominent hill, near the top. There was a chill in the wind, and Elke wrapped her wool cloak around herself to conserve what she could of the afternoon's fading warmth.

"If I'm right," Lor said carefully, rubbing his chin and looking off to the east, "it would be around that next hill there." He nodded in the direction he was looking.

"In less than an hour, there won't even be twilight," Elke said brusquely. "If we want to have a fire tonight, I think we need to stop chasing will-o'-wisps and just start our own."

Lor nodded slowly, his eyes still facing east.

Elke continued. "Listen, I was up on that hill, too, and I didn't see anything. I still haven't. No smoke, no glimmer of light, nothing."

"You know it's hard to see past the edge of your nose out here in the Bosk. And a good woodsman can make a fire with hardly any smoke at all," Lor said. "I know I saw something."

Elke opened her mouth to speak but thought better and closed it. The sun was heavy and red like an overripe fruit that had fallen to the earth, the clouds as orange as falling leaves.

Abruptly, Lor burst out into laughter. "All right, I guess it does sound stupid, doesn't it?"

Elke nodded without a word.

"Shall we just forget about the whole thing?" Lor asked.

"Well," said Elke, "we don't have to forget about it. If you really want to go over there and try to find this fire of yours, we can do that, but it's just that right now it's—"

"—it's getting dark, and we're in the bloody Bosk. I know."

"I'm not saying it's a bad idea," she said.

"I understand. It's all right," Lor replied softly.

"And we can go if you really want," said Elke.

Lor shook his head. After a pause, he looked up at Elke and smiled. "Well, gorgeous, we've got a little light left. Do you want to gather firewood or set up camp?"

Elke smiled. "I'll go for firewood, and you can start working on something for us to eat. You know I'm no cook."

Lor feigned shock. "Then how have you been conjuring up the feasts we've had these last weeks? If you're not a cook, you must be a sorceress."

"Not a sorceress," she corrected. "A priestess—haven't you seen my burnt offerings?"

Lor laughed and dismounted. He began to unpack their saddlebags as she walked off towards the trees to find kindling. She chuckled to herself about her joke, pleased that she had been able to make Lor laugh. Quick wit was not always her strong suit.

As she wandered through the woods looking for good dry wood for kindling, Elke wondered if she had been too hard on Lor. She hadn't seen anything, but it was true that his eyes were better than hers. They were also a deep, rich, beautiful shade of green. Her own were green as well, but kind of a dirty greyish green. His were like glittering jewels. True, his face was a little weather-beaten and worn, but beggars can't be choosers, as her mother had told her, over and over.

Lor was different than other men: he wasn't put off by Elke's towering height and powerful physique. She thought it must be because he was tall and strong himself, but sometimes the biggest men wanted the daintiest mates. Elke hadn't been able to figure out what Lor wanted in a woman, since he flirted with everything in a skirt. So, he probably didn't mean anything when he called her gorgeous. But at least he treated her the same as he treated everyone else. And that was enough, enough that she found herself wishing for an extra hour of daylight so that she could have gone with Lor to look for his fire.

Elke looked around, her arms now laden with firewood. She realized she had climbed to the top of the ridge. She turned to the west to watch the sun set over the wild, forested hills. The clouds were streams of pink and orange fire. Once she had heard a bard tell a girl that this was what dragon's breath looked like—she believed him of course, the foolish child.

She turned again to go down the hill while there was still some light and stopped cold. There, just around the next hill, just where Lor had said it must be, was a glint of light, winking at her from out from among the trees like an impudent, naked child. Elke charged down the hill to where they had tied up the horses.

She burst into the hillside meadow where Lor knelt by the pots, preparing the meal, and breathlessly blurted out, "I saw it!"

"I knew it!" Lor jumped up and pounded his fist into his palm. "I knew I saw something!" He threw his fists up into the air, his eyes flashing with triumph. Slowly, his fists opened, and he cast her an inquisitive glance. "So…"

"So, we're going—now!" Elke declared.

Lor crowed with excitement and then began to quickly repack the pots and foodstuffs into their saddlebags. "So," he asked, "same approach as always?"

"Yes," said Elke, strapping on her heavy sword belt. "You take the horses and circle around to get behind them with your bow."

"And you walk right up and knock on their front door," said Lor, "so to speak."

Elke grinned savagely, pulling her bright steel helmet over her long blonde hair. She fit her bracer and shield on sun-browned arms crisscrossed with white scars. Elke stretched, flexed, and then gripped forearms with Lor in a fierce warrior's handclasp.

"Thank you for believing me, about the fire," said Lor.

Elke nodded. "Of course."

Lor smiled, and then mounted his horse, taking the reins of her own steed in his left hand. "I'll be close," he said. "If something goes wrong, just call to me."

Elke nodded impatiently and began to walk. He nudged the horses forward and continued alongside her. She rolled her shoulders and shook out her arms, preparing herself.

"If there are problems—" Lor began.

Elke chuckled cruelly and inhaled deeply, throwing back her massive shoulders and shaking her head. "If there are problems, they will not be mine."

Lor shook his head and smiled. "You're such a brute."

"That's what they pay me for," said Elke. She drew her sword and bared her teeth menacingly. Lor shook his head and chuckled. He turned the horses and headed off south into the woods ahead of her.

The light was almost gone now, but Elke knew where her path lay. She followed the curve of the hill around to the south and then to the east. She was in the valley bottom now, and there was a small stream to guide her. All the same, she became more and more nervous as the light waned away to nothingness, and she still saw no glimmer of fire. She began to wonder if she had turned herself around in the dark.

So it was that, when Elke did finally see a faint light, she wasn't sure at first that it wasn't her imagination, but she strode toward it anyway, slowly. As she approached, she saw a figure seated near the fire. She decided on a show of good faith and approached the campsite from an angle that put her across the campfire from the figure, so that he could see her clearly.

As she stepped out of the trees, the figure spoke up in a raspy voice that spoke of many years. "Stop right there, swordsman. Put away your weapon."

Elke slowly sheathed her sword in her scabbard and began to move towards him.

"Don't take another step, forward or back, or I'll put a crossbow bolt right through that shiny chain mail shirt of yours." The figure held up a large, heavy crossbow and pointed it at her heart. "Now take off the sword belt and put it down. The shield, too." She complied, moving carefully.

There was a moment's silence before the man spoke again. "A woman, if I'm not mistaken," the figure declared.

"Yes, a woman," Elke replied. "And although I am armed, I am an honest traveller and mean no harm. These are dangerous parts for a lone person, man or woman. I saw the light and decided to see if I might share the fire with fellow travellers."

"Yes, I'm sure," the man said. "But if you are a traveller, where is your horse? Surely you do not walk through the Neverlands, do you?"

"I tied up my horse a ways back in the forest. If you will allow me, I will go and get her. I do not want to leave her tied up too long out there without someone to watch her."

"I will not allow you," the man said. "Because then you will go and get your brigand friends to come slit my throat and take my purse. I may be able to fend off one of you, but I can't take a whole pack."

Elke quickly reviewed her options and briefly considered the possibility of calling for Lor. Even if he had circled around the long way, by now he must be close by.

As if reading her thoughts, the man said, "And don't think of summoning your friends, either. If I even see you take a deep breath, I'll put this through your lungs before you can so much as call out."

"Well," said Elke, "I very much doubt you can do that, but I have no friends to summon and no desire to see if you really can plant that pretty flowered branch in my chest."

"You see that you keep that in mind, because I could kill you and disappear into these dark woods before your friends can get here."

Elke shook her head. As long as he was talking to her, he wasn't carrying out his threat. "This is strange," she said. "May I sit down?"

The man nodded, and she walked a few steps to her left and sat down on a fallen log. She tried to see the man's face, but he wore a hat with a large brim that kept the flickering firelight from revealing much of his countenance. If she was not wrong, though, his face was lined and weathered to match his age-worn voice. "If you don't trust me to stay," she said slowly, "and don't trust me to go, what does that leave me with?"

The stranger chuckled. "That is a problem."

"Is there no way," Elke asked, "for me to win your trust?"

"Well, keep talking and perhaps you will convince me to let my guard down for a little while."

Elke smiled; this was, of course, her plan.

"But for now," he said, as he patted his crossbow with his left hand, "don't do anything that might give me cause to let this bolt fly. Once it's gone, I can't call it back, for better or worse."

Elke laughed. "For better or worse—like the arrow of love." If she was lucky, she could steer the topic to things everyone likes to talk about, especially lonely old men.

The man chuckled and repeated her phrase. "Like the arrow of love." He put his crossbow in his lap, folded his arms, and leaned back. "Like the arrow of love."

Elke smiled. She put her gloved hands on her helm and asked, "Do you mind if I take this off?" He shrugged impassively, and she pulled it off. She intended the gesture to be friendly and disarming, but as the firelight hit her bare face, the man sucked in his breath with a hiss. "Is something wrong?" Elke asked.

"Green eyes…" he muttered. He sat up straight again and picked up his crossbow.

Elke cursed at herself. "Yes, I have green eyes," Elke admitted casually. "Is that unusual in these parts? Have you never seen them before?"

"Oh, I have seen green eyes before."

"But they seem to discomfit you somehow."

There was a long silence before he responded. "You are a stranger to these lands, are you not? You have the look of Ciweriya about you."

"I was born there," Elke said. "Green eyes are common in the North. And the West."

"Not here," said the man. "Not on this side of the Bosk." His voice trailed off into the quiet of the night.

Elke said nothing.

"Have you ever heard," he asked abruptly, "of green-eyed trolls?"

Elke shook her head. "I have seen and slain trolls," she said, "but I have never paid attention to the colour of their eyes."

"Of course you haven't. Why would you?" He laughed bitterly.

"Trolls have six-inch teeth, and hides like crocodiles," said Elke, "so you can hardly mistake me for one, green eyes or no green eyes."

"You know less than you think," the man retorted sharply. "Green-eyed trolls are not like other trolls. They are far more dangerous."

"How so?" asked Elke. Her sword was only a few paces away. She tried not to look at it.

"Because they can change their shape," said the man. "The legends say they can wear any face they wish."

"Then why not change their eyes?" asked Elke.

"That's the one thing they can't hide," said the man.

"So, this is why you can't trust me," said Elke.

He laughed. "Well, it's one reason." The firelight reflected off the man's smiling teeth, although the wide brim still hid much of his face. "In these parts, it pays to be cautious. You never know who you're going to run into."

"Agreed," said Elke. She thought of Lor waiting on the hill with his bow. "Tell me more about these green-eyed trolls," she said, with a smile as charming as she could manage.

"The creatures we call green-eyed trolls are more cunning than any other people that walk the earth, but also more vain," said the old man. In the flickering light of the dim campfire, his face was obscured—nothing more than a bushy grey beard and a wide-brimmed hat.

"They delight in their own craftiness," the old man said, "but cannot be content unless their victims recognize their superiority—whether by praising them or cursing them, it makes no difference."

"My sister's son was like that," said Elke. "He was always being whipped, but it never made a difference. I think he liked the attention. And if he got away with something wicked, he would boast about it until his mother heard. He could never keep his mouth shut."

"Too clever for his own good," said the old man. "Very like the ones of whom I speak. In the stories, this was always their undoing. Have you ever heard the story of Clodwick and the reluctant bride?"

"My mother told me the tale of Kludevig and the seven tasks," said Elke.

"It is the same," said the old man. "It is a very old tale, and remembered now mostly in pieces. But I know the whole of it."

The old man stopped, expectantly. Elke had always hated children's stories, even as a child. And she had no desire to hear this old man ramble. But neither did she want to end up on the receiving end of his crossbow. If only Lor would show up—but perhaps he had already been found by something out there in the dark.

Elke forced herself to smile. "Please," she said, "share your tale with me."

The old man grunted with satisfaction. "Long ago," he said, "a noble Prince of Guern, named Clodwick, desired a certain maiden for his bride. She was a lovely young lass, with long black hair and beautiful green eyes. Though she had no family, he loved her and would take her to wife. But she said that he did not truly love her.

"Clodwick asked the maid what he should do to prove his love. She said nothing would prove his love because he did not love her. But he begged her to set him a task, and so she did. He ventured into the deep of the Bosk and brought her back a goblet from the Silkie Queen. She told him that she was glad for the gift, but again said that he did not love her.

"Again Clodwick begged her to set him a task. And so she did. Six times the maiden named a great labour, as your mother taught you, and each time he returned triumphant only to have her deny him as before.

"After the seventh, Clodwick asked her how she could know that he did not love her. The maiden told him that she had a secret, a terrible secret, and that if he knew, he would surely not love her. Clodwick swore that nothing could cool the fires of his love, and the maiden consented to be his wife, promising that once they were married there would be no secrets between them.

"So they were wed. And that night, Clodwick asked his new bride to reveal her secret. She said that as his wife, she would tell him, but as her husband, he must never speak her secret to another living soul. He agreed. And in an instant, she assumed her true form as a green-eyed troll. Terrified, he killed the monster with his bare hands. And the next morning, Clodwick proclaimed to his people that his beautiful bride had been slain—murdered, by a green-eyed troll."

"How terrible!" Elke murmured quietly. "But a fitting end to the story, I suppose."

"Terrible indeed," said the old man. "But it was not the end. For Prince Clodwick, maddened with hate, plotted a terrible revenge. And on a certain night, the Prince and his conspirators arose and slew everyone they could find with green eyes. And as you can imagine, it ended as a mad slaughter, neighbour killing neighbour until the whole of Guern was consumed by war and bloodshed. Clodwick's mad pogrom nearly destroyed his kingdom, but he did succeed in purging his land of the green-eyed trolls. And since that day they have been become mere legends.

"And even these legends are fading, leaving behind only fragments and remnants. In certain islands in the west, for example, witches and herb-women all have green eyes, because green is the colour of magic—the colour of lost things, hidden things, dark things, strange things."

"Strange things indeed," said Elke. She shifted uncomfortably.

"Not quite like the tale your mother told you, was it," the old man laughed.

"No, not quite," said Elke. "In her story, Kludevig was a hero. In yours, he was…"

"A villain?" asked the old man, in a carefully neutral tone.

"Perhaps," said Elke. She rubbed her arms. "Certainly no one to be admired."

The old man grunted in satisfaction.

"After all," continued Elke, "what kind of fool would keep pushing for a secret that his love clearly did not want to reveal? If only he had been content, they would have been happy together."

"You think that's happiness?" the old man asked. "You would prefer to content yourself with the illusion of love than to embrace the truth?"

"What is illusion? What is truth?" Elke said. She gestured at the fire, now dying down to coals. "We live by firelight, and when we look out into the dark you might see a spear where I see a tree branch. But in the end, there is nothing but shadows."

"Then we need more light!" said the old man, angrily. He stood up and kicked at the fire, sending sparks up into the darkness. "Truth is truth. Let us not complicate things." The firelight glinted off the metal tip of his crossbow bolt.

"Truth is truth," Elke agreed. "And light is light." She tried to keep her posture relaxed. "Speaking of—shall I put some more wood on the fire?"

The old man chuckled. "No, you just stay right where you are."

Elke shrugged, and tried to smile. She had to keep the old man talking. "I suppose I can't blame the Prince for wanting to know the truth. It's natural. Human."

"Very human," said the old man.

"And after all," said Elke, "he was being deceived. She—the creature, I mean—was the real villain of this story. Of course."

"Of course," the old man said.

"She started it all," said Elke, "by saying that he didn't love her. When the truth is that she was the one that didn't love him."

"What do you mean?" the old man asked.

"Well," said Elke, "you've said that these creatures love to play tricks on men…"

The old man said nothing.

"… which you can see from the way she tormented him," Elke continued. "You know, by making him do all those tasks. And then, telling him she had a secret that she would only reveal after they were wed. It's like you said, she was just playing with him, to prove her own superiority."

"So, it was all a cruel joke?" the old man asked.

"Well," said Elke slowly, "if she really had loved him, she never would have made him do all those things. And she never would have mentioned her secret, much less told it to him. It was too much for him to bear, obviously."

"But how could she have remained silent if she loved him?" the man demanded.

"If she truly loved him, how could she have spoken of it?" shot back Elke.

"But to know is to love and to love is to know. That's what the words mean! You cannot truly have the one without the other."

"No," she said. "You are older than I am—"

"Older than you might think."

"—and have probably loved many times—"

"Fewer than you might think."

"—but I do not agree with you, older and wiser though you may be. I do not know if one person can truly know another. I am not even sure there is something to truly know." Elke stopped to try to bring together unruly thoughts. "We wear masks," she said slowly. "Different masks for different days, different people, different places. Love is wearing the mask that your beloved loves the most."

"But he only loved the mask," the man cried out, as if in pain.

"Masks are all we see, all we show each other. Can we fall in love with anything else?"

"But that is madness!"

Elke laughed out loud. "Love is a kind of madness."

He smiled, and his teeth shined in the unsteady light of the fire. "So, you think the troll acted foolishly?"

"She was a fool to mention it, and he was a fool to ask her."

"How so?" the man challenged.

"Well, to my way of thinking," Elke began, "it's just another way for her to keep him at a distance. If he couldn't accept the secret, she would be out of the obligation to love him, and she could go home at the end of the day, saying, 'Well, I did my part, I told the truth, and he was the one who couldn't accept me as I was. It's his fault because he didn't really love me.'"

"And you think this is true?"

"Well, it's nonsense of course, but there's lots of women out there like that. And men, too. Especially in my line of work, I run into lots of them. They've been hurt before, and so they're afraid of being hurt again. It's natural; I feel it, too. So, they show off their ugliest side, their most horrible secrets, and then when things don't work out, they still come out with their fragile pride intact. Telling a nasty secret like that is... well, it's just like dogs barking or cats hissing—they're afraid, and so they try to frighten off what frightens them."

"No!" The man angrily shook his pointed finger at her. "It's not like that at all!"

"Sir," Elke said, "I am not trying to offend you. But it seems that nothing I say pleases you. Maybe it would be better if I left. I could even leave my sword, to show I mean no harm. I am no bandit. I am just a woman, lost in a strange place, who saw a fire on a cold night and sought human companionship."

"What offends me," the old man said, "is that any person can believe what you do."

"I think this is the strangest conversation I ever had," said Elke. "Please sir, just let me leave in peace."

"No," the old man said. "Not until you tell me this: how could she let him stay, let him think that he loved her, when he did not even know her name, her true face? It would have been a torment to her—to continue the charade and wonder if he could ever really love her. She had to tell him. She had a responsibility, and a need."

Elke said nothing.

"Talk," the old man said. He levelled his crossbow at her.

"I begin to see your point," said Elke.

"Liar," the old man spat.

"You hate me for agreeing, and you hate me for disagreeing," said Elke. "What do you want me to do?"

"I want you to speak the truth!"

"The truth," said Elke, "is that he was living a beautiful dream, and she rudely awoke him. Love is a gift, and you must take it as it comes. To try to have it on your own terms is selfish and stupid."

The old man sighed heavily. "I grow old," he said quietly. "I grow old, and my stories do not even mean what I used to think they mean. It appears, young woman, that you are perhaps wiser than this battered old teller of tales. Tell me then, what should she have done with this prince?"

"She should have known that he could never love the truth and let him remain enamoured with the illusion. It is not much different than what we do every day, men and women alike."

"But can a man love a lie?"

"I do not know," Elke said with a grin. "I am not a man."

"No, I did not think so," said the man. He lifted his crossbow again and aimed it at her chest. "I am sorry."

"No," she interrupted. "I am not a troll. I was only making a jest—meaning that I am a woman, not a man, and so I do not know what fool things men think in their hearts."

"Your tricksome lips want me to believe so," the old man said, "but I see danger in those pretty green eyes of yours."

"You do not trust me yet?"

"On the contrary," he said, "I have trusted you, and far too much. It is a dangerous thing, to trust. Did you not learn even that from my tale? Monsters such as yourself are far too crafty and devious for the likes of me to tangle with. And so, it is best for me to be rid of you, before I let you get close enough to put steel in my poor old bones."

"You're serious—you really think I'm one of them?"

"I know my own kind."

"Then know me! Know me as one of your own!"

"I thought I could, once. But there's nothing to know, isn't that right? Just masks."

Elke's thoughts raced as the man raised his crossbow to his shoulder and prepared to fire. "Think for a moment, sir, before you do something foolish! As you said before, once an arrow is flown, you cannot bring it back!"

"But arrows flown do not always kill. Sometimes they only wound. Beware a man wounded, my dear." He smiled grimly.

"You told me no one had heard anything of them in hundreds of years—and who knows if they ever even existed in the first place. Do you really think they're still around?"

"It would appear so, my green-eyed beauty."

"But, if they were so powerful and tricky, wouldn't you think that this whole green-eyed business is just a ruse?" She talked slowly, trying to stall as long as she could. "Why not spread the rumour that the only thing that gives them away is their green eyes, and then watch the chaos ensue as innocent people are torched and slaughtered? Or if it were true, wouldn't they have been working for the last five hundred years to change this one trait, through breeding or sorcery or whatever means are available to them? Five hundred years is a long time, and perhaps the fact that no one has heard anything about them just means that they have become even more adept at hiding. Couldn't they be among us still, and not just as green-eyed folk?"

There was a long pause, and then the man smiled slyly. "It is possible. And just the sort of thing one would expect to hear from an innocent green-eyed traveller trying to keep a suspicious old man from putting crossbow bolts in her belly. Or," he added, "from a green-eyed troll wearing the face of a woman trying to lull a wily and wary veteran into letting down his guard. Perhaps that's what love is all about—letting your guard down. Like a Prince of Guern once did. A dangerous thing, love."

"Love? Why do you talk of love?" Elke cried desperately. Her plan was falling apart and Lor was nowhere to be seen. "I don't even know you! You are a stranger to me!"

"A stranger, yes. Even now you do not know me." He clenched his teeth. "And you never shall!" the man cried fiercely.

"I am no troll! I am no monster!"

"Troll or not, you are a monster."

Although her eyes remained locked on the shadows under the wide brim of the man's hat, Elke's thoughts reached out to her sword. It was fifteen feet away, too far away for her to get to without getting feathered by the man's crossbow. Her mind began to search out other avenues. She needed time. "You are mad," she said calmly.

"I was once."

Elke slowly spread her hands wide. "Sir, I beg you, stop a moment and think about what you are doing." She carefully shifted her weight as she sat on the log, preparing to rise to her feet. She measured out her words in the most reasonable tones she could manage, with as much professional detachment as she could muster. "If you think I am a danger to you, why not simply tie me up and wait until morning. Certainly I am no more danger to you tied up than dead. And if you believe that I have friends in the woods, as you said before, then a hostage is much more useful than a corpse." She measured the distance between them.

The man laughed. "Do you even know who you are talking to?"

"No, I must admit that I don't. As I said, I am a traveller, a stranger to these parts." She thought of her mail shirt and mentally tried to gauge the weight and power of the crossbow in the man's hands. She cautiously began to stand.

"Don't," he warned.

"I mean no harm for you or anyone else this night." She continued to rise to her feet.

"You'll be dead before you move another inch."

She spread her hands demurely and raised her eyebrows in a mute plea. With a wry smile, she gestured to her immense form. "But, sir, can you not see? I am just a poor, helpless little girl."

The man threw back his head and laughed, and as he did so, Elke jumped to her right and rolled towards her sword and shield. Caught off guard, he still twisted and fired the crossbow. The bolt shot through her left thigh as she jumped, but she rolled out and had her scabbarded sword in her hands when he rushed her.

He was tall and powerfully built and moved much more quickly than she expected from his grey beard, but she used his momentum against him, seizing his outstretched arm and throwing him behind her.

He came up with a long knife in his hands and a wild look in his eyes, which she could see for the first time glinting in the firelight. They were a deep, rich green, and glittered like emeralds.

"You are dangerous, my darling, but I am prepared," he said menacingly. "Your kind are a plague; you only live to deceive and tear down. But tomorrow belongs to me and my kind. Farewell and good night." He settled into an experienced fighter's crouch, knife held low and arms spread wide for balance.

"How many times must I tell you?" Elke growled. "I am no monster!" She tossed the sheath off her broadsword and tried to find a stance that would not put too much weight on her left leg.

He circled in close. Suddenly he feinted, dodged her counterstroke, and delivered a savage kick to her wounded thigh. She almost collapsed with the pain, but instead threw herself at him, knocking him to the ground. Between the shock of the kick and the impact of the fall, she lost her sword, and the two of them rolled across the campsite, struggling for control of the knife. He used his legs to clamp down on her wounded thigh and squeezed ferociously. She gasped but struck his nose with her forehead repeatedly until he lost his grip on both her and the knife. With his better mobility, he dashed for the knife, but she grabbed his legs and pulled him back to where she could grapple with him.

He turned quickly and put strong hands on her throat to strangle her. Fortunately, Elke's well-muscled neck protected her for a few moments, while she struck his temples again and again, hammering his skull with her powerful fists. She began to despair, but as her vision went black from lack of air, she felt his fingers relax from her windpipe. She struck down his hands and punched him once more, as hard as she could, in his chest right below the sternum. His breath rushed out in a horrid gasp, and he crumpled into a ball, bleeding from the nose and ears.

Elke pushed him away and struggled to rise to her feet. She staggered a few feet away and supported herself against a nearby tree, taking in the air in great gulps as the adrenaline flowed away and her body was assaulted anew by the painful awareness of the damage it had suffered. She heard a faint, gurgling chuckle behind her and awkwardly turned to face the man lying in a heap on the ground behind her.

"Do you know who I am?" he mumbled. "Do you know who I am? You've killed an old man, my darling. A very old man."

Elke said nothing but coughed roughly as spasms wracked the muscles of her throat.

"An old, old man . . . Do you . . . know . . . my name? . . . I have . . . a very . . . old . . . name . . . Ancient . . ." He trailed off into incomprehensible murmurs, as bloody bubbles spat forth from his mouth and nose. Elke lowered herself carefully to the earth, crawled to the man's side, and cut his throat. Then she crawled back to the tree and watched him quietly die.

Elke pulled herself erect, held to the tree's low branches to keep from collapsing and drew in a deep breath. "Lor!" she called out, as loud as she could. "Lor! Lor, I am hurt!"

She held herself up against the tree and waited for the hoof beats of the horses. "Lor, I am here! Come, I need help! Lor, help me!" She sat down on a log and looked at her wounded leg. She ripped some of the fabric from the tunic that covered her mail shirt. "Lor, come quickly, bring the horses! I need a poultice and bandages!" She grimaced and pulled out what was left of the crossbow bolt, almost fainting with the pain. Blood began to pour forth from the wound, and so she wrapped the tunic scraps tightly around her thigh to stop the flow. "Lor!"

She found a staff at the campsite that she could use as a crutch and began to hobble through the woods. The light of the fire was behind her, and as long as she didn't go too far, she could always find her way back. "Lor, where are you? I need you! Lor, I'm hurt!" As she was about to turn back and limp back to the camp, she thought she heard the nickering of horses. "Lor? Where are you?"

She searched about in the darkness until she found two horses tied to a tree. "Lor? Are you here?" She examined the horses and the saddlebags and was astounded to discover that they were her own. "Lor?" She began to wonder how far she had wandered off from the campsite but turned and found she could still see the fire.

"Lor!" She called and called, until her voice was gone from shouting.

Elke looked back at the fire. She saw the body lying there, and those beautiful, deep, emerald-green eyes staring blindly up into the star-flecked darkness. She took a step forward, her heart in her throat, and then stopped.

"Damn all tellers of fairy tales," she said hoarsely. Then she mounted her horse and rode on through the night, thinking of princes and monsters, and of the murderous sack of lies men call love.

From the Author

As you might be able to guess, I wrote this story back when I was single. Now that I am married (with four adorable little monsters), I kind of want to go back in time and tell my old bachelor self to try listening to some more cheerful music. Then again, if past me had spent his days bouncing along to upbeat K-pop, maybe he would never have written this story. And I actually quite like it, angst and all.

I also really like the protagonist, Elke. She's fierce, capable, stubborn, and despite her best efforts has a little love and a little hope left in her heart. Elke started life as a throwaway D&D character, but grew into the heroine of some of my very favorite fantasy stories. Every one of those stories has taught me a little more about her, about her world, and about myself. I hope I get the chance to give her a novel some day. I feel like both of us would learn a lot.

Writing this story, I learned about an ancient race of shape-shifting trouble-makers called green-eyed trolls. They're tough, cunning, and very hard to kill. They're also vain and self-important, which I guess is an occupational hazard of living long enough to see civilizations rise and fall.

This is one of the reasons I like writing Lor. He's complicated. He has secrets. He plays at being open and transparent, but his whole life is about disguise and pretense. In fact, I've written him into a number of my other stories. And if you poke around a bit, you might find him. Like Where's Waldo, if Waldo would brutally kill you for spotting him. So… exactly like Where's Waldo.

If that sounds like your kind of game, you can read more of my stories on Patreon, here:

https://www.patreon.com/johndpayne

If you'd rather play with some of my game writing, you can find it on DriveThruRPG, here:

https://www.drivethrurpg.com/browse.php?author=John%2
0D.%20Payne

And if you'd like to read a novel from me, try this one:

https://books2read.com/u/3JRKKg

Happy reading!
–JDP

About the Author

John D. Payne grew up on the prairie, where the tornadoes and electrical storms play. Watching the lightning flash outside his window, he imagined himself as everything from a leaf on the wind to the god of thunder. Today, he lives with his wife and family at the foot of the Organ Mountains in New Mexico, where he focuses his weather-god powers on rustling up enough cloud cover for a little shade.

Stalk him on Twitter @jdp_writes.

Patronize him at www.patreon.com/johndpayne.

Taking the World by the Horn

by
Sam Knight

Taking the World by the Horn

I am here, Margie. Do you remember me?"

The gentle voice roused the old woman enough to flutter her eyelids. Rheumy, faded blue eyes searched the hospice room, but saw only the blur of subdued colors.

"Over here." The voice spoke with a rich, yet subtle accent.

The woman, white hair thin and wispy against her pillow, struggled to turn her head. A large, dark maroon blur contrasted against her normally bright room, blocking the light from the windows.

"Margie? Do you remember me?" the blur asked.

At the sound of her name, Margie felt the world come into focus in a way it hadn't in years. Her vision still failed her, but she knew where she was and why she was here. Hot tears formed and trickled down her withered cheeks. Life was so cruel, but the cruelest thing of all was the way it stole the memories of who she'd been and what she had done.

Her mouth was dry, and licking her lips didn't help, but she tried to speak anyway. Little more than a rasping croak, her words were unintelligible, even to her own ears, but her visitor seemed to understand.

"It's all right, Margie. I will help you remember. Here. Take hold."

A warm, smooth cylinder, with ridges like finger grips, pressed into Margie's hand. Stiffly, arthritic knuckles complaining, she closed her fist around it.

A lightness of being, like the first kiss of the warm morning sun, enveloped her old body and her pain began to fade. Her unquenchable thirst vanished, followed by the lifting of joint pains and the heaviness of gravity pulling down upon her tired body, and then, mercifully, the weariness that had been in her soul for as long as her feeble mind could recall.

She took a deep breath, feeling her old ribs painlessly expand to their limits, and sighed contentedly.

The object in her hand tugged at her to stand. Margie, relishing the absence of pain, held tight and used it to rise. Unable to remember the last time she had been on her feet, it took her another moment to realize the room around her was now sharp and clear, and that the object in her hand was the pearlescent horn of a claret-colored unicorn.

Letting go of the unicorn's smooth spiraled horn, she stared into the equine's blue eyes, enjoying the disparity between the vibrant sky blue and the softer wine color of the creature's coat.

"I think I should be disquieted by the fact I am standing here talking with a unicorn, but... you seem so familiar. I feel I know you." Margie's voice came out strong and grew stronger as she spoke, surprising her with not only its timbre, but with the use of eloquent words she had not heard herself speak in far too long.

"You do know me. You've just forgotten." The large head nodded in agreement, amusement shining in its eyes.

"What is your name?" Margie reached out and stroked the smooth coat behind the attentive ears of the creature. It gave gently under her fingertips, like the richest velvet.

"You once called me Jerry."

Margie nodded. She didn't remember, but it felt right.

A quiet, steady, electronic tone caught her attention, and she shook her head irritably. "That damned machine goes off and tells them I'm dead at least twice a week." Margie waved a hand at the monitor. "It will take twenty minutes before they can be bothered to come and check."

She froze as she noticed the body lying on the bed.

Peering closer to be sure, her mouth made a little wrinkled 'o' and she put a thin hand to her chest in surprise. Taking a step back, she looked from the body on the bed to the unicorn.

She stood straight and squared her shoulders. "Well. It's about time. Whoever said you could die from boredom was most certainly wrong."

The unicorn nickered in amusement.

Looking down at herself, Margie was pleased to find she was wearing her favorite summer dress. One that had been lost many, many years ago. She smoothed the pleats, relishing the feel of the fabric under her fingertips, and then did a slow twirl, lightly lifting the hem out, away from her shins. Satisfied, she smiled up at the horned equine.

"Now what, Jerry? Isn't there supposed to be a bright light leading the way?" Her countenance darkened. "Or am I not taking the elevator up?"

"Do you remember the movie you loved as a child?" Jerry asked. "The one where, at the end, they take the elevator sideways?"

"I think so. Yes. The Chocolate Factory."

"It's a bit more like that, rather than actually up or down. But there is something we need to take care of first."

"Hmph. Isn't there always?"

"Yes. It does seem that way, doesn't it?" The unicorn lowered its head and pointed its horn away from Margie. "Climb up."

"In a dress? I think not."

Cocking a blue eye at the woman, Jerry stared at her, unblinking.

"What? Are you just going to wait until I acquiesce? I assure you, while living, I was the best at this game. At this point, when I doubt I will be suffering from the need to eat, sleep, or urinate, the best you can hope for is that we stand here staring at each other for all eternity."

"Fine." Jerry turned away and headed for the door. "You can walk then."

"Why can't we just fly there? I'm a ghost now aren't I? Aren't there certain privileges to be afforded the living-impaired?"

"Just as everything else, they must be earned," Jerry answered from the hallway, still walking away.

"I'd say I've more than earned mine."

"Have you now?" The unicorn's voice faded, leaving Margie standing alone in the room with her corpse.

She looked back to the withered body on the bed, unable to recognize anything of the face she had seen in the mirror her whole life. Supposing she should have felt sorrow, regret, or something looking at her own lifeless body, she made up for the lack of feeling by cursing the attending staff instead.

"I see they are in a real goddamned hurry to check on you, aren't they?" she told the body. "Fat lot of good it did you to save the world. In the end, the world didn't give a damn about you. They abandoned you, left you here to die." Margie let her eyes wander the bland room. "Not a flower in sight."

Someone walked by in the hallway, obviously ignoring the steady warning tone of the machines hooked up to the body.

Shaking her head disgustedly, Margie turned her back on her earthly remains and followed the red unicorn.

"Long walk, wasn't it?" the unicorn asked as it came to stop in front of a grave. Tall trees and groomed grass filled the cemetery. "What was that? Three days?"

"Do you have someplace you need to be?" Margie retorted. "If I'm holding you up, please feel free to excuse yourself."

"As a matter of fact, I do have someplace I need to be, but I have a promise to fulfill first."

"If you are implying that promise was made to me, I have no memory of it. Therefore, it means nothing to me, and I release you from it."

The unicorn snorted. "As much as you might wish to dismiss it, the promise was made to someone much more important than you, and you have no power over it."

"More important than the first President of the United World?" Margie answered absent mindedly as she noted the grave they had stopped in front of. "Who could that possibly be?" Her voice trailed off as she stared at the name of her deceased ex-husband, etched into the smooth, black granite.

"A little girl."

"Hm?" Margie looked back up from the grave to the unicorn. "Oh, pshaw! Children don't remember promises of anything but ice cream and Disneyland."

"Perhaps not. But I do." The unicorn turned and nodded towards the grave. "This is the first time you have ever been here."

Margie turned her eyes back to her ex-husband's name.

"You were too busy to attend his funeral," the equine continued. "What kind of message do you think that sent out to the world?"

"That I was dedicated to keeping peace and eradicating hunger," Margie snapped back. "This is old news. I've had this conversation before."

"Yet, you *never* found the time to come here."

"What was the point? He was dead."

"He gave up his life for you."

"What? Ludicrous. He died of cancer."

"He wanted to be a leather worker. He could make beautiful things out of leather."

"That was beneath someone of his station."

"Of your station, you mean."

"You arrogant—" Margie whirled to confront the unicorn, but it was already walking away.

She looked back to the grave, pursing her lips in irritation. "I should be angry at you, leaving me like you did. But in the long run, you did me a favor. You always were holding me back."

"Actually, he was the one who carried you forward." The unicorn's voice drifted back to her as it walked out the cemetery's iron gates. "All the way up until you stopped talking to him."

Margie noticed her reflection in the polished headstone. Even as a ghost, her eyes were hard as her mouth was stern. She recognized the cold disapproval of her husband settling into place, deep down inside of herself, making itself right at home in her soul, as if it had been made to be there. It was a feeling she hadn't had for a long while.

Looking at the date on the grave, she realized that feeling had been gone for nearly fifteen years.

"So where are we now, Ghost of Christmas Past?" Margie asked as the red unicorn stopped in front of a non-descript house.

"Oh, you can still talk. I was beginning to wonder. Three months is a long time to hold your tongue."

"If you can't say something nice…"

The unicorn nodded and kept quiet.

From behind the wooden privacy fence surrounding the backyard came the sounds of a little girl squealing with delight.

"Whose house is this? Tiny Tim's? Are we just going to do the Dickens thing for all eternity?"

They stood in silence and listened to the laughter as the red unicorn pointedly did not answer. Rolling her eyes, Margie went to look over the fence.

"Oh, yes. I see. My daughter and her child. Thank you for reminding me they were not a part of my life. I feel so much more enlightened now."

"That is your grand-daughter and *her* child. Your daughter passed on eight years ago."

"And no one told me!" Margie glared at the unicorn.

"Actually," the unicorn held her gaze, "you told your staff to never... how did you phrase it... 'never let me hear another word about my mooching, no-good, low-life relatives again.'"

"I didn't mean my daughter!"

"No. You didn't. But you didn't make that clear, did you? And I think, after the way you publicly disowned her for marrying her high-school sweetheart, and then berated your husband every time you found out he had been in touch with her, your staff could be forgiven for the misunderstanding, don't you?"

"That boy was a no-good pot-head."

"One-time experimentation does not usually lead to a lifetime of—"

"That's what they all say! Everyone wants forgiveness for their trespasses so that they can trespass again."

The unicorn turned and began walking away again.

"Where are we off to now? How many more things are we going to go look at so you can try to show me the error of my ways, and I can show you how you just don't see the big picture?"

"Do you have someplace you need to be?" The unicorn tossed Margie's own words back at her. "If I'm holding you up, please feel free to excuse yourself."

Margie came up alongside of the unicorn and stopped. They had walked for so long she had stopped paying attention to the passing of night into day, let alone the scenery they walked through.

The twelve-foot-tall statue towering over them brought a smile to her face.

"Finally. Someone shows a little respect." Margie nodded in approval.

"Enjoy gazing upon your own likeness?"

"*Oh! You can still talk!*" Margie mocked the unicorn. "I was beginning to think you'd run out of ways to criticize my choices in life."

The unicorn hung its head low, the shimmering horn nearly touching the bare dirt at the base of the statue. His words were little more than a whisper. "Forgive me, for I have failed. After all these years, at the hour you needed me most, I will be the first one—the only one—to abandon you. And I will leave you truly abandoned. You deserved better."

Margie snorted. "You think you are the first to abandon me? Everyone has abandoned me. There is no one in my life who did not abandon me!"

"Although you accuse me of arrogance, Margie, it is you, again, who is arrogant." Raising its head high, the unicorn met Margie's eyes. "I was not speaking to you. And, as a point of matter, no one, ever in your life, abandoned you. You abandoned them. Every last one."

"How dare you!"

"How dare I?" the unicorn murmured, lowering its head again. "Yes. How dare I. How dare I dream of the days when I ran free through the fields of flowers, carrying on my back the one person who ever saw me for what I was. For what I could be.

"How dare I dream that I could be important enough for the first President of the United World to remember me? When she doesn't even care about her own family, how dare I wish she could care for me? That she would have anything left for me when she has nothing left for anyone… How dare I?"

The unicorn scuffed the ground with a front hoof.

"You can stop pretending now," it said. "You and I both know all of your memories came back when you left the physical world behind. You have made your choice clear. You choose not to remember me, or what I stood for in your life. I have no choice left but to respect that. I am sorry for delaying you."

With a wave of its opaline horn, the unicorn revealed a well-worn cobblestone path leading off towards a distant glow in the sky.

Margie stepped onto the path with a determined stride. After two steps, she stopped and looked back. "If you weren't talking to me, who were you talking to?" she insisted.

"I was talking to the little girl you once were. The one who made me promise I would always be her friend, that I would always warn her when she started acting like her father."

"Well, you certainly failed there, didn't you?"

"No. I didn't. I kept my promise, and you know that. I always told you. Every day. Hundreds of times a day. But you chose to ignore me, Margie. You abandoned me. Just like you abandoned everyone else in your life."

"No. That's not true."

"Yes, Margie. It is. Anytime someone close to you disagreed with you, you left them behind."

"A lot of people in this world disagreed with me. It goes with being a leader."

"You know what I mean, Margie." The unicorn flicked its tail. "You left behind your husband because he wouldn't leave your daughter—his daughter—behind."

"He divorced me!"

"After years of you refusing to talk to him. Just as you refused to talk to your daughter, because she married someone you didn't approve of."

"He was a *loser!*"

"So were you, Margie. Remember when you tried marijuana, back when they legalized it?"

"That was different."

"Why? Because it was you?"

"No! Because…"

"No point in lying to someone who has been with you the whole way, is there?"

"You were not with me the whole way. You abandoned me, too! When the war forced us to move into the shelters, you abandoned me!"

"No, I didn't, Margie. You stopped listening to me. You decided to put aside your childish things and move on. It was a conscious decision, remember? You actively started ignoring me."

"Because you weren't real! How could I worry about cherry-colored unicorns while I was trying not to get raped and murdered by roving gangs?"

The unicorn dropped its horn to the ground again, this time letting it touch the dirt. "I never asked you to worry about me, Margie. I just needed to be there for you. That was all I needed." A silver tear ran down the unicorn's nose and fell to the ground, leaving ripples, as though the earth were a reflection in water.

"I united the world! I didn't have time for pretend friends. I didn't have time for anything!"

"I know that, Margie. We all did."

The unicorn shook its withers and raised its head. Turning, it walked away.

Margie looked down at the path she stood upon and then out at the distant light it led to. It wasn't as warm as she'd expected. Nor did it call to her, as she'd been led to believe it would. It just was.

It was merely another destination. Nothing more than another goal. Another worthless achievement to move past.

"Wait," she heard some small part of herself call out, her voice nothing more than a whisper. Something inside grew too taut and snapped, breaking whatever had held the emotions back. And the tears flowed. "Wait! Cherry Jerry!" she called, loud this time.

Margie stepped off the path and toward the retreating unicorn. The unicorn twisted its neck to look back at her.

"I don't really have someplace I need to be," Margie said. "If I'm not holding you up, I was wondering if… if you would like to find a field of flowers to go riding in?"

Jerry nickered and turned to face Margie. "It's about time."

"I know, right?" Tears glistened on Margie's cheek.

The unicorn lowered its head and offered its horn as a handhold.

Hesitating as she climbed up, Margie blushed, and then realized her dress had turned into riding pants. She took a deep breath, wiped tears away, and steadied herself again. "Sorry. It's been a while."

"It will all come back to you."

As she settled upon Jerry's back, Margie looked to the path leading towards the light. "How long will that wait for me?"

"Remember what I said about the sideways elevator?"

"Yes."

"Well, you just pushed a different button, and we won't be going that way. Hold on."

Jerry reared up onto his back legs with a gallant whinny, waving his front hooves as if they were going to climb up into the sky.

Margie squealed with joy and held on tightly as Jerry dropped back to the earth and raced towards the setting sun in search of a field of flowers.

From the Author

My Facebook page states, "I am an author who refuses to be pinned down into a genre. If the idea grabs me, I write it." This story, "Taking the World by the Horn," is a good example of why I feel that way. Most of my stories have been Weird Western, but not all stories need to be action or violence or even, dare I say... fun?

Sometimes I find myself writing something that just isn't quite like anything else I've written before. Personally, I feel that is a good thing, but it does make it difficult to place some of those stories.

Originally written in 2015 for an anthology requesting "red unicorn" stories, it was never submitted. In fact, up until preparation for this anthology, I had never shown it to anyone. Instead, I wrote two more and submitted the third story for that anthology. It wasn't accepted, rightfully so, as the editor felt it was more like part of a much larger story. And so it was. I may get around to that someday. If you are curious, that story is called "Pure as the Driven Snow," and is available as a stand-alone e-book.

Why didn't I submit this story? I honestly can't say, other than it didn't "feel" right. In truth, this one probably stood a better chance at being accepted for that anthology.

In the six years since it was written, "Taking the World by the Horn" never really felt like a good fit for other anthologies, but it finally felt right for this one. It felt like this was the right time to publish it. I hope you liked it.

If you did, you may also like "A Little Bird Told Me,"
www.books2read.com/u/bwYdgv

You can find other books with stories by me, and where to purchase them, here:
www.books2read.com/ap/xdeGQR/Sam-Knight

You can find my (mostly) complete bibliography here:
www.samknight.com/?page_id=1592

About the Author

A Colorado native, Sam Knight spent ten years in California's wine country before returning to the Rockies. When asked if he misses California, he gets a wistful look in his eyes and replies he misses the green mountains in the winter, but he is glad to be back home.

As well as having worked for at least three publishing companies, Sam has edited six anthologies and is author of six children's books, five short story collections, three novels, and over 75 stories, including three co-authored with Kevin J. Anderson, two of which were media-tie-ins: "Wayward Pines: Aberration" (Kindle Worlds, 2014) and "Of Monsters and Men", *Planet of the Apes: Tales from the Forbidden Zone* (Titan, 2016).

A stay-at-home father, Sam attempts to be a full-time writer, but there are only so many hours left in a day after kids. Once upon a time, he was known to quote books the way some people quote movies, but now he claims having a family has made him forgetful, as a survival adaptation. He can be found at SamKnight.com and contacted at sam@samknight.com.

Unlocking the Gate of Fear

by
David Boop

Unlocking the Gate of Fear

Love is the master key that opens the gates of happiness,
of hatred, of jealousy, and,
most easily of all,
the gate of fear.

—*Oliver Wendell Jones*

Arizona Territory

1870

*L*eopold Reinholdsson, renamed Leo Rheingold by the United States government, got up from the shelter that he and his partner, Farlan Wellmann—now Frank Wellman—had found to wait out the night in. The rocks formed a cave of sorts, enough to keep the snowstorm outside. It didn't make the night any less cold, but the fire Leo tended to during his watch helped some.

He kicked Frank lightly.

"Gotta sheet."

Frank numbly replied.

His cousin made for a good companion, and they watched each other's backs. They split everything equally, even when one or the other had a bad run, like Frank was currently experiencing. He knew it bothered Frank that Leo's catches brought more money than his did, but Frank was family, and having someone trustworthy to travel America with made it worthwhile.

Frank got up to a sitting position and grabbed his Sharp's from nearby. Just like the animals they hunted, trappers knew they were most vulnerable when squatting. Together, they stumbled through the snow-covered scrub brush that lined the Verde Valley foothills, until they got far enough away from the shelter to not accidentally step in his shit later.

Leo couldn't believe how cold it had grown since they arrived. Wasn't Arizona supposed to be a desert or something, like the Sahara? With each breath he took, he felt like a hundred little icicle shards went into his lungs. It was unnatural.

It took nearly five minutes for Leopold to get down to his long johns.

"Hurry up, will ya?" Frank entreated. "Da fire'll be out."

"So damn cold, dontcha know? Hard to get started."

Leo grunted, trying to rush, but then a sound from nearby stopped all other thoughts.

An animal—a predator—growled hungrily.

As they stood motionless, something moved around them. The noise bounced off the rock formations, making it hard to gauge how close or from where the hunter lurked. Its snarl—an eerie echo.

Ethereal.

Haunting.

"Get up!" Frank whispered.

Leo gathered his pants to bring them up with him as he stood, however…

The creature struck while he was still bent over.

Its large maw clamped over Leo's shoulder, teeth digging into his neck and chest. Steaming blood sprayed out far enough to hit Frank's boots. Leo screamed as the creature tossed him around like a rag doll.

With only sparse moonlight, Frank could only see its glowing yellow eyes. The monster, for he couldn't make out any recognizable animal, had to be the size of a small horse. Placing the rifle to his shoulder, Frank aimed for the spot between those eyes.

It paused long enough from rending his partner's flesh to study him.

Frank fired from only ten feet away, but the creature only blinked as the bullet bounced off its thick skull.

It dropped Leo and roared like no creature Frank recognized. From the scream, the world around Frank froze like a fresh coat of ice had covered it. Frank backed away from the encroaching freeze as the creature eyed new prey, and Frank knew he would be lying next to his cousin in moments.

Keeping his wits about him, Frank dropped the rifle, as there would be no time to reload, and, with speed only a man facing death could have, whipped out his other gun, tucked under his pelts. He ran forward and slid across the frozen ground to jam the gun's barrel down the creature's throat. He fired, hoping to send lead careening through the creature's organs.

A massive paw swatted Frank like a fly. Luckily, Frank's thick furs saved him from any serious damage. The creature coughed up the gun before turning and running off into the dark.

Farlan Wellmann, now Frank Wellman, crawled over to where Leo Rheingold, once Leopold Reinholdsson, lay twitching; the gurgling of life escaping his cousin's throat guiding Frank to him. And then Leo released a single word with his dying breath.

Frank dragged his partner over near the shelter and took up a pickax to dig Leo a grave as deep as he could. When he cleared about two feet of clay and sand, Frank wrapped Leo's head in a cloth, as was custom, and filled in the hole. He placed rocks over the grave to keep it from predators.

He kept alert the whole time but did not hear the haunting growl again. He stoked the fire as high and bright as he could throughout the night and, at day's break, started the long walk into Drowned Horse, the closest settlement.

Frank thought about what he'd seen and the final word his cousin spoke as a warning. He must have misheard, because Frank recognized that word, and it was no *thing* known to inhabit America, let alone the territories.

No! A *gulon* could not have made it all the way to Arizona.

No way in hell!

Sheriff Levi Forrest shot his fifth empty bourbon bottle off of the fence out back of the Sagebrush Saloon, and yet it didn't relieve his discontentment. The Sagebrush's owner let him do this from time to time, as a way to work through his frustrations.

Forrest faced a two-fold dilemma. Whereas a few years back his ratio of bullets to bottles was one to one, today it sat closer to three to one. His hand wasn't as steady. His eyes not as sharp. Not a good combination for a lawman protecting his town from the evil that all-too-often threatened it. Day was coming that someone, or some*thing*, got the drop on him... and thus the second issue.

Deputy William Ragsdale hadn't come along as quick and as clean as Forrest hoped when he had brought him on. He figured that hiring him young, as he did, meant that he'd have years to hone the boy's talents. Only, as Will grew into manhood, his tendency to let anger cloud his judgment had become an issue.

Just the other day, Will dragged a gambler out into the street by the man's collar and deposited him in a fresh pile of manure, all 'cause the cheat offered the deputy a bribe. Forrest arrived just as Will finished kicking the man senseless.

"I'm no crook!" Will screamed at the man while Forrest helped the card cheat up and sent him on his way.

"What's gotten into you?" Forrest demanded. "That's not how we handle this kind of thing."

"He thought me dirty, Sheriff. He figured I was like him." He shouted at the gambler's quickly retreating back. "I'm not! I'm not like you!"

Forrest noticed that Will's hand twitched near his holster.

"Let's go back to the jail and sit a spell, 'k?"

Forrest led Will to the office they shared, but the deputy would not sit. He paced back and forth, mumbling under his breath about being better than a damn cheat.

"Something's eating at you, boy?"

A storm flashed in Will's eyes as his head snapped up to stare at Forrest.

"I ain't no boy no more, Sheriff. What does it take to get a little respect from you?"

Forrest leaned forward in his chair and pointed to his chest. "Me? Whadda I do?"

Years ago, when Will was but a lad, he'd helped Forrest and the great tracker Kit Carson out of a mess. Seeing potential in him, Forrest started training him as a lawman. Will's naturally keen senses, quick draw, and previously level-headedness made him the perfect heir to the office. When Will's parents moved on to California, he stayed, and Forrest thought of him like a son. He made Forrest proud when he married his long-time love, Sarah. The couple had a little one recently, a girl. Will should be the happiest man alive.

"Now listen up, *William*. I don't know what's got you in such a state, and maybe you don't trust me enough to tell me, and that's your decision. But I won't allow Drowned Horse to get the reputation as a town that drags crooked gamblers into the street and beats them bloody. We've enough other stuff to overcome if we're to keep this town afloat."

Other stuff... like the curse.

Forrest stood and walked over to the lad. He placed a comforting hand on his shoulder. "So, I need you to get your head on straight, all right?"

Will looked as he might cry, but, as if sensing this, the deputy twisted out of Forrest's grip and marched out of the office.

"Well, that didn't go as planned," Forrest had said to no one.

But then little did in Drowned Horse.

Sixth bottle destroyed after the fifth attempt, Forrest stomped through the ankle-deep snow to have a drink and decide what to do next.

Drowned Horse sat nestled in an area named "the Verde Valley" for its lush vegetation, though none of that was right visible due to the snow coming over the mountains that boxed it in to the west and north. The Oak Creek came down from Flagstaff and became the Cottonwood Wash, which often got plugged with horse carcasses in the spring, thus the all-too-true name of the place Forrest called home.

But that was far from the most interesting thing about Drowned Horse.

Further back than anyone can remember, a curse had been placed on the area, stating that none who settled there should know a day's rest from the evils of the universe.

In Forrest's time as sheriff, he'd fought creatures from mythology, demons from hell, and things dropped down from the stars. He felt it was his calling to protect the settlers that chose to stay in the area, but could it be that William had developed second thoughts about the mission? He'd been so young when he wound up here that now, as a man with a wife and baby, maybe he wanted to leave and didn't know how to say it. Drowned Horse wasn't the best place to have a family.

It could also just be the unseasonably long winter they'd experienced. The boy, er, young man, could have a touch of cabin fever.

However, before Forrest could gather the wits around him enough to go talk to his deputy, the town's undertaker, Ram, bolted into the office.

"Sheriff? You're gonna want as to come see this."

Adoniram G. Craddick had inherited the business from his father, one of Drowned Horse's many unfortunate victims. Ram, who was similar to Will in age, impressed the sheriff when he sent his pappy to his final resting place in a very mature and professional way. It took something serious to shake the calm demeanor of the tall, broad-shouldered man, but Ram looked downright white, as if Satan himself had shown up to pay respects.

"It's going to be that sort of day, isn't it?"

Ram nodded, and the sheriff unlocked his special cabinet for those sorts of days.

There wasn't anything left that could be called a corpse, or even remains for that matter. The dark splotch in the impromptu grave looked more like what the butcher had left over when he finished making sausage.

Both Forrest and Will fought hard to keep their breakfast down. Not that either hadn't seen dead men before, but never so... chunky.

Pieces that could only be identified as once human by the bits of clothing or buckles, lay scattered around. Rocks that Frank must've used to cover the grave had been tossed about like skipping stones. Whatever thing unearthed Leo Rheingold's resting place must've been really big. The only thing that worked to their advantage was that the whole area lay frozen, even in the heat of day, keeping the scene intact, like it was sealed under glass.

Ram pointed to the desecrated grave. "Leo was a trapper with Frank, over there. They'd been heading up to Prescott, but the pass closed due to the storm. They bunked down with plans to try again this morning."

Frank waited in said outcropping, his knees pulled up to his chest.

Ram continued. "Frank walked into Drowned Horse at first light to fetch me and a cart, as to bring the body back for proper burial. When we got back here, though, the creature had dug up Leo's grave and ripped him apart."

Will spat. "Carrion eater. Must've had a hell of a nose, too."

Forrest agreed. No badger, wolf, fox or other grave digger would've dug that far down.

"*Vielfras,*" Frank called out, his German accent thick. "Leo call it 'gulon,' but my people known it as veilfras."

Forrest approached the trapper. He wore a pelt thick with fox, ermine, and wolf—many of which seemed to still be looking up at the Sheriff. Only Frank's face, covered in a long beard, identified him as human.

"What is a gulon, or veilfras as you call it?"

"Monster," Frank answered. "Would not have think such a thing come to America, but then I see Leo's grave and know to be true. Dey eat the dead."

Will joined his boss. "What's it look like?"

"Beeg. It gorge itself then quickly take a sheet before eating more. Da veilfras always hungry."

That worried Forrest. There were a lot of settlers spread out farther from town than he'd like.

Frank continued, "Could gobble up whole family, then eat the sheep later, dontcha know?"

"Sarah!" Will ran back to his horse, launching into the saddle and raced off.

Forrest barely got a "no. wait," past his gums before his deputy had vanished.

While the Ragsdale residence sat on the opposite side of Drowned Horse from where they were now, Forrest understood the young man's fears. It's one of the reasons the sheriff never settled down himself. Once Will made sure his wife and baby were safe, he'd come back. He would probably take them into town where others could look after them. Which, knowing the town, really didn't make them all that much safer.

"What, other than 'beeg,' can you use to describe it?" the sheriff asked.

Frank ran down its legendary traits from dog-like body, cat-like ears, to fox-like tail, leaving Forrest to wonder if it wasn't really a bear or something.

"Too fast for bear, especially in da winter. It stop the world with its breath. When it scream, it freezes everything around it."

Forrest thought that odd, even for some of the creatures he'd fought in the past. Well, whatever it was, Forrest needed to kill it. That was his job.

Ram motioned for Forrest to join him.

"I'd like to look at where Leo was killed. I found one of the scat piles Frank mentioned not far from here. He wasn't kidding. Huge pile between two trees, like it'd pushed the poop through a piping bag."

Forrest was sure he'd never get rid of that image until his dying day.

Forrest asked Frank to take them there.

"Why?" Frank looked at them both with trepidation. "Bad memories. Just want to leave."

"Well, we need a place to start hunting this thing, before it kills other people."

After some discussion, Frank agreed.

At the kill sight, blood-soaked snow had frozen into ice, pink as a lady's bonnet, to boot. Forrest crouched down to examine the gulon's tracks while Ram, carrying a knife that Forrest thought just a few inches short of a sword, circled out from the trampled area, searching.

Frank stared at the scarlet evidence, seemingly replaying the events in his mind.

"Shot it, did your undertaker tell you that? Hit right in da head." Frank pointed at a spot right between his eyes. "When that did nothing, then I ram my gun down its throat, shot again, but did not stop it."

Looking at a print in the snow, Forrest did mental calculations of the paw size to what that meant for the creature. "That's all a man can do. You're lucky to be alive." He looked up. "It's funny that you two come from the same place this thing originated from."

Frank, acting as if the question took a moment to register, answered, "I am, as you say, from Germany. Leopold from Denmark. His mother, half of each. He was cousin, of sorts. Both countries have same legend."

"Yeah. Strange coincidence."

Frank took in the sheriff, now aware that Forrest studied him.

"What? You think I do this? Bring veilfras here?"

Forrest stood up and then shrugged. "Maybe. Maybe not. I just don't believe in coincidences. People bring things to America, sometimes without even knowing it. They bring their culture, right? But also, their demons." Forrest spat on the ground. "You have demons, Frank?"

Frank nervously glanced to the sheriff's holster and back.

Ram arrived a second later. "Just as I thought. There's game carcasses scattered around, staked to the ground. Even tied to trees, but not like a trap. Just a lure. Someone tried to attract big game here. Maybe that person lured something he wasn't expecting."

Despite the cold, Frank's brow dripped sweat across his face.

"Wouldn't know anything 'bout that, would you, Frank?" Forrest asked.

Frank stared at each of them, going back and forth with shifty eyes. He stuttered, "N-not supposed to be veilfras. Just mountain l-lion. Something I could kill and make good money. My traps not catching what Leopold's were. He must think to cut me loose. I just wanted to..."

Forrest swore. "Dammit, man! This land is cursed! Evil draws out evil. Your greed must've brought the veilfras here, a nightmare from your own minds."

Frank looked back and forth between the two men, seemingly to gauge whether to run or shoot it out.

"Not greedy. Hungry. He not supposed to die. Maybe injured. Then must keep me as partner."

Ram took a fighting stance, knife extended, while Forrest's hand hovered near his piece. Frank's arms were hidden under his thick pelt. He could have a throwing knife, iron, or a rifle under there, Forrest couldn't tell.

The pelt parted and the double barrels of a shortened shotgun peeked out.

Forrest placed a bullet in Frank's chest. He could hardly miss at that range, and the pelts made him a big target. He dropped flat as a grave.

Ram hadn't even gotten a step forward.

"Jesus, Sheriff. What was he thinking?"

"He was thinking he could shoot me first, then you." He cocked an eyebrow. "Any questions?"

The undertaker shook his head.

"Good, now let's go bury the body, then we watch and wait."

Dusk had settled in by the time they finished filling in Frank's grave.

They scampered up a series of nearby boulders, to give them a bird's eye view.

Forrest positioned his four-bore rifle in a nice crook that would allow him to steady it. Not only because it was a beast to hold, but he knew he'd gotten lucky with Frank. The pelts had weighed down the man's gun as he lifted it to shoot the sheriff and undertaker. If Forrest hadn't hit him with the first shot, it would be he and Ram down there as gulon bait, not Frank.

When Ram set his Sharps rifle same as Forrest had, the sheriff felt relieved. He didn't want word getting around yet that his skills had started fading. Ram's rifle wouldn't have the range or the stopping power of the "elephant gun," as some called it, but it might be useful as a distraction.

As if almost on cue, they both caught movement through the brush near the grave. A dark shape crawled low.

It could still be a mountain lion, Forrest hoped, but all thoughts of that fled his mind when the creature reached the mound. Twice as big as any mountain lion Forrest had ever seen, Frank's description of the monster hit it pretty close, though Forrest would've said the tail was more whip-like than a fox's: long and sinewy with a tuft of fur at the end.

He and Ram followed it through their sights as it breathed on the mound, turning it brittle, and then cautiously chipped away at it with its large paws.

But as the sheriff made to tighten on his trigger, a noise drew all three of their attentions away from their tasks.

The sound of hoof beats.

Deputy William Ragsdale rode hard along the range to catch up with the party he'd abandoned, oblivious to the notion he would run right into the "always hungry" gulon.

Forrest didn't know how far a gulon could jump, but it could easily take down the horse and rider, making a meal of one, before squeezing out a shit and eating the other.

Ram made to get up, but Forrest held him down.

"That's my friend," Ram said.

"He's mine, too. But if we do this wrong, we'll miss our chance, and he could still die. This is a powder load, and I'll only get one shot off in time."

Ram settled back into his spot.

"When I say, shoot right in front of Will's horse."

Ram slowly turned his head to check if Forrest was serious. Seeing that he was, he returned to sight in the advancing deputy.

The gulon crouched, back end high lifted—an indication it prepared to pounce.

Forrest exhaled, and held the gun exactly at the place the gulon should arc.

He counted down from three as Will arrived at the intersection point.

"Now."

Ram fired a shot hitting the rocks right in front of Will's mare. Well trained, the horse darted the opposite direction as the gulon leapt. Forrest fired his gun, the boom shaking the foothills. Ram covered his ears, though Forrest had grown deaf to it.

The gulon took the large caliber bullet right in the side of the head. The force punched through, taking most of the skull with it.

The white of Will's eyes could be seen even from up high as they were. The now-carcass passed by him in the air, blood gushing everywhere. Will leaned forward to dodge the gulon's claws, which acted as if they didn't know the rest of it was already dead. Still, the gulon's ice breath hit the side of Will's head and hat, turning the blood into frosting.

Once clear, William brought his horse around; side iron drawn and ready for whatever came next.

The body of the gulon twitched, and blood gurgled out of it, soaking the late winter snow crimson.

Forrest was all grins as he walked up to his deputy.

Will punched him across the jaw.

"You used me as BAIT?"

Ram ran up between the two, placing a hand on Will's chest. "To be fair, he used Frank's body as bait. You just got between them."

Deputy Ragsdale paused, fists still balled, as he processed the new information.

"That trapper, Frank, is dead?"

Ram nodded. "He called the gulon here, intentional or not. When the Sheriff figured it out, he drew on him, and you know what that gets."

"Yeah, sucker punches aside." Forrest rubbed his chin.

"Still don't make it right." Will stomped around, still looking for an outlet for his fear-driven rage. He swung at the air. "Not right."

"Wouldya preferred I let the damn thing eat you?" Forrest felt like he, too, wanted to knock the young man down a notch. He'd been dealing with Will's temper all too long. "You wanted me to bring your body back to your wife; your baby girl growing up without her daddy? That sound better to you?"

"No!" Will said, "But I sure as hell didn't want to go back to her covered in blood. Not again."

The two angry men stared at each other, tensed, ready to come to blows when they began to laugh.

They laughed so hard, Forrest had to hold his side. Will bent over and grabbed his thighs, blood cascading off his hat like a waterfall which only made them laugh harder.

Ram looked back and forth between them, his expression indicating he thought them both insane.

Forrest composed himself first. "Yeah, don't want to have that conversation with Sarah again. She still hasn't forgiven me for blasting giant scorpion guts all over you."

"Well, how could she? She was under Ol' Stabby, too!"

They continued to laugh all the way back to Drowned Horse.

William Ragsdale calmed down somewhat soon after, Forrest noticed gratefully. They never did talk about what burned a hole in his deputy's soul, but in the end, it really didn't matter. Forrest's instincts told him his own time in Drowned Horse drew close to an end. The curse wouldn't be his problem much longer, and he could only hope he'd done right by the boy... and the town.

Sheriff Levi Forrest lined up five more empty bottles on the fence, feeling the cold right down into his bones.

It would be a long winter, and he needed to be ready for what came next.

From the Author

"Unlocking the Gate of Fear" takes place the first act of my *The Drowned Horse Chronicle* series, of which twenty-two stories (mostly) self-contained have seen publication to date. Set in and around the cursed town of Drowned Horse, Arizona, any resemblance to existing towns—cursed or otherwise that I might have lived in or around—is purely coincidental. Having told the tale of the citizens of Drowned Horse in no particular order, I realized that I'd created holes within the timeline and story arc of these characters.

One in particular was the relationship between Sheriff Levi Forrest and his deputy, William Ragsdale. I'd featured them separately or together in eight other short works and one novella. Yet, I hadn't explored how they'd changed toward the end of the arc. I needed a story that showed an older Forrest and an angry Ragsdale at odds with each other. As I often do, I sought out a creature to fight and wrapped around an overlay regarding trust... and the lack thereof.

I hope you'll enjoy.

DB
02/09/21

About the Author

David Boop is a Denver-based speculative fiction author & editor. He's also an award-winning essayist, and screenwriter. Before turning to fiction, David worked as a DJ, film critic, journalist, and actor. As Editor-in-Chief at *IntraDenver.net*, David's team was on the ground at Columbine making them the only *internet newspaper* to cover the tragedy. That year, they won an award for excellence from the Colorado Press Association for their design and coverage.

David's debut novel is the sci-fi/noir *She Murdered Me with Science* from WordFire Press. A second novel, *The Soul Changers*, is a serialized Victorian Horror novel set in Pinnacle Entertainment's world of *Rippers Resurrected*. David was editor on the bestselling and award nominated weird western anthology series, *Straight Outta Tombstone*, *Straight Outta Deadwood* and *Straight Outta Dodge City* for Baen. He's currently working on a trio of Space Western anthologies for Baen starting with *Gunfight on Europa Station*.

David is prolific in short fiction with many short stories and two short films to his credit. He's published across several genres including media tie-ins for *Predator* (nominated for the 2018 Scribe Award), *The Green Hornet*, *The Black Bat* and *Veronica Mars*.

Additionally, he does a flash fiction mystery series on Gumshoereview.com called *The Trace Walker Temporary Mysteries* (the first collection is available now.) He does a quarterly comic strip about a new author's experiences with *Sign Here, Please*, and runs an author-themed t-shirt shop called *Author-Centric Designs by Longshot Productions*.

David works in game design, as well. He's written for the Savage Worlds RPG for their *Flash Gordon* (nominated for an *Origins Award*) and *Deadlands: Noir* titles.

He's a Summa Cum Laude Graduate from UC-Denver in the Creative Writing program. He temps, collects Funko Pops, and is a believer. His hobbies include film noir, anime, the Blues and History.

You can find out more at:
Davidboop.com
Facebook.com/dboop.updates
Twitter@david_boop
and www.longshot-productions.net

The Serpent's Eye
by
Todd Fahnestock

The Serpent's Eye

*I*f you're looking for a hero, stop reading. This isn't a hero's story. It's not something you can tell your children to inspire them or to make your heart fill with loyalty for the empress. I once dreamed of such things, about swinging a sword and achieving great deeds. But I never fought the Slink Lord alongside the legendary Whisper Prince. I never rode to glory beside High Lord Denshell against the sea serpents.

No. When given the chance to serve my sworn lord or join his enemies, I chose the monsters.

Are you still with me? Be it on your head, then. I'm going to tell you what you don't want to hear, that your High Lord Denshell is a thief and a would-be murderer of little boys. And I swear to you that if you take his side, you'll face the same bloody end he did.

There were many steps that led to my moment of transformation. I look back on it like I had slipped on a slick rock while fording a river, then stumbled again and again until I finally fell over a waterfall. When you go over a waterfall, there's only one place you can end up. But I was just a boy. I believed I could somehow clamber back up that rushing spout of tragedy to the steady ground I'd once known.

The slipping first began when my father left Mother and me. That faithless dog trailed behind a rich woman to the capital city of Thiara and called it true love. Because he needed to. His new woman was of higher birth and greater fortune than my mother, and since Father had already squandered all of our money, I suppose he thought abandoning us was his only choice.

Whatever his sordid reasons, he left us alone in the house of my birth, with no money and no prospects. That was the end of my childhood, and it was the first of many events that dragged me over my personal waterfall, though I didn't know it at the time. I hadn't known much of anything back then. I didn't know the dangers of poverty, how the lack of money could strip you of your station. My life had consisted of attending to my tutors, attending Father's social functions, and spending time in our house with its big windows and tall ceilings, with its polished mahogany tables, chairs, and cupboards.

I loved that house. It always smelled of lilacs, Mother being a fiend for flowers. I remember dining on elegant meals from porcelain plates and dressing in finery. My fondest memory was of the sitting room, which had a rich rug depicting sea serpents twisting into symmetrical knots. I'd spent many lazy afternoons lying on that rug while Mother sang *The Sea Serpent's Wife* to me, that story about the girl who spends her days by the sea, letting her beautiful voice carry out over the waves until it accidentally attracts the attentions of a sea serpent who transforms her into one of its own kind, to be its bride forever.

I'm sure you know the one. Your mother probably sang it to you, too.

During those lazy afternoons, laying on soft, fanciful sea serpents and staring up at the high ceilings, I imagined everything a typical boy does. I imagined being a great hero, riding on a snorting stallion with an enchanted sword in my hand as I fought alongside The Whisper Prince, slaying Slink after Slink. I also imagined being a sea serpent, slithering through the waves of the sea. I wondered if it would feel like flying.

Of course, the actual sea serpents—unlike the artful monsters depicted on our rug—had killed dozens of men and women just that past summer, any who had dared to go near the Sunset Sea. The serpents were the scourge of Trimbledown, and High Lord Denshell had been trying to exterminate them for years to no avail.

Perhaps those daydreams were where my story began, but I think not. Every boy dreams; not every boy comes to a hard choice, as I did. Perhaps my story began the moment my father left, after which Mother and I had to sell everything we owned and—at the supposed grace of High Lord Denshell—move into one of his small huts by the sea. Except I made no choice then; I simply followed my mother like boys do.

And perhaps—no doubt you'd think this the most likely—my transformation began with the death of my mother. You see, High Lord Denshell had cunningly offered her a job as a sea hacker, and she joined a roving band of fighters who patrolled the coastline with hooks and hatchets, hunting serpents.

They said a serpent ate her whole.

Her death was another slip, another slide toward the frightening edge of that waterfall. But I didn't go over. I hadn't the courage yet to take control of my destiny. That choice still lay before me.

No, my story began when I punched High Lord Denshell's son in the mouth. I—and none other—made that choice. That was when I left my previous life behind forever.

When Mother took the job as a sea hacker, I'd felt such effusive gratitude toward High Lord Denshell for all he'd done for us. At first glance, his offer of a hut in which to live, and a means by which to earn a wage, seemed like pure generosity. But after I punched Mellistor, I finally saw the Denshells for what they really were: scheming jackals intent on robbing me. And they didn't care if I lived or died any more than they'd cared if my mother got eaten by sea serpents.

For you to fully understand why I did what I did, you need to know about the Serpent's Eye. No, it wasn't actually the eye of a sea serpent. It was an artifact, a ball of golden glass, as hard as steel, created by Faia magic two hundred years ago, and it was the only thing we'd kept from our old house.

The Serpent's Eye could shine as bright as the sun or go as dark as a river stone, depending on the time of day and the needs of its user. It could float of its own accord, and it tended to follow its master around, lighting her way. Mother had said it was a gift to my great-great-great-grandfather from the first emperor of Thiara, Baezin the Conqueror himself. She'd also said it was once a powerful weapon in the Benascan Wars two centuries ago, though that had never made sense to me. How could a floating lamp be used as a weapon? Still, it was by far the most valuable thing we owned, even during our wealthier days.

Father had tried to take it when he left, and Mother had fought him—had actually fought him. I'd never seen her raise her hand in violence against anyone or anything, but she'd drawn blood clawing at his face with her bare hands. He'd run from her, and that was the last time I ever saw him.

After that savage scuffle, after Father had gone, Mother had sat down with me and quietly told me that, though Trimbledown might forget our lineage, the empire never would so long as we kept the Serpent's Eye. She believed the artifact was more than just a light, that it had been given to our family for a purpose. It meant we were special, more special even than High Lord Denshell or Father's new lady or any of the other nobles in Trimbledown. Mother had said not even the nobles in Thiara, who rode their elegant, slender boats down their stone-sided canals, possessed such a powerful Faia artifact as the Serpent's Eye.

I think you see where I'm going. Yes, the Serpent's Eye was the true reason for High Lord Denshell's "generosity." It was why he gave us that hut by the sea at no apparent cost, why he pushed my mother into the dangerous job of sea-hacking. He'd wanted Mother out of the way. He'd wanted to take the Eye for himself.

It was three days after they told me Mother had been eaten whole by a sea serpent when the High Lord's son, Mellistor, spotted me in Trimbledown Square. I had stuffed the Serpent's Eye into a leather pouch and affixed it to my belt; I carried it everywhere with me, as I had no safe place to keep it. I even clutched it with my hand to ensure I always knew exactly where it was.

I was in the market at Trimbledown Square looking for a meal to steal. I had no money, I had no food, and without Mother I had no means of gaining either. I had to steal, or I was going to starve.

Mellistor must have decided it was time to take the Eye. Perhaps he thought his father would give him a hero's welcome if he returned with it.

My stomach had been growling for most of three days, and if Mellistor had guessed what I was actually doing in the marketplace, he would simply have waited for me to make my move, exposed me, and then accused me. He could have called me a thief in front of everyone and taken the Eye while I stood in shame-faced guilt. At that wretched point in my life, I would have been cowed enough to let him.

But he didn't do that. Instead, he strode up to me, no less than five of his friends behind him—he always had an entourage—and snatched the Serpent's Eye out of my hand, snapping the leather thong attached to my belt.

"Jyshen the shack boy," he said derisively, pushing me. "This doesn't belong to you. You're not highborn any longer. You owe rent, and you've no way to pay it. I'm taking this."

When he wrenched the Eye from my hand, when he snapped those leather cords of my pouch, something snapped inside me at the same time. It was like he'd ripped away my heritage, all ties to my previous life.

That snap released a coldness within me, coated my insides with a numbing frost. I didn't feel fear. I didn't hope for courtesy or kindness. All that remained was an icy, howling rage.

I hit him. I'd never hit anyone before, but I hit Mellistor with every bit of my strength. The stunned lordling yelped and dropped the Eye onto the cobblestones. I stunned him. By the Faia, I stunned myself, and that howling cold suddenly vanished, leaving me empty and uncertain. I stared at my fist, then at Mellistor, then back at my fist. I had no words. I'd never done that before. I'd never been that boy; a boy who would turn to violence.

Mellistor backed up, eyes wide with fear as he touched fingers to his bloody lip. But he saw my sudden astonishment, and it seemed to lift his courage. His fear twisted into fury.

"You'll hang for that, Jyshen," he whispered lethally.

He hit me once, twice. First in the eye, then in the mouth. Wham! Wham!

If he hadn't hit me, if he'd waited even a second longer, I think my astonishment at my own actions would have crumbled into terror, and I'd have run. Striking the son of the High Lord of Trimbledown meant jail time for a noble. For a newly orphaned boy with no money, it could mean death.

But Mellistor's two cruel blows brought back the howling cold inside me, and this time it overwhelmed me. I slipped for the final time and went over the waterfall. I saw what Mellistor and his father really were. I raged at Mother's death, at my precarious situation, at Mellistor's attempted theft. It suddenly felt like this wasn't just a scuffle between boys. This was a fight for my mother, for what was rightfully ours, for my entire lineage. If I didn't win this fight, I might as well just fade away.

I screamed and leapt on Mellistor like a mindless, rampaging Slink, my fists flailing. He hit me again, but I couldn't feel it. I couldn't feel anything. I just kept punching and punching until he fell to the cobblestones.

By the time I stopped, I was astride him, blood on my fists. He whimpered, holding trembling hands over a ravaged face. Before the rest of his stunned friends could react, I grabbed the Serpent's Eye and ran, weaving left to snatch a fresh fish from a vendor's cart while the man gaped at the bloody lordling and his cluster of gabbling friends.

I ran all the way back to my little shack by the sea.

Perhaps it was battle shock that made me so calm, but I prepared my dinner as though nothing had happened. I reflexively hummed *The Sea Serpent's Wife* as I cleaned and cooked the fish. It caused my split lip to throb, but I hummed anyway, with a mad vigor. I could hear Mother singing in my mind. And as long as I heard Mother's voice, I could somehow believe this nightmare was going to end, that she would return to me, that everything would go back to the way it had been.

After I devoured the fish, I took my wooden plate down to the sea and dumped the bones, warily scanning left and right for sea serpents. With a fistful of sand, I hastily scrubbed the crinkled, scaly skin into the water, then ran back to the shack. I placed the clean plate on the table across from Mother's plate, empty and unmoving for three days.

I glanced around, and my gaze fell on Mother's hatchet, leaning against the wall beside the open doorway to the hut. That was the pitiful weapon they'd pressed into her hand when they told her to go hunt monsters. They might as well have given her a wooden spoon for all the good it did her.

"Swallowed her whole. Ate her right there in the water," the rough man who'd brought the hatchet back to me had said. "Damned serpo. Wasn't a thing left 'cept this."

I stood up, pressed my scraped and throbbing fists into my head until it hurt. The sun had begun to set beyond the doorway, flicking flames over the tops of the waves and smearing orange across the sky. Soon, darkness stole the colors, and the Serpent's Eye rose from the table where I'd set it, illuminating the wooden plank walls with its soft golden light. I turned away from the doorway, turned away from the Serpent's Eye and its light.

They're coming for you, I finally thought, forcing myself to stop humming Mother's song and to look at my plight with honest eyes. *You hurt Mellistor bad, and no matter how much you hum, High Lord Denshell is coming for you. You have to run——*

A shadow slithered up the wooden planks on the wall in front of me, and the room filled with a cold, salty smell. I spun about and gasped.

A sea serpent had entered my little hut, ducking its head beneath the doorway and rearing up to almost touch the low roof. Green scales glinted in the light of the Serpent's Eye, and the monster's mottled lips pulled back to reveal shark-like teeth. It was as thick around as a full-grown man, and its seemingly never-ending body trailed out the doorway and onto the dark sand beyond. Its eyes burned gold, and I suddenly understood how my family's artifact, the Serpent's Eye, had gotten its name.

The monster hissed.

I stumbled backward until my shoulders slammed into the wall. There was nothing but a rickety table between me and this living nightmare. I couldn't breathe. The enormity of the creature froze me. My legs trembled, but as much as I wanted to leap out the hut's single window, I couldn't seem to make myself do it.

Beneath the monster, water splashed onto the floorboards, shooting from underneath its scales and creating a small stream upon which the creature moved. It slithered toward me on this self-made wave and drew itself up taller. Its jaws opened, and I knew I was about to die.

It struck, and I shouted, swinging my fists wildly...

But they swept through empty air.

The monster had struck, but it hadn't attacked me. Instead, it snatched the Serpent's Eye from the air above the table and recoiled to its previous position, the Eye clenched tightly in its jaws.

It felt like someone had poured ice water on my head, and my whole body shook. The creature's gaze stayed fixed on me as soft golden light leaked from between its teeth. The monster dropped low, twisted, and slithered out the door on its wave, splashing water against the doorjamb.

My heart hammered so hard it hurt. The briny stench hung in the air, nearly choking me. The monster had stolen the Eye!

Get Mother's hatchet, I thought. *Chase it. Kill it!*

But I froze as the serpent undulated down the beach until darkness swallowed it. It had stolen the last bit of my history, my family's birthright, the most important possession I owned. And yet here I was, too afraid to move, too afraid to chase it.

"Do it!" I shouted, and the ringing command shattered my fear. I shoved the table out of the way and snatched Mother's hatchet from the corner. Empty wooden plates clacked and rolled onto the floor as I lunged out the front door—

—and I pulled up short.

A half-dozen people were positioning themselves in a semi-circle outside the hut. Two of them held bright lamps that made me squint. At first, I didn't know what was happening. My befuddled brain thought maybe this was a band of sea hackers chasing the serpent.

Then I saw the thick-limbed, well-dressed High Lord Denshell at the back of the group, as well as Mellistor, who hung behind him like a wraith. The puffy, purpling bruises on his battered face were obvious even in the flickering light.

"Jyshen Grenlyth," High Lord Denshell boomed, his deep voice thumping my chest like a mallet. "Lower that hatchet!"

Paralyzed, I realized I was holding the hatchet in front of myself protectively. The head dipped at his commanding tone, but then I tightened my grip and raised it again.

The two lamp holders were just servants, but the tall woman on Denshell's left was clearly a fighter. She wore leather breeches, armor plates on her shoulders, a hard leather breastplate, and a longsword across her back. Her eyes were close-set and dark. She looked bored.

On Denshell's right stood another fighter. He was shorter than the woman, with loose pantaloons and an X harness over his bare chest like an imperial Highblade. His short sword and dagger were strapped to a belt around his waist, and greasy hair fell in his face, almost reaching his equally greasy mustache. His half-lidded eyes made him seem like he was daydreaming.

"There's a sea serpent," I warned. "It might still be near. It attacked me, and it took—"

"Shut up!" High Lord Denshell boomed. The intimidating rumble of his voice seemed to shake the very sand. "You've got a lot of cheek, boy. I show you and your mother mercy. I let you live on my land, and this is how you repay me? You attack my son? He lost a tooth, you little gutter snipe!"

"H-He tried to steal the Serpent's Eye—"

"That's a lie!" Mellistor interrupted, seeming to find the courage to step forward at last. Denshell put a hand in front of his son, barring him from coming closer.

"Get off my land, Grenlyth," the high lord said in a quiet, lethal voice. "Leave that hatchet. And leave the Serpent's Eye as payment for your crimes. Be grateful I'm letting you walk away. It's the last kindness you'll get from me."

"But the Eye isn't—"

"The Eye belongs to us now!" Denshell boomed.

"But I..." I stuttered.

"Fetch it and be quick, boy," he warned. "My patience is done—"

"The serpent took it!" I blurted. "Snatched it and... It went that way." I pointed toward the sea. Nobody looked.

"By the Faia, this is insufferable," Denshell growled. He made a jerky, angry wave with his hand. "Kill him! Throw his body into the sea for the serpents."

"High Lord Denshell, please!" I cried. I know I shouldn't have been surprised at his ruthlessness, but I was. I still wanted to believe there was justice in the empire, that justice came from the nobles, that they were the heroes I'd read about in stories. That little, frightened part of me still wanted to climb back up the waterfall.

The greasy-haired man chuckled. His short sword grated on its sheath as it came free, and he started toward me.

But the fighter woman crossed her arms. "He's a boy, milord. Spank him and send him along with a scar. He'll remember the lesson."

"Do your job," Denshell commanded.

"Milord—" she protested.

"Are you a warrior or a milk maid?" he barked. "You have your orders."

The woman sighed and reluctantly drew her longsword.

Tears welled up in my eyes, and my arms shook. The last of my illusions fell away. High Lord Denshell was no hero. These were thieves and murderers. I saw it clearly. I found true courage at last, and my spine stiffened. I stood up straighter, gripped the hatchet tighter.

I would stand alone against these villains like the Whisper Prince stood alone against the Slinks. I thought of Mother clawing at Father for the Serpent's Eye. I thought of my fists striking Mellistor. I hadn't known I could do that, but that's the boy I needed to be again.

231

I held the hatchet high and readied myself to leap at them.

A salty breeze blew past me, and the temperature dropped. The hairs rose on the back of my neck. I recognized that cold breeze, that briny scent. The sea serpent had returned!

The monster's horned head rose up behind the lamp bearer at the back of the group. Its golden eyes burned in the dark. Denshell's fighters didn't see it; they were facing me.

But one of the lamp bearers slowly turned. Perhaps he smelled the salt or he felt the chill of the creature's towering presence. Whichever, he lifted his glass-and-copper lamp, and he screamed. The serpent's jaws snapped over his neck, cutting off the scream abruptly.

"By the Faia!" Denshell roared. He turned, tripped over his own scrambling feet, and fell down. Mellistor froze, looking up at the serpent with horrified eyes while the other lamp holder ran up the beach, squealing like a pig.

"Kill it! Kill it!" Denshell piped, his voice suddenly high and tinny. He squirmed backward, arms and legs flinging sand like a crab as he tried to get away.

The fighter woman was the first to react. She leapt at the serpent, swinging, but the monster coiled beneath the whistling strike and bit deep into her thigh. She screamed and went down, her blade flinging away from spasming fingers. It flipped end over end and stuck point-first in the sand.

The greasy-haired man bolted, but the serpent shot after him, nipping his calf. He went down with a cry. The monster rose tall above him. Its head lanced down, biting again and again, on the man's back, on his neck. The fighter gurgled and went still, his last breath sighing across the wet, darkening sand.

The serpent doubled back, water jetting from beneath its scales and splashing all around it. It reared over Denshell next, who had just managed to make it to his hands and knees.

"No!" he screamed, but the serpent fell on him like a headsman's axe. His scream stopped.

"Father!" Mellistor keened. He stood frozen for a moment, just as I was, then he sprinted away in terror toward the sea. He must have realized that no escape lay in that direction, and he bolted along the shore. He realized that, too, was dangerous, turned again, and ran away from the water, feet scrabbling frantically in the sand. He finally clambered over a grassy hillock and vanished from sight.

The beach was silent now, except for the gentle splashing of the serpent's wave and the quiet slither of the fighter woman pulling herself pitifully toward her sword. Everyone else was dead or fled. Everyone except me.

The serpent rose up before me, bloody jaws dripping. I held my shaking hatchet high. The monster hissed, then turned and slithered toward the sea, riding its sloshing wave and taking the cold with it.

My hatchet descended until it hung by my side, numbly gripped in my trembling fist. Breathing hard, I forced my shaking legs to move. I took one step. Then another. I began to jog after the monster, then I sprinted. Huffing madly, I finally caught up to it at the edge of the surf. The serpent swiveled to face me. The Serpent's Eye hovered next to it, just above the water, casting golden light upon the monster and the wet sand.

I raised the hatchet. "You killed my mother!" I shouted like a war cry.

I swung with all my might, but the serpent coiled gracefully around the strike. I swung the other direction, but the hatchet was awkward, and my aim was poor. The blade glanced sideways off tough, green scales.

The monster loomed over me, golden eyes burning, plainly unworried by my attack. My swings were pathetic and empty, so I stopped, breathing hard from my efforts.

Why was I even chasing it, fighting it? The sea serpent wasn't the real enemy. It hadn't brought about the ruin of my house. It didn't even understand my pain. It was just a beast. There was no agenda in its golden eyes, not like the cunning, thieving High Lord Denshell. By the Faia, the sea serpent had exacted my revenge for me!

I looked back up the beach, back to where the slaughtered high lord and his guards lay, but I couldn't see them. There was only darkness.

My life had come down to a pile of corpses on a beach. Through a stroke of dumb luck, the monster had destroyed my enemies. All that was left for me were the repercussions that would follow. I had but three choices now. I could throw myself upon the mercy of the new High Lord Denshell, who would delight in hanging me. I could run away from him, in which case he'd delight in chasing me down.

Or I could let it end here, as it had for my mother, upon the jaws of a sea serpent.

Then let it be here, I thought. *Let the serpent take the Eye, take my life as it took my mother's. Let it kill me and deny Mellistor the pleasure.*

I dropped the hatchet, closed my eyes, and hummed *The Sea Serpent's Wife.* If I was going to die, it would be thinking of Mother.

I waited for the serpent to attack.

It didn't.

I opened my eyes. It was watching me, and as soon as we locked gazes, it let out a long, shuddery breath and reared up. It opened its mouth and, tucked just inside its row of deadly, shark-like teeth, two small fangs unfolded, long and thin.

The serpent moved in a blur. It had lulled me, and I didn't even have time to flinch before it sank those fangs into my forearm.

I gasped as poison sluiced into my veins. It burned up the length of my arm and into my chest, my heart. I could feel it killing me as it spread throughout my body. I fell to my knees, then onto my back.

Good, I thought. *This is what I wanted. This is better...*

My muscles became stiff, and my legs pushed together. My arms slapped to my sides and they... stuck. I screamed in pain as my own muscles continued tightening, moving in ways they'd never moved before. They shifted beneath my skin, coiling around my chest, my waist, my legs, around and around like they were tying me up. I opened my mouth to scream...

And it came out a hiss.

The pain stopped abruptly, and I knew something was horribly wrong with me.

I craned my neck and looked down at myself. My arms were gone. My legs were gone. I thrashed sideways and felt the muscular power of my new, sinuous body. I saw the glimmer of my own green scales.

I whipped my head around to face the sea serpent, looked into those burning golden eyes, which watched me steadily. The serpent hissed, took the Serpent's Eye from where it hovered over the wet sand, and passed it to me. I took it in my sharp, new teeth.

"I returned for you as soon as I could," the serpent hissed, and I was stunned to hear Mother's voice in that hiss.

"Mother?" I hissed back, incredulous. The Eye from my mouth, almost hit the water, then slowly rose to hover next to us. *"You're dead. The serpents killed you!"*

"Not so," she hissed. *"They did not attack me. They felt the mark of The Serpent's Eye upon me, felt it in my blood, just as it is in yours, and they accepted me. The magic of The Serpent's Eye combines with their venom, Jyshen. Their bite did not kill me, but transformed me into one of their own, just like the girl in* The Sea Serpent's Wife. *And now you have a choice, my son. You can remain this way, or you can become human again."*

"Become human again?"

"This construct of the Faia..." she indicated the Serpent's Eye in my teeth, *"is an artifact of great magic. It is a light in the dark, and it holds the power of transformation inside. It can undo what was done to us, if we wish. I came back to get it so I could become my old self one last time. To see you one last time as you knew me, that I might let you know what happened."*

"One last time?"

"Jyshen, I am bound to the serpents now. I made them a promise, just as the Sea Serpent's Wife did. It was the price of living, of returning to you. But you are not likewise bound," she said. *"You may stay as you are now, transformed, darting through the seas with me, just as you wished when you were little. Or you may return to your life as a young man."*

A new future opened up before me, one of power, not poverty. There was more I could do than die at Mellistor's hands or run from him. I could embark on an adventure that few humans had ever taken. I could become like mother and rule the sea... or I could lash myself to the laws of humankind, bowing to its petty lords with their thieving and their cruelty...

Excitement and fear coursed through me. It hardly seemed a choice at all.

"We will keep the Serpent's Eye," I hissed.

"The Eye will never leave our family," she said.

"May we return from time to time? Pay our respects to the new High Lord Denshell?"

"Respects?" she asked slyly.

"For every cruelty he visits upon his people, I will visit ten upon him."

Mother hissed approval, and it sounded like laughter. She nodded her great scaly head and plunged into the surf. I let go of the Serpent's Eye, but it hovered next to me. And when I dove after her, it followed, streaking along through the water and leaving a trail of churning bubbles behind it. The slithering motion of my new body came naturally, so much so that it felt like I had come home at last. Together Mother and I coursed through the waves, side-by-side. And I was right. It was just like flying.

As I told you, mine isn't a hero's story. I no longer dream of human glory or valiant deeds. When I think of returning to the dry lands of your kind, I dream only of bloody deeds. Ten for every one.

From the Author

The Serpent's Eye (previously published as *Ten for Every One* in *Fantastic Realms*) is different than my usual short fiction fare. Most of my smaller stories are components to established novels, backstory for a primary character we didn't get to see in the main story (like *Urchin*), "darlings" I had to kill because they didn't fit the main story (like *Threshold*), or supplemental side stories that aren't necessary to understand the core story, but are fun to play with (like *Pawns of Magic*).

While *The Serpent's Eye* is set in my *The Whisper Prince* series, it stands alone. It has no direct connection to the main characters of *Fairmist* or *The Undying Man*. It will not illuminate some Easter egg secret. It's just a story about a young man forced into a difficult decision in the often-cruel world of the Thiaran Empire.

I will say, though, that I liked Jyshen and his transformation a lot. It made me wonder how I might tie him into *The Whisper Prince* later. Sometimes following a random inspiration leads me to another. Perhaps Jyshen and his mother could make a cameo appearance in the upcoming novel *The Slate Wizards* as our nefarious villains sail across the Sunset Sea.

Hmmm, I think like that idea...

Anyway, thanks for taking a chance on *Particular Passages*. I hope you enjoyed all the varied stories as much as we the authors enjoyed writing them. I hope they did their jobs and took you away from normal life for a little while.

Cheers! And happy reading.

About the Author

Todd Fahnestock is a fantasy/sci-fi author of the bestselling *Tower of the Four*, *Threadweavers* and *The Whisper Prince* series. He was a finalist in the Colorado Authors League Writing Awards for the past two years, for *Charlie Fiction*, his time travel novel, and *The Undying Man*, book 2 of *The Whisper Prince*. His passions are fantasy and his quirky, fun-loving family. When he's not writing, he teaches taekwondo, swaps middle grade humor with his son, plays Ticket to Ride with his wife, scribes modern slang from his daughter and goes on morning walks with Galahad the Weimaraner. Visit Todd at www.toddfahnestock.com.

Facebook Author Page:
https://www.facebook.com/todd.fahnestock

Facebook Group, Quad Fahnestock:
https://www.facebook.com/groups/176249136990979

Fairmist: https://books2read.com/u/38RwAV

Wildmane: https://books2read.com/u/3yzyLL

Tower of the Four: https://books2read.com/u/49lG5X

From the Editor

Unlike most anthologies, this one was curated and edited with a light touch. The authors herein were given a chance to share a story they liked, the way they liked it. Often, when submitting stories to anthologies, authors are required to fit a central theme somehow. The stories all have to be love stories, or horror stories, or horror love stories that have vampires that are allergic to blood and love kale juice. This was not that kind of anthology.

As an editor, I found it incredibly freeing to go through the stories and not be looking for that one little line thrown in to make the story "fit in" with the rest, trying to decide if it was "enough" to fit the theme. Instead of dreading the moment when the author and I would have to discuss why they needed to make changes if they wanted to be included in the anthology, I made suggestions knowing that if the author didn't like them, they didn't have to use them. They got to retain their artistic vision the way they wanted it.

For me, it felt like a breath of fresh air to have a variety of stories, with a variety of themes, told in different voices and with different styles, and not to worry about making them all similar enough somehow to belong together in the same anthology. I hope the authors felt the same way.

And I hope you felt that way, as well.

If you did, if you liked someone's story, reach out and let them know. The BEST way to make sure your favorite authors will write more is to tell them! (Not to mention it will make their day!)

If you really liked this kind of anthology, let any or all of us know. Comments on our social media, our websites, or in an email all work. That is the best way to make sure we do another one. The second-best way is to tell other people about the anthology, so that they buy the book too. The third best way is to leave reviews. Not just at the place you bought the book, but anywhere you frequent online.

Seriously, that helps a lot.

I would like to take a line of ink to thank the authors, who were willing to take a chance on this kind of anthology. A special thank you to our cover artist, Rashed AlAkroka, who did such a great job (Did you notice the individual keys on the cover art relate to stories in the book? That was awesome, Rashed! Thank you!), and to Chris Mandeville, who brought him on board with this project. Also, thank you to Marie Whittaker and Todd Fahnestock for their input and suggestions, and a very big special thank you to Laura Hayden for her help, suggestions, and offering up the benefits of her online bookstore, **author, author!** which can be found at author-author.net.

May your search be that which brings you the most pleasure, and may your search be never ending.

Sam Knight
2/24/2021

Additional Copyright Information

CPSIA information can be obtained
at www.ICGtesting.com
Printed in the USA
LVHW111509250721
693631LV00004B/92